FLIRTING WITH FANGS

LAVENDER FALLS

BOOK THREE

ISABEL BARREIRO

Published by Isabel Barreiro

Copyright © 2025 Isabel Barreiro

All Right Reserved

Paperback ISBN: 979-8-9902878-1-5

Flirting with Fangs

Genre: Small town paranormal romance

Cover Design: Jennette Perdomo

❀ Created with Vellum

CONTENTS

For the ones who always felt like Eeyore on the inside,
you're deserving of sunshine.
Also there's nothing wrong with a little biting...

THINGS TO KNOW

This an **open door romance** book so there are **adult scenes.**

TW: Biting, depression

Spicy Chapters:
17, 23, 24, 28, 31, 25

Playlist:

PROLOGUE

LOLA

"I know what I'm doing," Flynn barked at me like a hellhound. I scoffed, irritation washing over me. I was so excited to be back in Lavender Falls after graduation. I finally finished vet school and couldn't wait to be working with the creatures of the town. I remember being nervous asking Ms. Heinstein for a possible job at her vet clinic. She had said, "let me think about," with a smirk that made me anxious.

When Lily, my best friend, said I would be Ms. Heinstein's assistant I was ready to explode. Although if I'm being honest, Ms. Heinstein has made me feel more like a partner than an assistant which I'm totally grateful for.

What's even more exciting is that she loved my idea of implementing more natural remedies for our patients. I've been partnering with Priscilla, the owner of Priscilla's Potions and Lotions, to come up with different medicines.

Everything was falling into place until I had to face Flynn Kiernan. Flynn was one of the bartenders at The Drunken Fairy Tale Tavern in our small town, and also one of the owners of Kiernan's Whiskey Distillery. He was also my rival from AHS, Alchemy & Horticulture Society club.

We were co-presidents and could never agree on anything. From debating which manure would mix well with magic to figuring out the best way to preserve the garden during harsh winters. I'd figured that now that we are adults, he would have grown up a bit.

And he did, in certain ways. Despite our banter, I felt my cheeks heat up as I stared into his honey brown eyes. His messy, dirty blonde hair was held back by a headband. He was giving total '90s heartthrob vibes. I hated the fact that he made my blood pump for different reasons. One reason was excitement.

I was Lola Luna, the clever, sunshine vampire. And this elf liked to rain on my parade. Something about Flynn just made me want to challenge him. I loved getting under his skin. He was so easy to rile up.

Flynn was also the man in charge of the community garden. Despite the fact he got on my nerves that man had a green thumb. I shook my head, not wanting my brain to start thinking about his fingers and what they could do. I mean he made pouring mulch look sexy. Mulch! Even when surrounded by the smell of pegasi manure I couldn't help but gawk at him.

However, since my idea for natural remedies was approved and he needed to grant me a bigger section of the garden he's been in a sour mood. Maybe it was because he grew up as the middle child and was seriously possessive.

What made matters worse is that Eleanor (*my other best friend, who is in charge of the **Spring Flora Festival***), wants us to work together. She had the brilliant idea to have a flower parade as a way to kick-off the event. It's a good thing that we're a magical town because I have no idea how we are gonna manage growing that many flowers. The Hollow Tree (*which helps nurture the magic of pixies*) was recently tied to our town's ley lines.

The tree was dying and the severing connection between the tree and our pixie population was wreaking havoc on our town's magic. Eleanor managed to save the day, but Flynn, the fairies, pixies, and I have been working overtime to heal all of the vegetation that suffered. We spent hours clearing away snow to turn over the soil, cleanse the water before every use and nurture the plants with potions.

Today, I noticed that he had overwatered the peonies and decided to bring it up with him. *Nicely.* Sort of. He was wiping down the bar when I popped in and onto a bar stool.

"I did not over water the peonies," he exclaimed. I rolled my eyes.

"Sure, *Ri-der*," I stressed my nickname for him. He huffed. He hated it when I called him Rider– after the male love interest from a certain Rapunzel movie. But he *really* looked like him. Of course, he didn't know that Rider was my favorite MMC.

"I told you that I'm not some prince," he said through clenched teeth. I leaned closer, enjoying his attempt to remain composed. There was a delicious flush on his cheeks.

"You're right. At least he's good looking," I said, teasingly. His nose scrunched. He leaned over to me and I sucked in a breath. He smelled like sunscreen and rainwater. I stifled a moan as I felt his breath sear across my neck. His lips brushed my ear lightly. For some reason everything he did made my senses heighten– and I am already a vampire.

"If you think I'm some sort of PG prince, you're sorely mistaken *Sunflower,*" he said in a low and gravelly voice.

"Are you more of a big bad wolf?" I teased, my heart pounding in my ears. The scent of arousal trickled in the air and I was ready to choke on it. This is why I pushed Flynn. I knew he was attracted to me. I could see the pupils in his honey eyes dilate, hear his heart race every time I got close, and I could fucking *smell* that he wanted me. It's been absolutely intoxicating ever since I moved back. He leaned away and I bit back a whimper.

"Bite me," he said. I tightened my jaw, forcing my fangs to retract.

"Don't tempt me Flynn," I said, pushing away from the stool.

"Lola," he said firmly. I fought back a shiver. I melted every time he used that tone. I sighed, turning back to face him.

"You know, for the festival we're going to have to find a way to get along. It won't be a competition," I pointed out. He crossed his arms.

"Not everything between us is a competition," he said. I threw my head back in laughter.

"Should I remind you that after I planted cilantro you decided to

3

grow some, and then used magic to increase the growth rate?" I pointed out.

"Greg needed cilantro for the flatbreads he was making," he said. I rolled my eyes despite knowing that Greg *had* been making more flatbread.

"And the reason you keep trying to get to the garden before me in the mornings?" I asked.

"I have to make sure the flowers are growing," he said.

"I understand that but I *see* you double checking my section. Do you not have confidence in my skills?" I asked.

"Well, I *did* study horticulture while you studied creatures." He dropped my gaze and reached for a glass. I shook my head.

"And yet *I* was the one who managed to regrow the chamomile, the lavender and peppermint. You know the ones we mostly needed for all of the healing potions," I pointed out. He grimaced, knowing I was right. He handed the glass he poured to Caleb whose eyes bounced between us.

"We're having a <u>floral</u> festival. It requires a shit ton of flowers," he said.

"I can grow a damn daisy, Rider," I said. There was a slight pause and then his lips stretched into a smirk.

"Shall we make a bet?" he asked.

"I thought not everything we did was a competition," I said. He tilted his head back and I felt the challenge in his gaze. I could never resist betting against him. "A bet about who can grow the most flowers?" I asked. He nodded, leaning against the bar.

"What do I get when I win?" I asked. He let out a chuckle that had my stomach twisting.

"*If* you win," he emphasized. "The winner gets anything they want."

"Anything can be dangerous," I said, smirking. I offered my hand.

"That makes it more interesting," he said, taking my hand in a firm grip. My heart skipped faster.

Flynn Kiernan was going down.

Flynn

Fucking hellhound's lair.

She had been sitting in my family's tavern, accusing me of over watering the peonies as if I didn't have a degree in horticulture. She'd stared at me with her big dark eyes, and I had looked away. Her eyes always held a sparkle that rivaled the night sky, enchanting me.

Every time I stared at her for too long I felt myself get lost in them. She had her natural hair down, creating a dark halo around her soft, round face. She always kept her hair down during the colder season.

Regardless she was achingly beautiful with whatever look she decided on. She leaned on the bar with a flirtatious smile. My eyes flickered to her full lips and I was once again tempted to kiss the senses out of her.

I've known Lola Luna my entire life. She was my academic rival. It all started in potion making class in the second grade when she corrected my ratio for a plant spell. Growing up as what felt like the middle child (there's four of us), I had a thing for wanting to prove myself.

Greg was the oldest and figured out quickly what he wanted to do in life. Caleb lived away with our father, though that didn't stop our mom from constantly worrying about him. Then there was my baby sister Bridget, who was the only girl. Bridget did everything with confidence even if she didn't know what she was doing. Sometimes I felt lost in my own family. The only time I didn't feel that way was when I was competing with Lola, working in the garden, or making whiskey.

I thought I was safe from my feuding days with her, but then she waltzed back into my life *and* my garden. The community garden was my safe space away from everyone, and now she was filling it with sunflowers and sage.

I hated it. I hated how she made me feel. Right now, she was walking out the door and I couldn't keep my eyes off of her retreating figure. Her megawatt smile, curves for days and mischievous gleam in her eyes were breaking me.

She strutted into town and it felt like a veil was ripped off of my eyes. I began noticing everything about her. The tilt in her head when she was concentrating. The way she lifted her chin up when she had a witty comeback. How she would work all hours of the day and night to help every being in need. Lola was slowly filling the corners of my mind and it set every single one of my nerves on edge.

"You're so fucking screwed," my brother Caleb said to me, breaking through my thoughts.

"I don't know what you're talking about," I grumbled. He rolled his eyes at me before glancing back at his girlfriend who was walking up to their apartment on the top floor. I smiled. I was happy those saps were finally together. Caleb had finally lost the icicle that he had stuck up his ass since getting with Eleanor. His blue eyes landed on me again.

"You've been wiping the exact same spot since Lola came and left," he said pointing to the bar. My eyes widened as I stared at the rag. *Fuck.*

"Whatever man, she's gotten on my nerves ever since we were kids," I said, tossing the rag into the bar sink.

"You're not kids anymore," he pointed out.

"She's in my garden," I retorted, like a child. A customer waved for a beer and I watched Caleb pour him a pint. I sighed, feeling the exhaustion hit me. I had woken up at the crack of dawn to tend to the garden. Ever since the winter festival, the garden has needed extra attention.

When the tree died, Eleanor ended up doing some magic and it was reborn as a sapling. It's been slow progress for the vegetation to regrow, even with magic. I've been having to keep an eye on the sapling.

"You could let her into *your* garden," Caleb said with a smirk. "Oh wait you did…sorta." I reached back for the towel and whacked him with it.

"Caleb!" I hissed. He let out a laugh. Since being with Eleanor he's laughed and smiled a lot more. At first I thought it was fucking weird but after a few family game nights per Bridget's request, I've been getting used to it. He arched an eyebrow at me.

"You know you want to," he pointed out. I shook my head.

"All I need is to win this bet, and for the Spring Flora Festival to be a success without Lola and I biting each other's heads off," I said, crossing my arms. My brother patted my shoulder.

"I've heard vampires like to bite," he said walking away. I sighed and looked at the door that the sunshine vampire had walked out of. Sometimes I wished I could just give into my wants and needs. But Lola and I would never work. My phone blared, cutting off the storm clouds rolling into my head. *Priscilla.*

"Hey, what's up?" I asked Priscilla. Her next few words had me running out of the tavern and after Lola. "Lola!" I yelled. She was up the street.

"What's wrong?" she asked. She reached for my shoulder, but pulled her hand away before making contact.

"Priscilla called. We need to head to the garden. *Now.*"

✳ ◉ ✳ ◉ ✳ ◉ ✳ ◉ ✳ ◉ ✳

ONCE WE REACHED Boogeyman's swamp we took a turn away from it to the community garden. Priscilla was at the gate crying. Lola reached out to hug her.

"Q-quick, please," she said in between sobs. We made our way towards the back of the garden that bordered the Gasping Greenwood Forest. My eyes widened in shock.

"Oh no," Lola whispered. A trail of rot that started in the forest had slithered its way towards the peonies and nearby flowers. Just this morning they were a vibrant pink and now they were wilting and turning yellow.

The sound of a broken branch caught my attention. I took a step in front of the ladies. From the forest, a gentle animal with pure white fur stumbled out. This was fucking bad. The creature collapsed once it made its way from behind the trees. Lola pushed me out of the way and ran towards it. I reached out to pull her back, but her glare stopped me.

The creature eyed her. It was clearly too exhausted to move away. She bowed her head and crouched down, offering her hand. It snorted, which she took as a sign to get closer. Lola's hands were gently brushing its belly. The creature continued to stare at Lola, whose eyes glowed slightly.

"It's pregnant and it's dying," Lola said in a soft voice.

"I can't believe they exist," Priscilla whispered. Lola eyed the forest.

"Something has to be wrong for it to come all the way to town, to be close to us," Lola said, getting up. "It says death is coming," Lola said, facing me.

"How do you know that?" I asked her.

"What do we do?" Priscilla asked. My stomach twisted and my magic vibrated against my skin. I looked back at the peonies and dug my hands into the earth, closing my eyes. I let my magic seep out and connect with the dirt. Its warmth flowed into the Earth. I sucked in a deep breath, opening my senses.

Something was...wrong. I tapped into that feeling, trying to secure a connection. A sharp sting raced up my arm and I yanked my hand back in a gasp. Priscilla reached for my arm and with a gentle whisper I felt her magic cool the sting.

"A rot is spreading, and if we don't act fast the creatures and the vegetation could all be at risk," I said. Lola nodded and began walking away. "Where are you going?" I asked, grabbing for her wrist.

"Go do what you're trained to do and take care of the garden. I'm going to do what I'm trained to do and save this unicorn's life." There was a silver glow around her pupils. My eyes widened. I had never seen that happen to her. Why did I have the feeling that there was more to this vampire than I'd initially thought?

"I'll grab the gardening tools," Priscilla said, running off.

"Go Flynn," Lola said, pushing my shoulder.

"Can't we have one normal festival," I said, rolling up my sleeves and following Priscilla.

CHAPTER 1
UNICORNS BITE

LOLA

SOMETIME IN MARCH

I couldn't stop tapping my foot. Ms. Heinstein was on a family vacation across the ocean and I had already left her four messages because nowhere in my vet school training was I taught how to deal with a pregnant unicorn.

I'd been taking care of said pregnant unicorn since very late December, and she was going to give birth soon. At least I thought so. They really didn't cover unicorn pregnancy in magical vet school due to the fact that unicorns don't normally approach people. Like, *ever*.

Plants were still dying at an alarming rate and there was a mysterious rot growing across our town. It wasn't just the vegetation that was affected, it was also messing with the beings of the town. I was up to my fangs with sick creatures, from cats to pegasi to frogs.

Even though things have slightly calmed down since December we still haven't slowed down the rot that's been eating at the Gasping Greenwood Forest and our community garden.

I bit my lip as I stared into the unicorn's stall. Her fur was pure white since I had just finished giving her a bath, and with the sun peaking through the stall it added an almost glittery sheen to it. Her belly was round, and I could see the baby shifting inside.

Inhaling a deep breath of hay, sunshine, and dirt, I concentrated my eyes on my patient. Magic shimmered around the unicorn and an almost rainbow glow encircled it But despite the light of my magic, her aura was dim. The grass and fruits she had eaten were slowly poisoning her and she was still in recovery.

Her big dark eyes flicked up towards mine and my heart pounded as a surge of magic rushed through me.

Thank you for cleaning the stall, however, you smell.

"I'll stop stinking up your pen, I'll be back later today to feed you," I said with an eye roll.

Also, sorry for biting you.

I glanced at my wrist which had a bite mark around it. Naturally, I was stuck with a sassy unicorn. Who knew unicorns could be vicious? Damn humans and their fairy tales depicting them as gentle creatures. I closed the door to the stall that housed the unicorn, pegasi, reindeers, and other creatures. I walked into the vet building to check on some of the charts of the animals that had stayed overnight.

The vet clinic was cold and sterile, everything orderly and in its place. My desk, however, was not. It was littered with paperwork. I was the only vet in town this spring season, and I knew that one of the reasons Ms. Heinstein left me in charge was my magical ability to communicate with the animals.

Every vampire has a gift. Sure, we have blood lust, great eyesight, speed, and strength, but we are also born with an inclination. Contrary to Hollywood, you don't have to be bit to turn into one. Honestly, that sort of thing doesn't happen often. Most vampires are born vampires, like myself.

Some vampires are tech savvy– they could see the code in front of their eyes. Others have a knack for spells, or a special relationship with various elements. I could communicate with animals which made helping them and filling out charts easy.

I rolled my shoulders as I looked over the chart for a pegasus and sighed happily. Penny the pegasus was doing much better. She had gotten a slight stomach bug from eating the grass near the forest.

I had many things on my plate. One: I was in charge of the clinic, two: I had to help figure out what the fuck was wrong with the vegetation, and three: I had to work with Flynn on the festival.

Why is a vet solving a mystery about our crops and flowers for the spring festival? I'm a vet with a green thumb. Flynn might have studied horticulture but I knew my shit too and that got under his skin. There was also the matter of winning our bets. The first was to figure out what was attacking the town and the second was who could grow the most flowers.

Flynn and I have been in competition since basically the second grade when I pointed out a miscalculation in his potion recipe. We continued to compete and bicker until we went our separate ways in college.

When I moved back I noticed Flynn wasn't the same competitive, lanky teenager. Now he was a stubborn, brooding elf who made smelling like manure hot. I closed my eyes briefly remembering the smell of his arousal. It always sparked around me.

At first I was confused. Growing up, Flynn never really showed any interest in me in that way. I always found him cute and brilliant. He excited me. But he never seemed into me beyond our rivalry, and I was fine with that.

When I came back we started hanging around each other more because of our mutual friends. Our banter turned flirty and I found myself trying to catch his eye more often. I began to crave his conversation and nearness. Then I started to smell his need for me and it awakened a hunger.

I had no idea why he wasn't giving in. There would be these tender moments between us where I would get a glimpse of a different side to him, a side that made my heart skip a beat and my body melt. But each time, he would suddenly snap away like a rubber band, almost as if he was afraid of what could be brewing between us.

My lips stretched into a small smile. I will keep pushing him. Flynn had become a puzzle that I was dying to piece together. Speaking of

Flynn, it was almost time to clock out of work and make my way to the garden. My stomach twisted with excitement. Lately it's been doing that whenever I've had a chance of seeing him.

CHAPTER 2
GETTING DIRTY

FLYNN

The wind outside lightly tapped against my greenhouse creating a soothing melody. The air around me was thick with humidity and heat as sweat trickled down the back of my neck. I glanced around at the different shades of green that were scattered around me. Everything was growing in decent condition.

My eyes caught the window and I couldn't help but stare at the Gasping Greenwood Forest. The trees seemed to hang low, as if too tired to hold up their branches despite being in the middle of spring.

I grunted as I plucked some sage that I needed for my latest whiskey recipe. I loved being in my greenhouse. I savored the feeling of getting my hands dirty and I especially enjoyed making whiskey. I was happy that my siblings never had any interest in the family business because it was one of the few things that made me stand out to my father.

My family owned Kiernan's Whiskey Distillery and I was one of the main product developers. Ever since my dad allowed me to try whiskey at 16 I've been hellbent on creating different recipes to appeal to every kind of person. Not everyone likes whiskey, and by the stars I was one of those people in the beginning.

Today I was working on a new recipe that incorporated sage. The last one was apple crisp and before that, orange and mint. My siblings all sampled the prototypes. For a while I've toyed with the idea of using sage and I think I've finally figured out how. It had an earthy taste with a hint of mint. I needed to blend something sweet to bring out the notes of mint.

My phone pinged with a reminder to check on the flowers. During the winter season the pixie's Hollow Tree was dying and it had made the town's magic go erratic. The roots ended up fucking up the land and now I was trying to restore it– albeit with some help.

I laid the sage out to dry after giving it a gentle wash. I still haven't figured out what was wrong. Eleanor saved the Hollow Tree by helping it be reborn as a sapling. Everything looked okay but the rot was still spreading slowly. Plant life seemed to have remained in a state of mediocracy.

Sure, they weren't dying at an alarming rate but they also weren't exactly thriving. And on top of this, I have the stupid spring festival.

I shouldn't call it stupid, I loved all of the festivals in Lavender Falls. This time, I felt immense pressure. Eleanor wanted to do a flower parade. What do flower parades need? A shit ton of flowers. What do we not have? A shit ton of flowers. I've tried using my magic. Stars, all of the Earth fairies have too, and Priscilla has been creating amazing growth elixirs.

But those were only doing so much, there was something fucking things up.

I slipped my phone into my pocket and headed to the flower beds on my left. Walking through the garden I felt at peace. The tension eased off of my shoulders slightly as I took a deep breath. Growing up it was like everyone in my family had a place but me. I felt like an awkward duckling. The Lavender Falls community garden was my escape.

I made my way over to the peonies to check on their growth. Once a week they begin to wilt for who knows what reason. I had a mixture of whites and pinks, and their petals were still not all of the way unfurled. Once the flowers bloom to near perfection I harvest them and cast a freeze spell until it's time for the parade.

The sun was beginning to set as I stuck my hand in the ground and took a deep breath. The dirt slid between my fingers, the warmth of the ground slowly wrapping around my body. It felt a little hot but not too moist, the garden will need some water soon.

My brows furrowed as I felt a familiar sliver of darkness approach me. I pressed my hand further into the dirt, trying to follow it. If I could just reach it, I could feel what this rot was and where to find it. I bit my lip, sweat dripping down my face as my heart rattled against my chest. My stomach twisted. My magic didn't like this. It wanted to retreat. But I was almost there. I just needed-

"What are you doing?" A familiar voice said from behind. I gasped for air, tugging my hand out. "Fuck, Rider!"

I fell back on my ass and stared at the owner of the voice that's been plaguing my dreams. Big dark eyes glared at me and I bit the inside of my cheek to keep from laughing.

It was Lola Luna, the vampire vet with an annoyingly gifted green thumb. She was still wearing her scrubs. They looked comfortable in the way they conformed to her curves. The ankles of scrub pants were a bit short because of her height. She had her braids tied back with a scarf and her skin was glowing against the setting sun.

"That is not funny," she said with annoyance. My lips automatically twisted into a smirk at her irritated tone.

"Did you hear me laugh?" I asked. She rolled her eyes and a part of me was thrilled whenever that happened. I loved riling up the sunshine vampire, watching her show different emotions, especially around me.

"I could see it in your eyes," she stated. I bit back a snort. One thing I always forgot about vampires was how easily they could read people. She continued to wipe away the dirt that I accidentally flung on her. "What were you doing anyway?" she asked. I glanced back at the peonies.

"The peonies need a little more water," I said, curtly. She raised an eyebrow.

"And you had to stick your entire hand in the dirt to figure that out?" she asked. I sighed, getting up and dusting my hands off.

"I just had to check things," I said, hoping that would be the end of it.

But with Lola, it never was. I turned my back on her and reached for the watering can.

"Well I'm just going to check my section. Make sure I'm still winning," she said, turning away. I scoffed. *This woman.* We've been at odds with each other ever since we were little.

My eyes flickered over to her, quickly catching a glimpse of her backside. I glanced at her side of the garden where she had planted roses. Some were red, some yellow and some pink. I hate to admit that they are blooming gorgeously.

"No one is winning yet!" I called out to her. She waved a hand.

"We'll see about that!" she said, getting on her knees in front of her plot of land. My mind began to wander. *Fuck.* Don't think about that.

I moved onto the next section when my eyes wandered back to her. She tightened the ribbon around her braids and I swallowed. She patted the ground gingerly and examined the stems of her roses.

The sun kissed her dark skin, bringing out her golden undertones. She reached for her own watering can and when she lifted her sleeve my eyes caught on something. I instinctively made my way back to my greenhouse.

After a few minutes I made my way back towards Lola with a bowl in my hand. She was pulling out some weeds when she finally looked up at me. My heart tripped at the sight. When did she become so beautiful? When did she start making me nervous and scattering my thoughts? I could have sworn the corner of her mouth twitched as if she'd read my mind.

"Yes, Rider?" she asked. Did she sound out of breath? Her lips were slightly parted, her tongue poking out to lick her full bottom lip. I held my hand out to her and she eyed me suspiciously. I motioned with my hand again. She pushed it away and stood up with an aggravated sigh. "What? I need to finish this," she said. I reached for the wrist I saw earlier and pushed up her sleeve further.

"This is a bite mark," I said, running my fingers over the indents on her skin. She hissed slightly. It was probably still tender.

"I'm a vampire, it'll heal," she said, tugging her wrist away.

18

"Shouldn't it have already?" I asked. Vampires had incredibly healing magic. Lola's nose scrunched up.

"Well, yes but…look it's not a big deal," she said, trying to pull away from me again. I bit the inside of my cheek. Lola could easily move out of my grasp, she was much stronger than me. And yet here she was, feigning weakness.

"Why hasn't it healed yet?" I pushed for an answer. When I glanced up her eyes were staring at the ground. Her nostrils flared slightly before she closed her eyes.

"I was stressed this week and so I've been skipping meals," she said softly. My stomach twisted at her confession. I wanted to tell her she should be taking better care of herself but it didn't feel like my place.

I gently rubbed my thumb across her pulse. She relaxed into my touch and it felt like a shot of victory. I began rubbing the paste I made on top of the mark. Her heartbeat was slightly fast. I wondered if it was because of my touch. Either way it doesn't matter. It would never work between us. I shut out my thoughts and focused on the task at hand. She eyed me curiously.

"What is that?" she asked.

"Crushed plantain leaves mixed with water. Has antibiotic and anti-inflammatory properties," I said. Her skin was soft beneath my fingers.

"Really? That is so cool. I wonder if I could use this at the clinic," she said. I looked at her and her eyes were sparkling as they stared at my hand working the herbal medicine onto her skin. It was cute how she got excited over these things. I bit the inside of my cheek. When the fuck did calling Lola cute become so easy for me?

"Yeah well next time don't piss off the unicorn. You're supposed to be a vet," I said. Her eyes snapped up to meet mine. There she was. I preferred Lola when she was biting off my head. That side of her I could handle without getting lost in a fantasy.

"One: how did you know it was the unicorn? Two: while I am a vet I can't always predict what a creature is going to do," she said. Her pulse fluttered beneath my fingers. I grunted and forced myself to let go of her wrist. Her heartbeat was rattling my senses.

"Just let it dry for a bit and you can wash it off later," I said, turning away.

"I hope I can wash it off before my date," she muttered. I clenched my jaw.

"You have a date?" I asked. There was a bitter taste in my mouth. I've seen Lola go on plenty of dates since returning to Lavender Falls. For some reason she preferred having them at my brother's bar. Each date was a stab to my gut. I was hoping the feeling would go away, that I would reach a point where her dating others wouldn't affect me because it shouldn't.

"I hope they can see past your competitiveness," I said, hoping to shove the jealousy down. It was a weak jab and she knew it too, because she barked out a laugh. It was deep and throaty. A tiny thrill shot through me knowing I got a laugh like that out of her.

"Some people find that attractive," she said. She batted her eyes at me and blood began flowing south. People did find that attractive– my rivalry with Lola made my heart race. "Anyway what matters is that the date ends the way I *need* it to," she said with a smirk. The tips of my ears felt warm.

I bit back a response, it would only provoke her more. I grunted and walked away. I wasn't going to continue this conversation. It always ended the same way: we argued until we were at each other's throats, and that's when the feeling of wanting my mouth against her throat would kick in. I needed to focus on the garden until my shift at the tavern tonight. I glanced back at Lola who was looking over my plot. I shook my head.

This vampire was going to be the death of me.

CHAPTER 3
THE JAKE DATE

LOLA

I was sitting impatiently at the tavern waiting for my online date to show up. My leg was bouncing up and down and my sundress was beginning to feel too tight. The last time I was in a relationship I was in college and my ex was a sweetheart– a bit too sweet. Since then I've tried dating others, but all of the men I've met have either been too full of themselves or wanted someone like their mom.

I stared at the empty seat across from me. I was always told that after graduation life would be difficult. Between finding a job and your place in the world it could get lonely. It didn't help that I knew what I wanted and that no one seemed to live up to that standard.

I wasn't even asking for much. Someone honest, who was decent at communication. Someone who cared for me and made me feel like the heroines in my romantasy books. Hot, adored, wanted, and thoroughly fu-

"Stood up, eh?" a deep voice said, sliding a glass of water in front of me. I pursed my lips and flicked a braid over my shoulder before I looked into the warm brown eyes of Flynn Kiernan. He wore an olive green shirt that stretched across his broad frame, and a black headband pulled back his wet hair. Taking a quick sniff he smelled like pine. My nose twitched, that was different.

On his days in the garden, he smelled like sunscreen and rainwater. When he spent more time working on his whiskey he would smell like citrus. But tonight it was pine and something else. His scent had notes that were darker, richer, and sexy. My canines ached to stretch. This was different.

His eyes wandered down, taking in my attire. The top of my dress dipped into a low V and was a rich lime green that made my beautiful dark skin shine. When he finally met my gaze again his cheeks were stained with pink.

"You look good in green too, Rider," I said. His hands tightened at his hips and I smiled inwardly. I laid my cheek in my hand before looking up at him from beneath my lashes. "Do you think I look good in green?" I asked, gesturing to my dress. He swallowed and I watched his throat struggle.

"You-"

"Lola?" A voice asked, cutting Flynn off. I bit back a grimace at the interruption. My eyes flickered to a man shorter than Flynn. Which meant he was shorter than me. He had tanned skin and his dark hair was brushed to one side. He wore a jersey of some kind. I stood up and reached out to shake his hand with a smile.

"Shit. I didn't think you were that tall," he said. I bit the inside of my cheek.

"Your profile says you're six feet tall and mine says I'm 5'9," I said, keeping the smile on my face. I could feel Flynn's eyes on me.

"I am six feet tall," he insisted. Flynn snorted. I tried not to make a face. I didn't need to hear Jake's heartbeat to know that he was lying. You would think as a warlock that he would know not to lie to me. We were practically the same height but for some reason people were sensitive about these things. Whatever made him sleep better at night I guess.

"Right," I said, hand still in the air. He gave me a weak handshake which made my stomach tighten. My dad always said that people who respected each other gave firm handshakes.

"Hi," he said, sliding into the seat.

"So what can I get you," Flynn said, giving Jake a bored look. Jake glanced at the bar quickly.

"What do you suggest?" Jake asked.

"Whiskey," Flynn said. Jake made a sour face.

"Whiskey is like gasoline," he commented. Flynn's lips twitched into a smirk before he glanced at me and raised an eyebrow. Despite our bickering, we both shared a love for whiskey. This man just landed his third red flag. First was being late and second was lying about his height.

"Whatever you have on tap is fine," Jake said. Flynn nodded.

"Whiskey for you, Lola?" Flynn said with a mischievous smile. *This fucker*. Jake's nose twitched.

"The water is fine, Rider," I said. Flynn grunted before turning away.

This was going to be a mistake. I knew it. Jake eyed me up and down and I fought back a chill. I was too good for this man. His eyes glanced around the room until he found the TV behind me that was playing some sports game. I could see the date unfolding in my head.

He would try to engage in small talk as the game behind us went on. His focus would be split between the game and I until I would excuse myself to the bathroom, make my way to Caleb, pay the tab and nurse a drink at the bar. He would forget that I existed as he cursed and cheered at the tv. It's what always happens. He grunted loudly, bringing me back to reality. I was still on this hellhound date.

"So you're an animal doctor?" he asked as his eyes skimmed the menu. I took in a breath. His true character was beginning to reveal itself, finally.

"A veterinarian," I corrected. He grunted.

"A doctor for animals, not humans? Too hard?" he said, jokingly. My hands clutched at my dress. I was used to this, people who would ask why animals and not humans. As if one was harder than the other. To be a human or an animal doctor requires hard work. This was his fourth red flag, no one belittled my job. I worked fucking hard to get to where I am.

"I prefer animals to humans, who have a tendency to be irritating, hypocritical, and judgmental," I said, flashing him a smile. Jake's face flushed in embarrassment. *Good*. "Anyway, you're in finance right?" I asked.

"Yes. It's a good job-" his eyes flicked over to the tv. "That was a fucking bad pass!"

✻ ● ✻ ● ✻ ● ✻ ● ✻ ● ✻

Twenty minutes later Jake was eating tacos, his eyes glued to the tv and ignoring me, just as I'd predicted. He yelled at the screen again and I leaned to the left to avoid being sprayed by his saliva. My eyes wandered around the tavern that was bustling with people in their post work routines.

Flynn was behind the bar, pouring a beer and my eyes tracked his movements as his muscles bulged. Lifting fertilizer must really be a workout. He could probably lift me up just as easily. His eyes met mine and he smirked as he glanced at Jake. I scowled.

Did my date fail? Yes. I didn't mind, they usually did. I just hated that it failed in front of Flynn. I excused myself from the table and Jake barely registered it. I headed towards Bridget who was standing behind the register. Bridget was Flynn's younger sister. She was 21 and extremely pretty with her blonde hair and brown eyes. She was taller than me and could throw anyone over her shoulder.

"He sucks," she said. "And not in the way we want him to." I giggled. While Bridget had the delicate features of an elf, she had a smart ass mouth. It's why she was my favorite Kiernan sibling.

"Sadly. Can I pay the bill? He's more interested in the game than me," I said, biting back the hurt.

"He should pay," she said, firmly. I shrugged my shoulders.

"Yeah but he seems to be enjoying the game. Why not throw in some free food," I said. I was being nice, too nice and I knew it. But the date was my idea anyway. *I* had reached out to *him*. At this point, I just wanted to wash my hands of this day. Bridget shook her head and I tapped my phone to the scanner.

"At least let me get you a drink– on the house for putting up with that dude," she offered. I smiled. Who was I to say no to a free pity drink? I slid into the corner bar stool where I would be tucked away from wandering eyes (including Jake's). Bridget turned to her brothers and I silently hoped she would ask Caleb to make my order.

Caleb's blue eyes glanced at me with a nod. I sighed. The last thing I wanted after getting bit by a unicorn, dealing with a puking pegasus, and pulling more fucking weeds from my rose garden was to listen to Flynn making jokes about my disaster date. He's already sent me knowing looks, I didn't need to hear it too.

Caleb moved to stand by Flynn who was flirting with some pixie. I swallowed hard. Flynn's eyes flickered to his brother and his eyebrows furrowed as he watched Caleb make a drink. I reached for my phone and texted my girls.

> The date was a disaster. The man couldn't look into my eyes for five seconds before wandering back to whatever game was playing on the TV.

ELLIE

> Online dating is wading through a dump filled with flying donkey shit that's on fire.

LILY

> I tried it for five seconds and said no way. I'd rather babysit baby griffins.

CRYSTAL

> I've heard horror stories

I had been best friends with Ellie and Lily since we were young. They were the women I could always count on to have my back. Crystal was Ellie's little sister and they recently reunited over winter. Eleanor was dating Flynn's grumpy brother Caleb, and Lily was dating her best friend Celestino.

They were all so cute that it made me want to puke. But in a happy way because I was happy for them. They deserved to be loved and cherished. I sighed. So did I. Was asking for romance too much? I just wanted someone to notice and care about me.

CRYSTAL
Should we do a girls night?

I smiled. Crystal was introverted much like Lily, so it was sweet of her to suggest one and surprising. I think we were slowly opening her up– that or her new friendship with Sailor.

Well after getting a bit by a unicorn today I say yes

LILY
Oh my stars! Are you okay?

ELLIE
Shit. Did you bleed?

CRYSTAL
Do you need anything?

It wasn't that deep. The unicorn apologized and Flynn rubbed some medicine on it even though I'm a vampire and I would have healed myself

ELLIE
He rubbed you?!

LILY
He RUBBED YOU????

NOT LIKE THAT

CRYSTAL
But he could...

Crystal don't be like your sister

ELLIE
Hey! I'm not a bad influence!!

Before I could respond someone tapped my forehead. I looked up from my screen to see Flynn. My mood quickly turned sour.

"Didn't last long?" he said, holding out a drink. I glanced at Caleb who shrugged his shoulders. I took the cold drink and placed my phone face down. It was futile to think I could avoid Flynn. I should have gone to The Plastered Pixies to avoid his gloating.

"Most men don't," I said. Flynn leaned his elbows on the bar. I met his eyes again. His gaze wandered around my face. They seemed darker in this lighting, I could barely see the flecks of green.

"Emphasis on *most*," he said.

"I feel like you're suggesting that you aren't like the rest," I said. His cheeks pinkened and his heart rate tripled. My stomach tightened as his scent shifted.

"Possibly," he said. I snorted.

"A possibility? So in theory you would last. But how are we going to test that?" I teased. I wanted to see how far I could push him this season before he caved.

His eyebrow twitched as his lips twisted into a thin line. He wasn't going to rebut because that would concede to trying something with me, which he was against for whatever reason.

I shrugged my shoulders, twirling my straw before taking a sip of my whiskey cocktail. Flynn's eyes glanced at my wrist which had healed quickly. My brown skin was once again smooth.

"Thanks for that by the way," I said, holding out my wrist. He nodded. Caleb handed him a basket of fries and he placed them in front of me. "What are the fries for?" I asked.

"Fries make things better," Flynn said, glancing away. I bit into a fry and my shoulders eased. He was right. The crunchy, salty goodness did make my day slightly better.

"Very true, Flynn. We can agree on that," I said. I waited for his eyes to meet mine again. They did, and softened slightly as I took a sip. "Thanks for the drink."

"Caleb made your drink," he said, his eyes hardening again. His wall was back up. I fought back a smirk. Maybe Caleb did. But I could tell Flynn did something too, because there was a hint of honey beneath the mint.

"Anyway, tomorrow is trivia night. I hope you're prepared this time," he said. Flynn looked over at my failure of a date, whose eyes were still glued to the tv. His nostrils flared and his scent shifted to something darker. It was either anger or annoyance. Either way, he was upset at Jake. I smirked. Oh charming, grumpy Flynn, you are so screwed. *And hopefully I will be too.*

"Game on, Rider."

CHAPTER 4
TRIVIA NIGHT

LOLA

I was sitting at a table in Siren's Saloon with my favorite ladies. Tonight was Trivia Thursday and therefore my favorite night. The pirate themed bar was packed with beings. Ellie was dressed in a short skirt with a pink halter top, her pink hair had returned to its natural color of auburn. Lily was dressed in mom jeans and a distressed top, while Crystal was wearing black leggings with an oversized Frankenstein graphic t-shirt.

"To trivia night!" Lily said.

"And booze," Ellie joined.

"And us," Crystal said softly.

"To beating the boys," I sang happily. We erupted into giggles as Sailor brought us a tray of food. Sailor was the only other siren in town besides Carrie, who owned the bar. He was a close friend of ours who helped save the town during the winter.

I liked Sailor a lot. He was a ball of sunshine and great on the dance floor. I was pleased he was looking more like himself. To help save the town, him, Ellie and Caleb had to go to his hometown. Sailor was from a small seaside town called Coralia Coast. According to Ellie it was all awkward.

Sailor didn't talk much about where he was from and we didn't press. But now his tan skin was returning to its normal glowy complexion and his blue eyes sparkled. He ran a hand through his blonde locks before glancing quickly at Crystal, a faint blush on his cheeks.

"Okay we have fried cajun shrimp, french fries and lemon pepper wings," he said. "Lola here is a cup of venison," he said, handing me a styrofoam cup of blood. I smiled, grateful.

With how busy things have been I've been neglecting that part of my diet. I didn't need to rely solely on blood, but I did still need it. Like how humans need water.

A waiter came by with a separate order of chili cheese fries and Sailor placed it in front of Crystal. She looked up at him in confusion.

"I-I didn't order this," she stammered. Sailor nodded.

"Yeah but you said it's your favorite, so, here you go," Sailor said. Crystal nodded and took a sip of her ginger beer.

"Sailor, are you joining the guys or just hosting?" I asked. Sailor often traded between competing and hosting when it came to trivia night at the Siren's Saloon. He offered a charming smile.

"Oh I'm with team Magic Men tonight. Are the Divine Divas ready?" he asked. We all looked at each other and nodded. I loved trivia night. Yes, because I was pretty damn good, but it was also a fun way for all of us to get together weekly despite our busy work lives.

Lily was in charge of random facts because she had a brain filled with the most peculiar knowledge. Ellie was the queen of pop culture. I ruled science, and Crystal was in charge of music.

Across our table sat the guys. Each of them was one of our rivals for trivia. Sailor versus Ellie and Crystal. Lily versus Celestino. Caleb was there for support, random interjections and mainly to be with Eleanor. Which left Flynn. He was all mine.

My eyes skirted to where he sat, drinking a beer. His brown messy hair fell forward in slight waves. He wore a beige button down shirt that was loosely tucked into nice, fitted jeans. His brown eyes looked dark in the pub's lighting and when they met mine my whole body heated up.

Since moving back and being thrown into work I found myself looking forward to Thursdays. Thursday I could hang with my friends and let loose.

But a secret part of me enjoyed it for another reason. A tiny piece of me looked forward to fighting with Flynn. I enjoyed being able to use my intelligence in a fun way, one that didn't involve tests or charts. And Flynn provided a constant challenge.

"Alright, who's ready for trivia night?" Carrie's voice rang throughout the pub. We sat excitedly in our seats. My eyes cut to Flynn who already had a delicious smirk on his face. I rolled my eyes, biting back a smile. At the moment there were four groups participating in trivia night.

"Y'all know the rules. Wait for me to finish the question. First hand up answers and no funny business, meaning no powers. I'm a siren. My eyesight is better than some of you paranormals," she said, glaring at team Magic Men. Celestino awkwardly coughed while Sailor absent-mindedly looked around.

There were two incidents that required Carrie to implement rules. The first was when Flynn and I kept cutting her off on her questions and she threatened to feed us to some sharks. The second was when Sailor used his reflexes to lift Celestino's hand to answer a question.

"First question. What are the seeds on a strawberry called?" Carrie asked. My eyes widened and I threw my hand up. "Flynn."

"They're called fruitlets," he said. I groaned inwardly. Crystal patted my arm with a small smile.

"What 2007 show involves a pastry chef bringing people back to life?" Carrie asked. From the corner of my eye Lily's hand shot up at lightning speed. "Lily."

"Pushing Daisies!" Lily said, happily. I shook my head. Our witch has always been obsessed with that show. I think she watches it every year. Carrie added a point to our name. I sat back in my seat and took a sip of my drink.

"Who sang the song "Guess Who I Saw Today"?" Carried asked. Crystal jumped in her seat nearly making me spill my drink. The tables laughed. "Crystal."

"Nancy Wilson," Crystal said with a faint blush on her cheeks. Carrie nodded.

"Sailor, you should have been faster," Flynn said.

"You boys are slacking," I teased, taking a bite of shrimp.

"Just you wait, Sunflower," Flynn smirked. His eyes were bright with a mysterious thrill that sent my body buzzing.

"Who is the mascot for Miami's futsal team, The Falling Iguanas?" Carried asked. *Oh fuck.* I knew who was going to get this. Carrie pointed at our enemies table.

"Iggy the iguana," Celestino said, confidently.

"Are bananas radioactive?" Carrie asked. I stared at her in confusion. "Flynn."

"Yes," Flynn said. I looked at him and raised an eyebrow. "Some foods carry small amounts of radioactive elements. Bananas have potassium and a small fraction of all potassium is radioactive," he explained. I stared in wonder.

"No way," I said, turning in my seat, my interest immediately peaked. Flynn's eyes glowed in excitement.

"Brazilian nuts are as well," he said with a gentle smile. My heart squeezed. This is why I always looked forward to trivia night. It was in these moments, when we weren't arguing but just two supernatural beings sharing a love of science, in these brief seconds Flynn would let down his guard and allow me to truly see him. I got a peek behind his grumpiness and saw a man who was loving and bright.

Flynn was the type to be annoyed at Caleb for spending too much time with Eleanor while also telling him he would take his shifts if he wanted to have a date night. Carrie snapped her fingers refocusing our attention on the game. I ignored the girls' stares.

"Alright you two, back to trivia. Do platypuses sweat milk?" Carrie asked. My brain must have short circuited because my hand went up a second later than Lily's.

"They do," Lily said with a grin. I glanced at Celestino quickly who was staring at his girlfriend in adoring shock. I leaned across the table.

"How did you know that?" I asked her. Lily giggled into her drink.

"I watched a lot of Phineas and Ferb and got curious about them," she said.

"That's my Posey," Celestino said proudly. Sailor pushed his shoulder.

"Your *Posey* is the enemy for at least twenty more minutes," Caleb pointed out.

"I only call her that, remember," Celestino said. Lily blushed at her man.

The rest of the night continued with everyone going back and forth. Occasionally I would glance at Flynn who would be speaking to the guys, flirting with the waitress, or playfully glaring at me.

I tried not to get jealous whenever he would throw a seemingly care-free smile at the waitress. She got to have his flirty banter sans attitude. Flynn helped her clear the table. I knew he was doing it because he himself did that same job occasionally but that didn't stop my stomach from twisting with jealousy. The waitress flipped her hair over her shoulder as she laughed at whatever joke he said. Crystal bumped my hip and I offered her a smile.

We all stood around the bar as Sailor poured us more drinks. "Well boys I guess it wasn't your week, was it?" Eleanor said with a smile. Caleb slipped an arm around her waist before whispering something in ear that made her bat her eyelashes.

"Victory tastes good," Lily said, sipping her drink. Celestino kissed her cheek and I redirected my attention to Crystal.

"You were on it with the music facts," I said. She smiled shyly. While Eleanor was a bright, sassy ball of sunshine, Crystal was slightly reclusive.

"I honestly surprised myself," Crystal said. Sailor handed her a cup of water with a princely smile.

"I did get you with the 98 Degrees fact," Sailor teased. Crystal rolled her eyes.

"I would have gotten it but you're a siren and therefore stupidly fast," she grumbled. I wrapped my arm around her shoulders.

"Next time we'll team up to take Sailor down," I said, holding up my fist. Crystal grinned and bumped my fist with a nod.

My phone buzzed in my pocket. It was a notification from the clinic. I had the cameras set up to detect motion. The unicorn was ready to give birth at any time and the Pegasi were still throwing up, although they were doing better. I patted Crystal's shoulder and motioned that I would be right back.

I made my way to the back of the bar, near the bathrooms where there was less noise. Checking the cameras, I saw the unicorn pacing back and forth in her pen. I chewed my lip. I wished I knew more about unicorns.

But even the best vets in the world didn't have much information. Unicorns rarely came in contact with anyone. They kept to themselves, deep in the forests. The fact that she had come to town and was letting me take care of her and her unborn child was a mystery.

I knew Flynn suspected that there was something wrong in the forest. Our garden was slowly rotting, and I was getting more and more injured animals in the clinic. I patted my braids on the side of my head, switching to the pegasi camera. They were still fast asleep. That was good. I switched back to the unicorn.

"Everything okay?" I looked up to see Flynn standing in front of me. The smell of pine invaded my senses. His heartbeat was steady and his body was relaxed.

"Just checking on the unicorn. She's still recovering and has been a bit antsy lately," I said, eyes flickering back to the camera. Flynn leaned forward slightly and his warmth washed over me. I bit the inside of my cheek. My pulse picked up at his nearness.

"I know a few herbs that might be able to help," he offered. "She's having stomach problems, right?"

My lips twitched and I met his gaze again. His pupils slowly dilated and a faint blush surfaced across his cheeks. His scent began shifting. What had started as just his new cologne (*a mix of pine and sandalwood*) was now laced with the scent of his attraction. I took a deep breath, enjoying the way it tasted on my tongue. He had no idea what he did to me.

"You would help me?" I said, setting a bait. He rolled his pretty eyes at me.

"You're using the garden for those remedies anyway. Might as well use me for my knowledge," he said. My face broke out in a smile as his eyes widened in realization of what he just said.

"Just your knowledge?" I asked, taking a step forward cautiously. I didn't want Flynn to snap away like he usually did. He stood his ground, a tick in his jaw. *Good.* Him pushing me away only made my vampire side want to go after him more.

"Lola," he warned. I shivered.

"Do use that tone with me again, Flynn. It gives me tingles in all the right places," I teased. Beating him at trivia felt like foreplay and now I was ready for more. The corner of his lips quivered. "Come on. You can flirt with the waitress and not me?" I said, knowing that I was revealing my jealousy.

Flynn's eyes sharpened and he stepped forward causing me to step back and hit the wall behind me. Now I had him hooked. The music was still blaring but it felt like we were in our own bubble. My chest brushed against his and my body tightened.

"Do you want me to flirt with you Sunflower?" he asked as his fingers grazed my cheek. I felt our pulses jump, nearly in unison. My eyes widened. This was not Flynn. Flynn was never this bold with me. Maybe the drinking and the heat of the game caused him to forget himself.

Regardless I was grateful because this is what I've been wanting. I wanted a sign so I didn't feel like I was losing it or just imagining what I was sensing.

Without hesitating I nodded my head slightly. He took another step forward, our chests pressing against each other. His body was deliciously warm against mine. His eyelashes fluttered as his eyes traveled down my face to my lips. I clutched my phone against the wall.

"Should I flirt with you? Drive you frantic with desire? Have you *beg* me to kiss you?" His voice caressed my body. I blinked, regaining my composure. My tongue swiped against my bottom lip.

"If anyone is going to beg, Flynn. It's going to be you," I said, slightly breathless. The scent of arousal between us was making my fangs ache again. This is what I've been wanting, craving. It was intoxicating and I needed more.

His finger traced down my neck and I bit my bottom lip to keep the whimpers at bay. Everything he did heightened my senses and now that he was touching me I felt like a live wire. I had never felt this attracted to someone in my entire life. There was a desperate need to lose myself in him. My fangs were begging me to taste him.

"I think I could have you on your knees," he said, as his finger made its way back up my neck.

"You would look much better on your knees, Pretty Boy," I said. My hand moved to push a strand of hair behind his ear. His pulse picked up again.

"I shouldn't be doing this," he admitted softly. He finally looked at me and I saw something I never thought I would see on Flynn Kiernan.

Wistful.

This was definitely not the elf I knew. Grumpy, intelligent, flirty, sarcastic, and humorous were his usual states of being. This was different. I wanted to erase this look from his face. I hummed, my fingers playing with the hair at the nape of his neck, encouraging him, bringing his focus onto me.

"Flynn. You're making this feel like a challenge and you know I'm competitive," I said, hoping to break the spell that clouded his eyes. His eyes sparked and I couldn't help but smile. He was slowly coming back to me.

"Is this another bet?" he asked. I took a quick breath. The elf was slowly making me crumble in the back of this bar. I tilted my neck, giving his hand more access before staring into his eyes again. I don't think he even realized the importance of me offering my neck. The fact that I didn't hesitate to do so told me that what I was doing was right. My instincts were right. As a vampire I was taught to trust my senses. They would lead me to the truth, always. And the truth was, Flynn was *mine*.

My tongue darted forward to lick my bottom lip. My fangs had grown slightly and I offered him a smirk. I felt his pulse pick up once again, blood rushing.

"Is it a bet if I win?" I said, dropping my tone, luring him in. He let out a dark chuckle and I couldn't help but grin.

"You think you'll win?" His lips teased my ear before pulling back to look at me.

"I like being on top," I said. His eyes widened and I could tell he liked that. Someone called out his name from behind and in a flash Flynn ripped away from me. He ran a hand through his hair and I could tell whatever bubble we were in had popped. Flynn was retreating.

"Flynn," I said. He stared at the bar before looking back at me. "I hope you've realized you've given me a taste of you," I said, crossing my arms. He snorted, shaking his head. His brown eyes darkened as they focused on me.

"You want a taste, Lola Luna? You're going to have to do more than flash a fang to make me break," he said. I shrugged my shoulders.

"Then that's the bet. Let's see who ends up giving in first," I said.

"And what is the prize?" he said. My phone vibrated again. I glanced at it quickly. I needed to check on the unicorn. I walked towards him and patted his chest.

"Each other," I said. Flynn was going to be mine by the spring festival.

CHAPTER 5
SMALL TOWN TALK

FLYNN

"So I heard you and Ms. Luna were getting pretty cozy on trivia night," My older brother Greg teased. The tips of my ears heated. I glared at him.

"I don't know what you're talking about," I grumbled, handing him a bundle of cilantro and dill. He nodded as he took them.

"Did you forget we live in a small town, Flynn?" he said with a mischievous glint. I rolled my eyes.

"There is nothing cozy between Lola and me," I said. My brother once again nodded, his eyes giving me a cheeky look. "Greg," I warned. He ran a hand through his growing gray beard.

"What? You think no one knows about you two? Did you forget you weren't the only people at Siren's Saloon on Thursday," he said. I shook my head. There wasn't anything between us.

Sure we had an endless rivalry and a multitude of bets constantly going but there was no *us*. There couldn't be an *us*. We had too much shit happening. My hands twitched because I knew the real reason I was keeping her away from my heart.

I don't know what compelled me to get close to her that night. It was a mixture of seeing her on a date, exhaustion and alcohol. I had a sour taste in my mouth thinking about that Jake guy. The man couldn't give Lola two seconds of time before his eyes wandered up to the stupid game. For phoenix' sake he had a goddess sitting in front of him and a stupid football game was more important.

"How's the new whiskey coming?" Greg asked. I shrugged my shoulders, watching him maneuver around the kitchen with ease. He began kneading some dough. His hands moved instinctively, reaching for more flour. Greg was always in his element when he was baking. He knew what he wanted to do from a young age. He had always been self assured and reliable. I rocked on my heels.

A floating feeling worked its way through me. I felt untethered, lost within my own family even though I knew it was wrong to feel that way. My brother Greg was the head pastry chef of Grandmother's Patisserie. Caleb co-owned The Drunken Fairy Tale Tavern.

Growing up cursed made our mother worry about him all the time. Due to an accidental spell casted by my sister he wasn't allowed to lock lips. That is, until last winter when Eleanor helped break it. My sister Bridget had just graduated, and while she didn't have an idea of what she wanted to do in life no one worried about her. She was headstrong and stubborn like the rest of us and excelled at everything.

Each of my siblings had a certain amount of attention and talent, and that made me feel like an outsider. I thought that I needed to constantly prove that I was important, that I should be looked at for just half a second longer. I grew up relentlessly helping out because I wanted to be needed. Greg shot me a smile and my stomach twisted.

I hated when I had these thoughts. I would beat myself up for thinking this way. I had a wonderful family that cared about me and stood by me. Mind you, I was successful in my own right. I was the lead developer at our family whiskey distillery. I ran the community garden and I was occasionally a bartender at my brother's pub. My family *was* proud of me.

And yet somehow I still felt like I had one foot on the path and the other in the unknown. It was stupid to be locked in this swirling cloud of self-loathing. I shook my head. Shaking off this feeling was a constant mental struggle, one that I didn't need right now.

I needed to check on the baby Hollow Tree. Something is still poisoning the grounds of Lavender Falls and I need to uncover what it is before the spring festival.

"It's going. Just trying to nail this flavor combo," I said.

"Lola could help you," Greg offered. I sighed. He wasn't going to quit.

"Greg, I don't have time for all of that. I have a shit ton of work to do," I said. He pointed to a package of honey bread and I tucked it under my arm.

"Do you not remember everything that Caleb and Eleanor went through last season? They still found time," he said. I rolled my eyes. "Multiple times, according to the town gossip."

"That was different," I said. Greg snorted.

"Please explain how, the last time I checked you didn't have a curse," he said as he folded dough into loaves. I swallowed. That was true. Unlike Caleb I had nothing keeping me from Lola. Only myself. I just wasn't in the right place for a relationship and she deserves someone better.

"Listen, I have to go check on the tree," I said.

✳ ❖ ✳ ❖ ✳ ❖ ✳ ❖ ✳ ❖ ✳

THE GASPING GREENWOOD FOREST, despite the name, wasn't typically that scary. However, lately the rot has given it a slightly more haunted feel. Patches of dead leaves hung in the corners of the trees where it should be sprouting new growth. You could barely hear any creatures skirting around.

We've all been working overtime to heal everything and I have a theory. What Eleanor did to help the Hollow Tree be reborn as sapling worked. However, I think there was a piece of rot from the original tree somewhere in the ground. A piece of root must have broken off. I just haven't been able to locate it yet.

Priscilla thinks I'm correct but the forest is so massive we haven't figured out how to track it all. Every time I check my garden, I dig my hand into the ground. I have an inclination towards natural magic. The closer I am to it, the deeper the connection I can make. Just when I think I'm going to touch the rot and find it my magic weakens and I'm forced to break away.

The Hollow Tree was near Hale's Lumber Industry, which was owned by Eleanor's family. They'd had a rough patch but Eleanor's father has been a big help with trying to solve this mystery. Just as I was entering the clearing where the sapling is, Eleanor's father walked by.

"Hello Flynn," he said curtly. Mr. Hale had the same tan skin as Eleanor and his auburn hair was graying. I nodded.

"Any updates?" I said, pointing to the tree. His lips twisted.

"I think your theory is correct, but I'm not sure why we're struggling to track the source of it," he said, crossing his arms. "I don't know how it keeps evading us."

I glanced at the sapling. It was about two feet tall now with growing branches and baby leaves. The trees surrounding it almost looked hunched over as if protecting it.

"Once we can figure that out we will be fine. But stars, is it destroying crops fast," I said. Every day something in the garden wilted and every day we had to use potions and spells to keep the rot at bay.

Hale's Lumber Industry was providing fresh soil and wood for us, thankfully. We had to build raised garden beds for everyone. Mr. Hale turned to look at the tree but his eyesight went further. He was staring deep into the forest as if trying to locate something.

"It's almost time for the festival. Hopefully we'll figure it out by then," he said. I nodded.

"Hopefully," I said, my hands fidgeting at my sides. We didn't have enough flowers for the parade yet. I needed this issue gone before the festival.

"This town is resilient. I have faith that everything will work out as intended," he said. There were plenty of moments where I forgot that Mr. Hale had grown up in Lavender Falls. He spent so much time away being an egotistical, arrogant ass. But ever since the winter he's displayed less ass-like qualities.

"Thanks by the way. Maybe you're not such an ass," I said, easily. Like Caleb and Bridget I had no issues with speaking my mind. Greg on the other hand was a bit of a softy. Mr. Hale glared at me. He opened his mouth and closed it for a second.

"Your statement is valid as I have shone parts of me that are..." he trailed off.

"Ass like?" I said with a grin. Mr. Hale sighed.

"Yes, yes. Anyway, back to work. I'll keep you posted," he said walking away. Mr. Hale wasn't the nicest person according to Eleanor, Lily and Celestino.

I wasn't really around them enough to know much about him growing up. I just knew that Eleanor and him had a massive falling out once she had attended college. Because of it she spent years away from her sister. All was well now that he was going to therapy and saw the error of his ways.

I quietly knelt in front of the tree and placed my hand at the base of the trunk. There was a trickle of electricity as my magic jumped from my fingertips and into the ground. Instantly my magic cracked through the dirt and weaved its way in.

First it wrapped around the roots of the Hollow Tree, double checking that everything was intact. The roots were consuming proper nutrients, the water levels felt good, and the growth rate was steady. My magic released the tree and I focused on the surrounding vegetation.

I took a deep breath. I focused on ignoring the weeds, grubs and other organic matter. I was searching for something sickly and grimy. My fingers twitched. I felt a trickle of something towards the left of the forest, near the Cosmic Campground. Cosmic Campground was a tiny part of the Gasping Greenwood Forest that was used for camping, stargazing and bonfires.

A sharp pain rang up my hand. "Fuck," I grunted. I yanked my hand out of the dirt and fell backwards. My heart pounded in my chest as I stared at the ground. My hand shook slightly. Well *that* was an interesting development. That little fucker shoved me.

CHAPTER 6

WOAH, NESSIE!

FLYNN

I was walking out of the forest when I noticed there were a few sprites gathering around Boogeyman's Swamp. The swamp water was a deep blue color, and bubbling. My brows furrowed as I got closer. I noticed Carrie was kneeling by the water.

A sprite flew up to me, her tiny face was scrunched up with worry as she pointed at the water. Carrie pulled her red hair back into a bun.

"Hey! What's up?" I asked. Carrie dipped her hand into the water. She was the owner of the Siren's Saloon and was from Coralia Coast, like Sailor.

"I think Nessie has made her annual trip to Lavender Falls but she seems off," Carrie said. Her green eyes were focused on the water. Looking closely, I saw green scales breaking the surface of the water. Nessie loved visiting Lavender Falls every spring.

A hundred years ago Nessie was kidnapped and taken across the states to show off. One of Carrie's ancestors (who founded the Siren Saloon) had saved her and since then, she'd vowed to visit the town that gave her freedom.

"Call Lola, Flynn," Carrie ordered as her fingertips brushed Nessie's scales. I nodded. Taking out my phone I stared at it. *Fuck.* I didn't have Lola's number. I had Celestino's who most likely had hers. Was she at the clinic or the garden? Double fuck. My heart rattled against my chest. I shook my head and called Celestino.

"What's up Flynn?" he asked.

"I don't have Lola's number. Nessie is here and she isn't looking well," I said. Celestino cursed.

"Got it. Wait, why don't you have her number?" he asked. I rolled my eyes.

"Call her now, please," I said, ignoring his question.

※ ● ※ ● ※ ● ※ ● ※ ● ※

TEN MINUTES later Carrie and I had our pants rolled up and we were both in the water. Carrie was rubbing Nessie's neck. Nessie's head reminded me of a garter snake. She had blue green scales in different shades all around her body. She was basically an underwater dragon and yet she was the sweetest thing.

Right now however she wasn't looking so sweet right now. Her eyes were droopy and her pupils dilated. I wasn't a vet but even I knew that something was off. She popped up to the surface of the water to let Carrie rub her forehead before diving back down and swimming in circles.

"I'm here!" Lola called out. I turned around to see her, running with a tackle box, her braids swinging side to side and wearing loose black scrubs. She stared wide-eyed at Nessie. "What happened?" she asked. I turned to Carrie who had stepped out of the water.

"I'm not sure. The sprites stopped me and pulled me over. The water doesn't feel sickly but there is definitely something off. I think Nessie is sick," Carrie said. Lola nodded and placed her tackle box at the edge of the water before removing her shoes. Water sloshed around me as I watched the girl I knew transform into a powerful, brilliant woman. She squared her shoulders before stepping into the water.

45

"Hey Nessie. It's Lola, remember me?" she said softly. Nessie popped up her head and snorted some water. Lola gave her an endearing smile and I couldn't look away from her. She glided her hands side to side in the water. For a second I stopped breathing as her eyes began to glow. Her breathing shifted, matching Nessie's who slowly swam towards her. "What's up my beautiful Nessie," she asked.

Nessie tilted her head and let out a noise. Lola nodded. *Could she understand her?* Something began itching in the back of my head. Vampires tended to have an affinity for something. *Some nature or tech and some–* Her shoulders tightened and her eyebrows scrunched in the middle. Something was wrong. I took a step towards her.

"Oh. Okay. Well I can help with that," she said. For a second her eyes flashed with worry. She glanced at me. "This is not the kind of wet that I want to be," she mumbled.

"Lola, *focus*," I said, pointing at Nessie who was emerging further out of the water. Fuck, Nessie had to be at least 20 feet tall. Water rained down on us. I glanced at her belly which was protruding. Nessie's head once again began swaying.

"I am focused and I can tell you that I was not prepared to dive into the Boogeyman's Swamp today," she said. Nessie's head dropped and her eyes closed briefly.

Poor gal must have had a rough trip on her way to Lavender Falls. We always enjoyed having Nessie here every spring season. She swam in a circle again, trying to get comfortable.

"Are you okay?" Lola asked. I glanced over at her, as she pulled her braids into a bun. My hand was still trembling slightly from when I was in the forest.

"Something happened when I was checking up on the tree," I said, flexing my hand. Lola's fingers gently lifted my hand and a flush crawled up my face.

"What happened?" she asked, softly. Her fingers began massaging my hand and my body relaxed. The leftover magic from getting zapped had tensed up my muscles. I could feel Carrie's eyes on us, watching.

"Um...I got zapped," I said. Lola's eyes widened.

"Stars, by what?" she asked, her fingers tracing circles on my palm. Slowly the trembles faded.

"I have a theory-" I had begun to say until I heard Nessie whining again. It was a high-pitch sound that sounded painful. Lola moved back towards Nessie who let her pat her head. I took a step forward as Nessie dived under the water. Water rose up then fell from the sky as she lifted her head back out of the water.

"Does Nessie look a little green to you?" I asked. Lola rolled her eyes. Nessie's head hung above Lola and her throat moved. My eyes widened.

"Flynn. It's Nessie, she's always green. Although she is also-" Before Lola could finish her sentence, I shoved her away as chunks of fish began raining down on me. Lola looked at me, her dark eyes wide with horror.

Sloshes of saliva, ocean water and fish guts coated my body. I stood in the water, arms out as if that would keep more of the inside of Nessie's stomach from coating my soaking body.

"She's what, Lola," I said through gritted teeth. The last thing I wanted was half digested fish in my mouth. Lola winced.

"Nessie is pregnant."

CHAPTER 7
ONE SHOWER ONLY

LOLA

I didn't laugh. I wanted to laugh but I didn't. It took every ounce of self control to not laugh at Flynn who was now quietly brooding and covered in Nessie's guts. I glanced back at the Boogeyman's Swamp. I wasn't surprised that Nessie was visiting us. She always did, every spring season. She was a part of the spring festival. People thought of her as an animatronic and she would do fun rides for the kids around the swamp.

What worried me was that she was pregnant. She looked tired and squeamish, hence the puke. But given the fact that our soil isn't in the best state I doubt that the swamp's water is in good shape either. I scratched the back of my neck. I would have to talk to Priscilla about a way to keep the water of Boogeyman's Swamp clean. I glanced back at Flynn.

Despite being covered in stomach parts his skin was beginning to take on a glow from working out in the sun. My mind raced back to both of us being in water. His face was twisted in concern for Nessie. It made my heart flutter to see how much care he had for magical creatures.

And then he shoved me out of the way. Flynn cared. He did. I wasn't sure why he was hiding it. Why didn't Flynn call me? I bit the inside of my cheek.

Beings eyed us as we walked by and some of them even held their noses. I didn't blame them. Flynn reeked. It took everything in me not to gag. But as a vet I was used to funky smells like this. What *didn't* help was being a vampire with a sensitive nose.

"Nessie has a stomach ache," I said to the townsfolk as we walked back. I didn't want them to know about Nessie's pregnancy until I had a better read on the water and knew she would be okay.

In a few minutes word would get around that Nessie was in town and had puked on Flynn. Which meant people would be sympathetic towards Flynn's attitude. He did his best to shrug his shoulders and give people a helpless smile. His eyes would soften at people walking by, and a gentle laughter would occasionally huff out of him. The second they were past him the facade would drop and so would my heart.

I didn't realize how good he was at pretending. Now I wondered if it was something he always did. Lily had a tendency to wear a mask, hiding herself away from the world. Has Flynn been doing the same? I could see that the more the fish guts dried on his skin the more agitated he became.

Highwayman's Haunt was in view which meant we were almost to my apartment. When I decided to move back to Lavender Falls I had become accustomed to living on my own and thus moved into my own place. My parents hesitated before I mentioned that my bedroom could be turned into a library. Granted I did a whole powerpoint presentation and devised layout plans to convince my mom.

I motioned to Flynn to follow behind me into the alley way where there was a separate staircase leading up to my apartment. Once inside my place I ran to the bathroom.

"The shower can be a bit finicky. I have to get the plumbing fixed," I said as he stood outside the bathroom door. I looked over at him quickly. His eyes were scrunched in the middle and his lips turned downward in almost a pout. He looked adorable. When did Flynn become adorable? I twisted the knobs in opposite directions.

"What's wrong with it?" he asked, crossing his arms, grimacing at the feel of his skin.

"Well I switched the shower heads and some of the water spray out haphazardly so that's why it's facing the direction of the wall and then for some reason hot is cold and cold is hot so I have to dial them at the correct rotation so it's at a good temperature," I said, stepping back and closing the curtain.

"Why not get it fixed?" he asked. I rolled my eyes.

"Maybe because I've been busy between every creature getting sick and the community garden," I said, a slight bite to my tone. I sighed. "That was rude. It was a long night with the unicorn," I said. Flynn nodded and I reached under the sink for a towel.

"You take a shower first," he said. I shook my head.

"You're literally covered in guts. You," I said. Before I could step out Flynn closed the door leaving me alone in the bathroom. Of course he would be stubborn. I bit back a smile. Flynn Kiernan was secretly a knight in tin-can armor. I bet beneath his grumpy exterior and erratic charm was a heart waiting to be loved.

✻ ❀ ✻ ❀ ✻ ❀ ✻ ❀ ✻

I TOOK the quickest shower of my life and wrapped myself in a robe before stepping out. Flynn was standing behind my couch, staring out the window. My chest ached. He definitely should have showered first.

He was standing there, unable to touch anything, probably bored out of his mind. I tilted my head in curiosity. His eyes had a sunken look and his face was painted in loneliness.

Something in his expression made me ache to wrap my arms around him and ease his worries. I'm not quite sure when these feelings for my rival started but I think they've always been there, below the surface of every bet, smirk and smart remark.

He flexed his hand and I remember him mentioning how he was zapped. I bit my bottom lip in worry. Despite the pain he must have been in he stopped to help Nessie and protected me from getting puked on. I tiptoed towards him and lightly brushed his elbow. His eyes widened and he pulled back in surprise.

"You can go now," I said, gaining his attention. Flynn's cheeks slightly flushed. He nodded silently and I stepped out of his path.

"There is a towel on the sink. Take as long as you need. I do suggest scrubbing twice to get the smell out. Trust me. And then you can use my lotion afterwards," I said. "I'll see if I can find some clothes for you while I put yours in the wash. Just drop them outside the door."

"Okay," he said with a strangled tone. He avoided meeting my gaze which only made me hunger for it more.

Once the door closed I sucked in a giant breath. This was the first time I had a man over at my apartment that I wasn't related to or in a platonic relationship with. This was the first time *Flynn* was here and what I've been feeling lately was anything but platonic. Even though we were separated by a door I felt him in my space. His presence was like a warm embrace.

I glanced around my one bedroom apartment. It was clean. Too clean. Probably because I was beginning to spend nights at the clinic. Which reminded me that I needed to pack an overnight bag again. My stomach growled. I haven't had lunch and neither has Flynn most likely.

"One thing at a time," I said, out loud. There was a thump behind me and when I turned around Flynn was closing the door, his bare shoulder in my eye-line. I bit the inside of my cheek. Flynn Kiernan was showering in my shower. He was naked in my bathroom. The thought made my blood pump faster and my fangs stretch. I closed my eyes briefly. First, his clothes needed to go in the wash.

✳ ❖ ✳ ❖ ✳ ❖ ✳ ❖ ✳

AFTER HANDLING his clothes I grabbed some leftovers. Rice, Lily's *carne guisada* and some bread from Godmother's Patisserie. I was grateful I had some food in my fridge. It was looking sparse with the amount of hours I was spending at the clinic. While that heated up I went back to the bathroom and knocked on the door.

"I found some clothes," I called out.

"Come in," Flynn said. When I opened the door a puff of steam came out. My nose twitched at the smell. The entire bathroom smelled like sage and citrus mixed with Flynn's natural scent. This was a horrible idea. I definitely should not be here.

A thin curtain separated us and my body trembled. His smell was invading my senses and it made my blood hum underneath my skin. I wanted to yank the curtain back, step into the shower and kiss him, bite him. My blood was calling for him. My heart hammered in my chest. Never had my blood, my magic ever called to another being with such intensity, or at all really.

"Lola?" he called out, pulling me back to the present.

"It's a shirt from my dad and some old sweatpants from college," I said, placing the clothes on the sink. The water died down a bit as I assume Flynn moved away from the shower head.

"College?" he asked. His voice was deeper than I'd heard it. My nose twitched. Did his scent shift to jealousy or was I just lacking sleep? I stared at myself in the mirror, cheeks slightly flushed. My braids were piled on top of my hair. I needed to get them rebraided soon.

"Um. They're an ex's. It's all I have that will fit you while your clothes are being cleaned. I have some lunch for us too," I said. I didn't wait for a response and hightailed it out of the bathroom. I sucked in a deep breath once back in my living room.

A second longer and I would have jumped into the shower. I was so fucking screwed. I thought winning the bet would be easy. I thought I could make Flynn cave but I didn't account for the way this elf man reeled me in. Whether it was his scent, his honey eyes, his brain or his snarky attitude I couldn't wrap my head around what kept drawing me closer to him.

What I did know was that I could easily lose this bet.

CHAPTER 8
APARTMENT

Flynn

While she was in the shower I did my best to focus on everything I needed to do and not on the beautiful vampire that was wet and naked behind that stupid door. I needed to check on the garden and possibly head back to the Hollow Tree for another round of magic. The last time I was there I was so close to figuring out where the rotten root was.

I told Lola I would help find whatever herbs she needed for her clinic. I grimaced. A baby unicorn and now a baby Loch Ness monster on top of her having to be extra careful with the vegetation she feeds the creatures of the clinic. I couldn't imagine the stress she was under.

My hands clenched at my sides. I cringed at the feeling of dried guts on my skin. I should have showered first. But my concern at the moment wasn't the fact that I was covered in monster puke– it was Lola. My heart thumped against my chest.

Lola was taking over my thoughts and I wasn't sure how I felt about it. On one end, I wanted to push her away. She was someone who poured joy into life while I lived with my head in a storm cloud. She was pulling me towards her orbit and I was nervous about raining on her sunshine. But another part of me craved her light.

My eyes wandered around her apartment. She had pictures of the girls and her family everywhere, along with knick knacks. Her coffee table was littered with books about science and gardening. The corner of my lips tugged up. She had always been studious.

I continued to peruse, trying to learn more about the girl I once knew, now a woman. Her apartment was immaculate, spotless. I cocked my head to the side. It was too clean. It looked like something out of a magazine. *Has she been sleeping at the clinic?* I bet with her nightly visits she must be.

The door creaked open and I could feel her stare on me. It heated my skin and gave me goosebumps. I just needed to get through this and leave before I tugged her against my body and kissed the stars out of her.

✳ ❖ ✳ ❖ ✳ ❖ ✳ ❖ ✳

I TUGGED at her dad's shirt. It fit me fine and I didn't mind wearing it. I liked Lola's dad. Just like Lola, he was warm and kind with the biggest smile. And he liked my whiskey. He was one of our best customers. Actually, now that my body and brain were clean of fish guts I remembered that I had an order for him to pick up sometime this week.

What I *didn't* like was the fact that she still had (and most likely wore) her ex's sweatpants. Which was why I was sitting at her dining room table with my lower half wrapped in a towel.

I sat across the table from Lola Luna having lunch and realized that this was the first time we were sharing a meal together…*alone.* The times we had eaten together were always due to school or our group of friends.

But this time it was just us, in her apartment, and it was giving me warm fuzzy feelings. I snuck a glance at her as she dipped her bread into the *carne guisada* to grab a piece of beef.

From this vantage point and unbeknownst to her, I could see how the past few weeks have been straining for her. Her eyes dropped slightly and her shoulders were tight. Her gaze met mine briefly and she gave me a smile. It felt like a punch to my chest.

Growing up, Lola was always like a ray of sunshine. To me she was a positive light in my bleak world. Lola gave smiles to everyone she met and every creature she took care of. She was the first to lend a helping hand, first to check up on others and last to help clean up.

But watching her now it felt...performative. She was trying her best to make her smile reach her eyes. She was trying hard to keep it together and that bothered me. It bothered me because I could relate, and I didn't want to see Lola's light dimmed.

I shifted in my seat, the towel rubbing against my thighs. Lola cleared her throat. I raised an eyebrow.

"Why don't you have my number?" she asked, before taking a bite of some rice. I tilted my head. I had everyone's number– except Lola's. "Tino called me," she pointed out. There was a flicker of hurt in her eyes.

"I don't think there's been a time where I've needed your number," I said, earnestly. "I never needed you for anything," I said. Her eyes dropped. I swallowed. That was the wrong thing to say. The pain in her eyes was more noticeable but she recovered quickly and stretched her lips into a teasing grin.

"Well I guess it would make sense for you to have it now, especially with the spring festival," she said confidently.

"Sure, or I could just keep reaching out to our friends or your dad," I said. Her eyes snapped to me, heated.

"You have my dad's number and not mine?" she said in shock. I chuckled.

"He's one of my best customers," I said, nonchalantly. Her lips twisted in a frown. "Jealous?" I teased. Lola narrowed her brown eyes.

"Yes, Flynn. I want you to have my number," she admitted. "With everything going on you should have it. What if you run into a wild creature? Or you somehow get stuck in quicksand?" she added quickly. Her fingers tapped against the table. Her eyes kept flicking between me and the wall.

Was she nervous? A tiny thrill ran through me at the thought that there was a possibility that she could feel for me a fraction of what I felt for her.

"Lavender Falls doesn't have quicksand." I crossed my arms and leaned back in my seat. I couldn't stop the smirk on my face from spreading. "Do you just want me to have your number?" Lola's eyes widened but in her true nature she once again recovered quickly, tossing her braids over her shoulder. I think I was beginning to understand her more. This confidence she wore on her sleeve was more of a shield from her real emotions.

"Yes I do. It'll make you caving in first, and me winning that bet easier," she said confidently. I chuckled.

"Think you can win me over with a couple of texts?" I teased. Her eyes traveled around my face, drinking me in. My hands twitched at my side.

We were flirting, and when we flirted Lola had a habit of making me lose all sense of control. Her tongue peeked out to swipe across her bottom lip. She was teasing me. Fuck, I wanted to kiss her. My dick was half hard under the flimsy towel just thinking about it.

"I can win you over in a number of ways. I just haven't decided which will be the most rewarding," she said. If I responded, she would have a better comeback and it would lead us down a rabbit hole that would end with us on top of her dining room table.

It didn't matter how much I wanted her, we weren't a good match. Lola needed someone who matched her energy. She didn't need someone who constantly had to work to be happy and struggled to find his footing.

"Sweatpants didn't fit?" she asked after a few minutes of eating in silence. I felt my lips twitch. I had been waiting for her to bring this up. I knew she would. I guess I was a hypocrite. I didn't want to respond to her taunts because at some point I would give in to her. But then I wanted her to notice me, to keep coming for me.

"Don't know," I said as she got up and took her plate to the sink. My eyes followed her on their own accord. She was back in scrubs again. She probably had to head back to the clinic or to the swamp to check on Nessie. The fabric curved around her ass and my dick twitched again. Fuck. Lola was making this hard.

She placed her dishes in the sink. A light bulb lit up in my brain. Our bet wasn't about romantic feelings, it was about the tension we had been harboring since her return. So maybe I *could* give in. Just a little.

"What do you mean you don't know?" she asked. She was scrubbing the plate when I came up from behind. My arms caged her in. Lola tensed briefly. I slipped the sponge out of her hands. She breathed in quickly and I wanted to growl at her reaction. She was definitely affected by me.

"You really think I want to wear your ex's clothes?" I said, my lips trailing her ear. She tilted slightly to the side, giving more excess. I was going to enjoy this now. She was going to cave first.

"Let me guess, too much room for you?" she teased. I pressed against her, our bodies flush. Lola froze. I bet she could feel everything. I knew she could and fuck did she feel great. "I see," she hummed, recovering her composure.

She turned around, our chest brushing against each other. She had a few shadows under her eyes. Her plump lips were slightly parted. I couldn't resist staring.

Fuck. Fuck. Fuck. I needed to stay strong.

"Flynn," she teased, her voice a whisper. As if she were a siren, I felt compelled to lean forward. It was dangerous how easily Lola could make me forget myself. A simple fluttering of her lashes, the gentle way her voice caressed my name and how her aura soothed my shadows. But it was for those same reasons that I kept a wall up.

I've grown up separating my emotions from my decision making and always being logical. I've grown up hanging back and not going after what I want.

From now on I was going to take this bet seriously. I was going to have Lola cave in to our desires. When those flames were fed and inevitably turned into ash, my heart would still be intact and we could go our separate ways.

Lola tilted her head up and I followed suit. My thumbs grazed her hips and her eyes fluttered closed.

"Flynn," she whispered. I could practically taste the mint of her breath. There was a faint buzzing noise coming from behind. "Bet those are my clothes," I said. My voice had darkened with need. She nodded, her brown eyes rooting me in place. I should have backed away but I couldn't, not yet.

"I might prefer you like this though," she said, eyeing me up and down. I sucked in a deep breath. I needed my control back.

"Like this?" I asked, pushing her to the side, breaking our connection. I reached for the sponge, continuing the dishes. This time she stood behind me, her chest pressing against my back. My stomach twisted. Her lips brushed the shell of my ear, the tiniest flick of her tongue sent my heart racing.

"Yeah, but naked is preferred," she whispered.

CHAPTER 9
WATER MALFUNCTION

LOLA

I have a pregnant unicorn and now a pregnant Loch Ness Monster. Ms. Heinstein, my boss who is on vacation, has complete faith in me and my abilities.

But I didn't want faith, I wanted her to come back and tell me what the stars to do. The mystery rot was still happening, and at this point I have a strong feeling that the second that I taste Flynn's lips it would be hard to let him go.

I groaned at this weight on my shoulders. My desk was covered in every book my mom had on Loch Ness monsters and unicorns. I was extremely grateful for my mom's connections but so far there wasn't much luck.

My mom was a professor at the local university one town over. She was one of the smartest people I knew. Unlike Lily and Eleanor's moms who moved to this town from Portugal, my family had been living here for three generations. My grandmother had moved over from Nigeria, and like most, our family came in search of better opportunities.

It worked out because my mom was one of the top professors at her school. My dad was one of the local doctors in town and he had met my mom in college. They took one look at each other and said their souls had finally found their home. The rest was history.

I smiled at our family picture that was taped to my computer. I grew up around so much love, and I wanted it for myself. My dad would randomly bring my mom history books and flowers to surprise her. My mom would make his favorite dishes and watch soccer with him. They cared for each other deeply and showed me what I deserved. I wanted to feel like a princess, like in the romance books I spent hours reading.

A knot was beginning to form in the front of my head. I knew my eyes were strained from the amount of books I had been going through since last night. Nessie would be giving birth in a few weeks by my estimate and while the water was *okay* in Boogeyman's Swamp, something told me we had limited time before it would also get contaminated. Which reminds me– I need to speak to Priscilla.

Before heading to Priscilla's Lotions and Potions, I stopped by to check on the unicorn. She was standing near the pegasi having some sort of conversation. I took a deep breath, centering my thoughts, and felt my magic surge as a connection with them snapped into place.

Pegasus 1: *The food has gotten better.*

Pegasus 2: *Thank the stars for that. But you feel that right?*

Unicorn: *Yes, and it's spreading. Do you think Doctor Vampire can figure it out?*

Pegasus 2: *She may be stubborn but she cares, so yes.*

I snorted and all three magical horses turned to look at me. If only the beings knew some of the things the creatures talked about. You think small town gossip is bad? You don't want to know about the time I eased dropped on a two timing cat. The unicorn huffed.

"Of course I'll figure it out. Flynn and I are working on it," I said. They all tilted their heads.

Pegasus 1: *Ah, the grumpy one*

Pegasus 2: *He has a great smile when he does smile*

Unicorn: *You've chosen a good mate*

"M-mate!?" I choked out. My face burned. "We're just sort of friends," I said quickly.

Unicorn: *What is sort of friends?*

She shifted on her feet. One of the pegasi snorted.

Pegasus 1: *These two legged creatures and their conflicting emotions*

Pegasus 2: *They fight a lot but it's obvious they care for each other.*

Pegasus 1: *All the time. He brings her our food and she gets annoyed saying she was going to do it.*

Pegasus 2: *One time he slipped in our manure and told her she needs to keep things tidy and she said well some of us have 16 hour shifts when you have three cats giving birth.*

I bit the inside of my cheek.

"It's not his job to bring me my feed. I'm the one that collects it," I pointed out. If they could roll their eyes I swear they would be right now.

Unicorn: *But isn't that a nice gesture? He obviously likes you. I've been around for a while, Doctor Vampire.* My heart thumped against my chest as I stared into her eyes.

Not everyone is lucky enough to have a mate in their life, let alone to keep one. Guard him well.

The unicorn's eyes glistened with unshed tears and my eyes roamed over her swollen belly. My eyes watered as her emotions poured into our psychic link. This poor unicorn lost their other half. I could feel it in every bone in my body.

"He isn't my mate. Anyway I just wanted to check on you guys before going to get some more herbs for your breakfast," I said. They each neighed, letting me know that they were fine. I quickly broke our connection, my body running high with too many emotions. Now I had to go see Priscilla.

✳ ✺ ✳ ✺ ✳ ✺ ✳ ✺ ✳ ✺ ✳

ONCE THE LAVENDER building with a pale yellow door came into view I knew I had arrived. Priscilla was *the* go-to fairy for all things potions, lotions, and natural remedies. She has been a major help in cleaning out rotting vegetation and supporting the regrowth of the garden.

The door chimed open and the smell of lavender and citrus soothed me. I took a deep breath. Priscilla's dark brown hair had traces of lavender and was tied up in a loose bun. Her amber eyes sparkled as she began tossing herbs into a bowl. Her lips moved as she softly spoke.

I glanced around at the never-ending jars and bowls of herbs and teas across the walls. The more the minutes passed, the more relaxed I became. I've always loved visiting this shop because it felt like a warm oasis that eased away my troubling thoughts.

"My lovely Lola!" Priscilla said, regaining my attention and opening her arms for a warm hug.

"Hey! How's it going?" I asked, giving her a gentle squeeze. She reached under her table for a box of tiny bags, each with a different label. Some were for stomach aches, some for blood pressure issues, so on and so forth.

"For the clinic! I took your recommendations and added my own knowledge and Flynn's to create some great tinctures for you," she said, beaming. My brows furrowed.

"Flynn?" I asked. Her eyes widened.

"Oh, I thought you knew! He came by yesterday with a bunch of different herbs and offered me some advice," she said. I stared at Priscilla with wide eyes. Against my own will, my heart swelled. I *knew* there was a heart beneath the rusty armor he wore.

"I'll make sure to thank him later. then. I really appreciate all of this," I said. I was so excited when I moved back to Lavender Falls and got the green light from Ms. Heinstein to implement more natural medicine for the animals. Thanks to Priscilla (and now Flynn), it was finally happening.

We've all had to monitor the rot, being mindful of the spread and making sure to harvest things earlier than usual. We've also had to build more raised garden beds and fill them with dirt from outside of town. It's been a team effort to keep everything going.

"I actually have a question for you," I said nervously. Priscilla settled the box on the table and gave me a warm smile.

"Ask away," she said, brightly.

"Nessie is back in town," I said, nervously. Priscilla beamed.

"I heard! How is she?" she asked.

"Pregnant," I said. Priscilla's smile faltered for a second. It was the reaction I was expecting. I really hope she is willing to help with what I am going to ask of her next.

"You've never helped a Loch Ness monster give birth," she said. I nodded. "And the rot might contaminate the water," she continued. I nodded again. "And you have a pregnant unicorn," she finished. I gave her one last nod.

"Well this spring season just got more interesting," she said with a laugh. Stars, was she right.

"You know any water fairies that can help monitor the swamp? I have a feeling she'll give birth soon," I asked. Priscilla waved her hand.

"I got you," she said. I sighed in relief. I wasn't used to asking for so much help but I knew for the safety of the creatures and the town that I needed to. I had a great, supportive community that I knew I could trust.

"Thank you so much. Maybe there's something we can add to the water. Lavender, rose, and chamomile?" I suggested. Priscilla's eyes began to glow with excitement. The wheels in her head were already turning.

"I can whip up some herbal bags," she said, already moving towards one of her walls of herbs. "By the way, how are you? I can't imagine having to help Nessie give birth," she said over her shoulder. I shrugged my shoulders.

"I've done water births before. Hippocampus's, selkies, dolphins and stingrays. But Loch Ness monsters? Nope," I said as cheerfully as I could. I didn't want to reveal just how nervous I was. I was seen as someone who was confident and could handle anything.

"I'll talk to some water fairies I know and make sure they're available to help," she confirmed. With the town by my side, I was going to be okay. I was going to get through this spring season. My phone buzzed with a text from my mom asking me to stop by Coffin's Coffeeshop.

❋ ❖ ❋ ❖ ❋ ❖ ❋ ❖ ❋ ❖ ❋

STEPPING into the medieval cafe I was immediately smacked in the face with the smell of lemon and rosemary. I glanced over at Madame Coraline, who was carrying a box of lemons into the kitchen.

"Lola, your mom is by the window," she called out. I grinned, shaking my head. I never understood how she was able to do that without turning back, but Madame Coraline was an odd, old witch that I've learned to never question.

My mom waved from her spot in the back by the window. Today was her day off and her table was littered with papers that needed to be graded. This semester she was teaching *The History of Vampires*, *Human Mythology vs History*, and her favorite, *Vampires in Hollywood*. I think her Hollywood class was just an excuse to watch vampire movies all day.

I leaned over to give her a big hug, and her scent of honey and clover eased the tension in my shoulders. She had a fresh twist out with one side pulled back by a pearl clip that my dad had gotten her as an anniversary gift.

"Hey there honey," she said with a wide grin. My mom always held this light air about her. She walked through life with a bright perspective and honestly, it was because of her that I could as well. "I heard about Nessie," she said, immediately reaching for my hand. I sighed at her comforting touch.

"She's pregnant but I enlisted Priscilla to help me out," I said. She nodded, her eyes waiting for me to continue. I knew what she was waiting for. "I will admit that I'm nervous. She's pregnant and I've never delivered a Loch Ness monster baby… or a unicorn baby for that matter. So it's a season of firsts, but I'm capable," I said, mostly trying to convince myself. Her eyes softened.

"And you're not alone. I found another book from a colleague of mine, a siren from the Pacific coast. It's a book about water creatures. I think it could be helpful," she said, sliding over a deep blue leather book. Its pages were wrinkled on the sides. Placing a hand on it my body tingled. It was definitely old and had a magical aura.

"I would talk to Sailor about this," she pointed out. I raised an eyebrow. "He's a siren. He might be able to help with some of the translations," she said. My eyes widened as I stared at the book. *Well, this got interesting.*

"There is so much about sirens that we don't know," I said, mostly to myself. My mother nodded.

"They're a secretive lot. Can't blame them though. I trust Sailor will know what is needed and who knows, you might learn something," she said. There was a bubble of excitement brewing as I eyed the book. Who knows what things I could learn from a book this old.

"Thanks mom. I really appreciate this," I said, earnestly. She waved her hand dismissively.

"Anyway that I can help, I always will," she said as her phone beeped. She glanced at it. My mom fought back a smile.

"What is it?" I asked, trying to catch her eye. She quickly sent a text back and I waited. She leaned forward and dropped her voice to a whisper.

"Mr. Hale has been trying to apologize to Ms. Rosario," she said. *That's interesting.*

During the winter, we were all shocked to hear that Mr. Hale wanted to rejoin the community in the town he grew up in. We all hesitated in accepting him, particularly Eleanor. But after admitting that he's been going to therapy, we've all noticed a difference in him. He's been helping out a lot with the town's needs– especially with everything going on.

Lily told us in secret one night that Mr. Hale has been trying to talk to her mom. They were a part of the same friend group and he was married to Eleanor's mom, Lily's mom's best friend. We all agreed that there was a lot we didn't know when it came to our parents and their friendship. There were probably secrets and stories between them. I mean, we all had our own so of course they did as well.

My mom had a twinkle in her eye and a sneaky grin. I crossed my arms over my chest. "You seem to be delighted by this," I pointed out. She shrugged her shoulders.

"I just think those two need to have a long talk," she said, nonchalantly. My mom picked up her pen, ending our conversation.

"You guys all hung out when you were younger, right?" I asked curiously. My mom nodded with a melancholy smile.

"We did. We were just like your friends with our own adventures, heartaches and love," she said, glancing at her phone.

Sometimes I forgot that my mom had a life outside of being my mom. It was a weird feeling, honestly. A mix of hurt because she was getting older and she had all these memories that I didn't know about and wasn't a part of, and happiness in knowing that my mom wasn't just my mom but also a kind, intelligent woman.

I smiled. I couldn't wait to talk to the girls about this. I slipped the book into my work bag and stood up.

"I see what you're doing mom," I pointed out. She raised her hands innocently.

"I don't know what you're talking about," she said. I giggled. I leaned over to kiss her cheek. "I love you honey," she whispered.

"I love you too mom. Give dad a hug for me," I said, turning away. She pulled me back and lifted a reusable grocery bag filled with Tupper-ware's. I smiled, gratefully.

"You have jollof rice and ofada stew," she said. My heart wanted to burst. I had been missing my mom's homemade food for a while and with the way I've been working my fridge has seen better days.

"Say hi to Flynn for me won't you dear!" she said, turning back to her papers.

"Mom," I warned her. She held a sneaky smile on her face.

"I've always liked Flynn," she commented innocently. My cheeks flushed.

"Everyone likes Flynn," I said, shifting my weight.

"True but..." she trailed off. A sorrowful look passed on my mother's face that made me sit back down.

"What's wrong?" I asked. Flynn had seemed fine the last time I saw him. Well, as fine as someone who was clearly denying his emotions *could* be.

"His mom worries about him. We all worry about our kids. It's a mother thing," she said, flipping through some papers.

"Is something wrong?" I pressed. My stomach twisted. Lily had a tendency to be forgetful when she was in work mode. Eleanor would try to control things. Caleb would shut down. Celestino would keep his feelings at bay. We all had a tendency to bury our emotions in work.

But Flynn and even Sailor were the ones that saw through all of us. They would point out what we were hiding from and help us bring it to light.

"I know you have a lot on your plate honey. But while you and Flynn work together, could you keep an eye on him?" she asked, sweetly.

"Of course," I promised.

"Also share my food with him. I know he likes it and he's been working hard," she said with a smile.

CHAPTER 10
THE HYPOTHESIS

FLYNN

The Drunken Fairy Tale Tavern was in full swing this Friday. My hands moved across the bar automatically, pouring beers and making cocktails. From the corner of my eye I could see Bridget was running around taking orders. Caleb was at the end of the bar making Eleanor her caipirinha. I bit the inside of my cheek.

Between talking to her father and what I've been sensing with my magic, I had a fairly decent hypothesis about what was killing the vegetation.

And if the winter season had taught me anything it was that I needed to tell my friends. Eleanor shouldered a lot of the responsibility when the Hollow Tree was dying, helping my brother break his curse *and* putting on the winter festival.

That tree had been around since the town was founded. I had a feeling the roots had run deeper and longer than we expected. I thought back to when I had my hands embedded in the dirt at the base of the baby Hollow Tree. The root was somewhere in the Gasping Greenwood Forest.

I just couldn't pinpoint where because the longer I kept my magic flowing into the ground the more painful it would become. Every time I tried to follow a path a shooting pain would go up my arm. It was like the fucker was protecting itself.

There was a tap on the bar. Lily was with Crystal, and I grinned at them. Crystal's eyes skirted around everywhere, her leg bouncing up and down on the bar stool as she sat.

"What can I get you beautiful ladies this evening?" I asked, my charm flipping on. Lily rolled her eyes with a wide smile and Crystal blushed. It didn't take long for me to notice how shy Crystal was. I looked around for Sailor. I also wasn't blind to the fact that the siren had somewhat of an interest in her.

"Tequila sunrise for me," Lily said with a sigh. I bet the spring festival was getting to her. She was prepping for another pub crawl, this time it was called Flower Power Bar Fest and the main sponsor was going to be The Plastered Pixies bar. I turned to Crystal who was chewing her bottom lip in thought.

"C-can I be honest?" she asked. I crossed my arms and leaned on the bar.

"Of course my dear," I said with a soft smile. Crystal huffed out a nervous giggle.

"I don't drink often so I'm not sure about my tastes," she said. I nodded in understanding.

"Sweet or sour?" I asked. This was my favorite part of bartending, figuring out orders for people, seeing if I could come up with their perfect drink. It was like a puzzle that I got to play while on the clock. It's also the same reason I enjoyed creating whiskey so much. Her bottom lip stuck out in thought.

"Sour," she decided. I nodded and leaned back.

"Have you tried any alcohol that you know you don't like?" I asked, reaching for the grapefruit juice. A smile tugged on her lips and her eyes narrowed mischievously. "Oh no. Why do you have that look Crys," I asked. Lily covered her mouth to hide her laughter.

"Whiskey," she said, beaming. I reached for my heart, pretending to be wounded.

"Crys! That hurts. How will I recover?" I said, dramatically. Crystal shook her head, laughing freely.

After a few minutes I handed Lily her tequila sunrise and Crystal a paloma. Lily hummed as she took a sip and Celestino wrapped an arm around her waist causing her to jump. He leaned in to take a sip and Lily swatted him away. He gave me a wink.

"Delicious as always Flynn," he said. Lily rolled her eyes as she leaned back into his arms. My throat tightened staring at them. They were an adorable couple, with the way Celestino was always affectionate and Lily blushed so easily at the attention. I focused my gaze back on Crystal who was trying her drink. Her eyes widened.

"This is great!" she said. I did my best to hide my smug grin. I had a feeling she would enjoy it.

"And now you have at least one drink you know you like," I said. Lily tapped the bar again.

"What is it?" she asked, her eyes narrowing. I knew I needed to be careful around Sailor with the way he was able to read energies. But Lily was someone I never had to watch myself around. Ever since she accepted her anxiety she has been in tune with her magic and senses. I knew it wouldn't take her long to figure out that I've been itching to talk to them.

"Do you think you guys could stay here, after closing? I want to talk about the Hollow Tree," I said. Celestino placed his chin on Lily's shoulder.

"Of course Flynn. Now if you would excuse me I would like to dance with a certain witch," he said, placing Lily's drink on the bar. The two of them twirled to the dance floor, leaving Crystal alone with me. Crystal's eyes followed the couple. I wiped the bar to fill in the silence as she sipped her drink quietly.

"How's Lola?" she asked. My hand stopped mid motion. Someone waved for a beer stealing my attention. She waved me away but I could see in her eyes she would be waiting for an answer.

How's Lola? I hadn't spoken to her in a few days and at the community garden we were like two passing ships in a storm. I scanned the crowd as I poured a beer. She wasn't here. If she was, I would have noticed.

I thought back to our lunch at her place. I wanted her. That much was obvious. I just couldn't do more beyond that. I couldn't be emotionally invested.

But fuck has it been getting harder and harder to keep my hands from reaching for her, squeezing her, feeling her.

At the garden I could hear her little pants as she pulled out weeds and I imagined how she would sound if it were my hands eliciting those noises.

My mind wandered to the stupid bet. A bet that, if broken, meant I could get rid of this itch to have her. But a bet is a bet and I was just as competitive as she was. If anyone was going to cave into secret touches it would be her.

I made my way back to Crystal. "I'm not sure. I haven't seen her around," I said. She nodded absentmindedly.

"She's been sleeping at the clinic lately. It's been hard to reach her," she said. My eyes slightly widened. So she was sleeping at the clinic? Alone? I knew Lola was strong, she was a vampire. She could probably beat me at arm wrestling.

But she was the *only* vet in town, responsible for the unicorn and Nessie's pregnancy, *and* the rot. Despite that, she did everything with a fucking smile and that made my chest ache.

"She's probably there right now," Crystal said. She looked at me and I felt my throat close up. "I hope she's taking care of herself," she said, sipping her drink.

* ❖ ❖ ❖ ❖ ❖ ❖ *

ELEANOR, Crystal, Celestino and Lily were sitting at the bar while Caleb and Bridget stood on either side of me drying cups. I wasn't the biggest fan of asking for help.

I was used to being the one helping others while also taking care of myself. I spent my whole life carving out a space for myself. I worked my ass off to be a whiskey developer. I dug my hands into the ground and read textbooks to get my degree in horticulture. But now standing before my friends I felt small. Lily met my eye and gave me a warm smile, encouraging me.

"Spit it out Flynn," Eleanor demanded. "I've got a date with a certain bartender tonight," she said with a smirk, looking at Caleb in a way that made me want to gag.

"We can all see you making eyes at my brother," I said. Eleanor smirked.

"Good, that should motivate you to hurry up," she said. The doors opened and Sailor walked in with a huff.

"I'm here guys," he said, catching his breath. Crystal got up from her seat and offered hers. Sailor gave her a warm smile.

"You sit," he said. She shook her head.

"You've been on your feet," Crystal said, cheeks flushed. Sailor's smile widened.

"One of you sit because Flynn needs to hurry up so I can take Caleb and f-"

"Okay!" Crystal said, shoving Sailor into the seat. We all broke out into laughter, easing the tension.

"Thank you M'Lady," Sailor said, giving Crystal a wink.

"So…" I trailed off, gathering everyone's attention. "I think I know what's causing the rot," I said. Lily reached for Celestino's hand. "I've been working with your dad," I said, gesturing to Eleanor and Crystal. Eleanor's eyes hardened and Crystal offered a smile.

"What do you think it is?" Bridget asked.

"While you did a great job Eleanor-," I said, hoping to not upset her. The last thing I needed was to piss her off and have her hit me with pixie magic. "I think a piece of the Hollow Tree root prior to your magic broke off."

"Fury fuck," Eleanor said. Caleb reached his hand over, taking hers.

"What do we do?" Lily asked. I took a deep breath.

"I need to figure out a way to find the root. Every time I dig into the ground and use my magic to track it I get a shooting pain up my arm," I said, clenching my fist.

"What do you mean 'shooting pain'?" Bridget's voice wavered. She hated seeing anyone in pain despite her tough attitude. Her heart was just as big as Greg's.

"You all know that I can connect to the Earth. Every time I try and I feel like I'm getting close it's like the root retaliates and shocks me," I said. "It doesn't want me to know where it is." Celestino cleared his throat.

"It's rotten which means it's dying. My necromancy magic plus yours might do the trick," he offered. I held my breath. I didn't want my shoulders to drop dramatically. I didn't want them to see just how much this whole situation was affecting me. Instead I swallowed and nodded my head.

"I can help find a backup tracking spell," Lily offered.

"Eleanor and I can be there for support since our magic is tied to the Earth," Crystal offered with a shy smile.

"I'll be there just to be there," Sailor said sheepishly.

"Bridget and I can handle your shifts while you work this out," Caleb offered. Bridget nodded.

"Guys this is too-" I started to say. Bridget lightly smacked the back of my head.

"You did this for Caleb during the winter when he had his curse. Let us help you," Bridget said with a frown. "I know you like doing things alone. We all do. Clearly we're siblings. But let us," she pushed. I still hesitated. Bridget's glare became even icier and I swallowed. For a little sister she was scary.

"Fine," I said, giving in.

"Great, now everyone get out of my bar," Caleb said, smirking at Eleanor.

CHAPTER II
WHOOPS ANOTHER BABY

LOLA

My head was pounding as I sat at my desk with my sad excuse of a salad. It was close to midnight and I was spending another night at the clinic. Priscilla had some of her water fairy friends tending to the swamp and checking on Nessie periodically.

The pegasi had all fully recovered from their stomach bug and were ready to start their flying exercises this week. They hadn't stretched their wings in weeks and needed to build back their strength.

I tossed the rest of my salad into the trash. As hard as I tried eating it, it wasn't what I was craving. I rubbed my temples. I drank my last blood bag two nights ago.

In today's day and age vampires didn't need to solely rely on human blood. There was animal blood and synthetic blood that provided similar nutrients to human blood. Vampires have existed for hundreds of years, across the globe. Each supernatural being had a history that was long and spread out. While many cultures have different stories of how we came to be, in reality our tale was a tragic love story.

There once was a warlock and a human who were madly in love. One night the human became deathly ill with a disease that had been plaguing the countryside. The warlock did everything he could to keep his beloved alive. He used dark magic and while he did save her, he ended up turning her into the first vampire.

And that is how vampires came to be. Werewolves shared a similar story. Now that I think about it, most supernatural beings came to be because of heartache, love or revenge.

My stomach churned, reminding me that my salad was simply not enough. I was supposed to pick up more blood from Griffin's Groceries but I didn't have any time to because someone had found a baby kitten in a tree that needed a deep flea bath and some warm milk. That kitten was now sleeping in a cage, happy and with a full belly.

I opened my computer to check on the cameras. The pegasi were sleeping and the unicorn kept shifting her weight around, trying to get comfortable in her hay bed. If I looked closely I could see that her belly had movement.

So far, she and the baby seemed to be in perfect health. My only thing was that I had no idea when the baby was going to be born. My estimate was a few weeks, near the Spring Floral Festival. I asked my mom for any books on unicorns and she's been talking to her colleagues to find some. The pain in my head increased again.

Flynn.

I hadn't seen him since that day at my apartment. My body tingled as it remembered the way he pressed against me while wearing nothing but a shirt and towel. I cursed at myself. I should have never made that stupid bet. It was obvious to me that Flynn wanted me. I could sense it. And for some reason he didn't want to give in. Instead he was beginning to enjoy making me lose my resolve.

"Fuck," I said out loud in frustration. He's been giving me just a taste of himself and it wasn't enough to satisfy me. I needed more. His scent was intoxicating and my blood roared to life every time I caught a whiff. My magic begged me to take him, to make him mine.

If Flynn was ever going to be mine it would probably be for one night; one *incredible* night. I rolled my eyes. I needed sleep. This was making my brain feel hazy.

A rustle filled the lonely clinic. My eyes flickered back to the screen of cameras. More rustling. There was nothing happening in the barn. I double clicked the camera that was recording the paddock. Near the edge where it was lined with trees something was moving. Goosebumps ran up my arms and my fangs grew.

It was well known that creatures liked to come closer to town to hunt but I'd be damned if something got a hold of any of my patients. A dark shadow poked out.

"Dragon's piss," I said. My heart was beating like a pair of sprite's wings as I made my way towards the double doors. Once I was outside I could smell dirt, sweat, fear, the quietness. The breeze was strong, stinging my hot skin. I stopped once I reached the paddock and slowly opened the gate. There was a deep groan. I closed my eyes and took a deep breath.

Deep in my belly I felt my magic push, filling my veins with power. When I opened my eyes I could see things more clearly. The hunched creature managed to hover over the gate and panted as it landed on the ground.

"No way," I whispered. I inched forward and even though I was about 15 feet away the creature was looking at me. Its eyes were filled with deep pain. It had the body, tail, and back legs of a lion, and the head and wings of an eagle.

A griffin. At my clinic– well Ms. Heinstein's. While griffins occasionally interacted with supernatural creatures it wasn't common. I've met a handful of them and they were incredibly kind. The creature groaned again.

I squatted down, averted my eyes and held my hand up. My magic slithered away from me, making its way towards the griffin. I needed to create a psych link that allowed me to communicate. I honed in on the taste of fear in the air pouring from the griffin.

"I'm a healer. I can help you," I whispered.

I know. Help, child. Please.

It grunted again and I made my way forward. I stared at its beautiful dark feathers glittering in the moonlight. I searched for signs of blood but found none.

"I'm going to touch you," I said softly. The griffin nodded with her beak. My hand ran over her feathers which were soft. Her heartbeat was erratic and her stomach kept contracting. Her lower abdomen was hard. *Kraken's crap.* The griffin was absolutely pregnant.

"I need you to squat and slightly lean forward. You can't do this lying down," I whispered before placing my hands under her.

Okay.

As gently as I could I helped roll her over. Now she could sit up properly to push. By the stars was this spring season filled with babies.

I'm afraid the forest has made me weak. I am not sure if I can push.

I sucked in a breath. This is what happened with the unicorn. She ate from the forest which had been slowly rotting causing a dip in her strength. I sucked in a breath. That meant I needed to help her push. My body was already straining against my magic. I hadn't drunk enough blood to handle this. *Fuck.*

I stared into the griffin's amber eyes. There was so much pain, and yet there was also trust. She trusted me to come over and help her. She said she knew I was a healer. I couldn't let her down. I had vowed to save every creature I possibly could when I became a vet. I took a deep breath and a new scent caught my nose. My head snapped behind me.

Who is that? The griffin snarled. I rubbed the back of her neck, calming her.

"A friend. A kind friend," I added quickly. "Can this friend help me?" I asked gently. The griffin looked from me to Flynn before nodding. "Flynn, please come here!" I called out. Flynn's eyes widened as he scurried over.

"Shitting stars," he said, taking in the sight of the griffin who was growling. "Sorry."

"I need your help," I said. He stared at me like I was delusional.

"Lola I-"

"Please," I begged. He sank to his knees, eyes determined.

"Tell me what to do," he said. I breathed deeply through my nose, his scent calming me. The more magic I used, the weaker I became. Flynn touched the back of my hand that was pressing against the griffin's belly. He arched an eyebrow and I gave him a tight smile.

"I'm going to press and rub down on this side. I want you to do the same. And Ms. Griffin you're going to push. Listen to what your body is telling you. Trust your body," I said.

My body wants these egg out of my fucking body.

Okay. We need to do this asap. I looked over at Flynn. His hair was loose and shaggy and his lips turned down in frown. *Why was he even here?* But the reason didn't matter right now. I was grateful that he was here.

"Flynn?" I said, softly. His brown eyes collided with mine and he nodded. He stared at me with unwavering confidence. I had never seen Flynn look at me that way. Tears pricked the back of my eyes.

"We can do this," he promised. My hands shook as I pressed and glided down her side. In unison we worked together. We began sliding our hands in tune to her pushes. Her feathers were soft between my fingers and I did my best to keep the trembles at bay.

The griffin grunted and after about fifteen minutes an egg popped out. Sweat began dripping down my neck and I felt a familiar woozy feeling settle in my stomach. I sighed happily and was about to remove my hands when I felt something. I bit the inside of my cheek. There was a ringing in my ear.

"There's another one," I grunted. Flynn nodded. Fuck I was absolutely going to pass out if this didn't happen fast.

Almost there.

The griffin grunted as if sensing my struggle and I held onto my magic with as much strength as I could muster. After a few more grunts, she relaxed under my hands. Our connection broke quickly. I sat back on my heels, gasping for air. The griffin turned her neck around and her eyes melted staring at her eggs. Two eggs. Flynn looked at me with wide eyes.

"Holy shit," he whispered. My stomach dropped and my skin felt cold and clammy. I blinked rapidly, trying to fight the shadows that danced around the corner of my eyes. I offered him a wobbly smile. "Lola, are you okay?"

The world darkened and the next thing I knew– I was out.

CHAPTER 12
BITE ME, PLEASE

FLYNN

My heart was in my throat watching Lola's eyes roll back and her body drop to the grass. I scrambled to catch her before she hit the ground. I lightly tapped on her face. Fury fuck, I should call someone.

"Lola I need you to wake up or I'm calling your dad," I said, my hand cradling her neck. Her nose scrunched. My heart skipped. She was awake.

"Please don't," she croaked out. I looked at the griffin who simply nodded towards the clinic. I nodded back. I think we communicated? I slipped Lola under my arms and lifted her up.

"I'm taking you into the clinic. If you stay awake I won't call your dad," I said. Her lips twitched.

"Are we going to make a bet," she mumbled. I groaned. *Of course* this woman would make light of the situation. Her eyes were still closed and her breathing was shallow. She gripped my shirt in her hands.

Once inside of the clinic she peeled her eyes open and pointed to a door. I pushed it open revealing a closet with a cot, pillow and blanket.

There was an open bag tossed to the side. I bit down on my cheek and my nostrils flared.

"Have you been sleeping here?" I asked as I eased her down, already knowing the answer.

"Don't give me that tone," she said, blinking her eyes. "It's either this or sharing some hay with the unicorn," she said. I pushed her braids over her shoulders and cradled her cheek in my hand, forcing her to look at me. Her pupils were slightly dilated and out of focus.

"Or you know, you could sleep at home," I said. She tried shaking her head, hands trembling at her side.

"I have to be here for the animals," she said. I sighed.

"You fainted Lola," I said sternly. She squinted at me and licked her lips before twisting them into a frown. She was attempting to glare at me and, while adorable, it also revealed that she was clearly too weak to.

"I'll be okay. You can leave," she said with a short tone.

"What's wrong?" I asked, sitting down on the floor. There was no way I could leave her like this. Lola's eyes flickered to the door, avoiding me. "Lola. Tell me. Now." I said, using the same tone. She scowled, crossing her arms.

"I-I fainted because I haven't drunk enough blood," she confessed. *Fuck.* Vampires needed blood as their main source of nutrients, in spite of being able to eat regular food.

"Griffin's Groceries is closed right now," I said. "Do you have any here?" I asked. She shook her head.

"I ran out like two days ago. Anyway, I'll be fine. You can go," she said, pushing me away. Her hands still had a slight tremor.

"Lola, you're literally shaking. You need blood. Let me call your parents," I said. Her eyes widened.

"Don't. They'll get upset and consider me irresponsible, which, I guess you could too but I've just been so busy that I didn't have time," she whispered. I swallowed. I had never seen Lola look so helpless. It made my insides churn. I knew she was working overtime– this was her busiest season. But there was no way she could continue like this.

"What if you drink mine?" I asked. Her eyes widened and she slid back on the cot, putting distance between us.

"No," she said firmly.

"Why not? Have you never done it before?" I asked. Most vampires were taught at a young age on how to drink properly from animals. I'm sure a being was similar. She swallowed and looked away from me.

"Yes, but it was a long time ago and under different circumstances," she said. "We don't feed from beings typically unless…there's some kind of relationship, due to the effects."

"When was the last time you fed on someone?" I asked, my heart leaping. She chewed her bottom lip before answering.

"College. Ex-boyfriend. We were…doing stuff," she admitted. She pulled a braid forward and began twirling it nervously. "Vampire bites can…give a euphoric feeling during-"

"Got it," I said, cutting her off. My heart was fully racing now and all the blood that she needed went straight to my dick. She pushed my shoulder again, urging me to leave.

"Go," she said. I clenched my jaw. There was no fucking way I was leaving her like this. Crystal was clearly giving me a hint when she'd mentioned that she hoped Lola was taking care of herself.

"How do you want me? Neck? Arm?" I asked.

"Flynn, no," she said. Her hands clutched her knees, as if she was trying to hold herself back.

"Lola if you don't decide I'm going to accidentally open a vein, and I won't know which one I'm not supposed to cut," I said. While her body began leaning forward she turned her head away. She was fighting herself. I moved closer to her, leaned over and reached for the back of her neck. I wasn't giving her a choice.

"Bite me, Lola," I said, tilting my neck.

"Are you sure?" she asked, one of her hands relinquished her knee and clung to my shoulder. Her resolve was weakening. I rolled my eyes and tugged her until she was a breath away from my skin.

"Fucking do it," I said in a rough whisper. She gently pressed her lips against my throat and goosebumps crawled over me.

The smell of sage and honey filled my nose. Her tongue swiped against me, tasting me and I fought back a moan. After another sweep I felt the sting of her fangs break my skin. I hissed lightly.

The pain was quickly replaced by a euphoric feeling. A buzz somewhat like being drunk hurtled through me. I sucked in a breath, my eyes closing. Both of her hands came around my shoulders holding me tight, and now all I wanted was to press myself against her. I wanted to feel our skins move against each other. Her hands dug into my shoulder blades and a small moan escaped my lips.

"Lola," I said, my voice coming out huskier than I wanted. Although I could feel my blood draining, I was filled with a sense of hunger. It was like my desire for her had grown into a fire.

I wanted Lola.

I *needed* Lola.

My hands slid down her back, squeezing. She sat up straighter, keeping her lips latched onto my neck and I tried to pull her flush against me. My cock strained against my jeans. I settled my hands on her hips and she whimpered.

She fucking *whimpered* and it was about to be my undoing. Another moan escaped me as one of her hands scratched my scalp. I wanted to pull her onto my lap and feel her cunt against my cock.

In an instant she pulled back, pupils wide, panting. A bit of my blood dribbled down her chin and she reached out to lick it. Fuck, that was hot as the stars. With her vampire speed she reached for me and for a quick second I felt her tongue on the spot where she bit me.

"T-there. It'll close and won't leave a scar," she stuttered. My eyebrows twitched. Why did not having her mark bother me? Already her skin was glowing, a faint blush on her cheeks and her body wasn't trembling anymore.

"How do you feel?" I asked. She placed the pillow in her lap, fingers crushing it.

"I feel great. You?" she said, looking away. Her chest was still rising fast and her lips were slightly plumped. I bet they would look good wrapped around my cock. I swallowed, squeezing my eyes shut briefly.

"Great. Are you sleeping here tonight?" I asked. She nodded. I stared at her cot, a heat of anger flickering through me. Lola deserved a good night's rest, not this plastic mesh. She was no good to these creatures if she didn't get enough sleep.

"I have to keep an eye on the griffin," she said. I pulled my phone from my jeans which now felt tight.

"Number," I demanded. "In case you need help again. You'll pick up more blood tomorrow right?" I said, eyeing her. She took my phone and rolled her eyes.

"Yes, sir," she teased. I closed my eyes briefly, ignoring what that little *sir* comment did to me.

✱ ❀ ✱ ❀ ✱ ❀ ✱ ❀ ✱

MY THOUGHTS DRIFTED BACK to last night and the feel of her lips against my neck. She was so warm and fucking soft against me. I wanted to peel off her scrubs and fuck her on that flimsy cot with her fangs still sunk into me. My fingers tightened. Lately she was invading all of my thoughts. Her, and that stupid bet we made.

While I wanted nothing more than to just give in and scratch this itch between us, the childish part of me didn't want to lose. There was a reason I called her my rival.

I was never into biting but something about it being Lola undid me and made me want more. Was it the vampire venom? Was it the mix of my own feelings? Her soft whimpers flooded my brain. I could feel my cock pressed against my pants. I groaned.

I was working a shift at the tavern again. I had the morning off to work on my whiskey recipe, but my greenhouse kept making me think of Lola. I did my best to focus on the herbs but all I wanted was to lay her on my work desk. So I escaped to the tavern and started my shift early hoping it would distract me from her but instead here she was filling the corners of my mind.

I stared at my hands. Lola was limp in my arms for a few seconds. I had never been scared shitless. Not when we were trying to heal the Hollow Tree. Not when we noticed the vegetation suffering. But watching her collapse felt like I was losing a piece of myself.

She was sleeping on a flimsy cot. Could she even sleep on that thing?

How did she expect to take care of others if she wasn't taking care of herself? I squeezed my eyes shut. This is why I didn't want to get involved. I was being distracted. I was wanting more.

"Just the elf I wanted to see!" A deep voice called out. I opened my eyes quickly and reached for a towel to wipe my hands.

"Mr. Luna! How are you?" I said, shaking the hand of Lola's father. He was around my height with a close crop fade and thick beard. He had his white coat tossed over his shoulder and a briefcase in hand. He was one of the doctors of Lavender Falls and was probably here for lunch, like usual.

"I'm doing good, son. I wanted to place an order for lunch for me and the misses," he said, taking a seat at the bar. I nodded. "We try to have lunch together twice a week, you know, keep the romance alive," he said with a wink. I felt the tips of my ears heat up.

"Medium rare burger, fries. Rice bowl with blackened grouper and two blood bags? We have rabbit, synthetic and venison," I said, remembering his previous order. Mr. Luna gave me a wide smile and huffed out a laugh.

"Sharp memory. Could we do one rabbit and one synthetic. Venison has always been more of Lola's favorite," he said. I nodded, trying to calm my heart at the mention of Lola. I definitely did not need to think about how she made me feel last night with her dad right in front of me.

I quickly handed the order to Tatiana and grabbed styrofoam cups of blood. When I was back, he had a slight frown on his face as he stared at his phone.

"Everything alright Mr. Luna?" I asked as I began re-racking the liquor bottles. He waved his hand.

"Oh nothing. Lola likes to send us updates on the animals. We've been worried since it's just her at the clinic," he said. I nodded. It was a tough season for Lola. "It's spring, so who knows what animals might pop up pregnant," he commented.

My heart sank. If I hadn't been there last night to help her with the griffin I'm not sure what would have happened. She would have been alone, passed out in the middle of the field. I pushed the synthetic blood closer to him and he smiled, taking a sip.

"I'm sure Lola will be fine. She's tough. Plus, she's not alone," I said. Lola had a slew of people who were ready to lend a helping hand at any moment, including me. Something sparkled in Mr. Luna's eyes.

"She's definitely not alone. But…" he trailed off. I raised an eyebrow, faintly hearing a ding. His food was ready but I waited for him to finish his sentence before going to grab it.

"What?" I asked, warily. He shrugged his shoulders.

"Sometimes when Lola has a lot on her plate she forgets things. You know. Like food and sleep," he said. He sighed dramatically. "She definitely gets that from her mother. Both are glorious workaholics," he said. I have become painfully aware of how Lola neglected herself for the sake of others.

CHAPTER 13
LUNCH AND LUST

LOLA

I fought back a grimace as my hair was tugged and then twisted. I did my best to keep my head in place. I glanced over at Lily who was getting her hair deep conditioned and trimmed. Eleanor was scrolling through her phone as Sophie painted her nails. Crystal was here getting a mani and pedi.

I bit the inside of my cheek. I hadn't told them about last night. I wanted to, but one: they would yell at me for not restocking the clinic fridge with blood, and two: they would go crazy at Flynn letting me bite him.

My body heated at the memory. His blood was warm and sweet. It had taken every ounce of self control to stop feeding. His blood fueled me in ways I couldn't imagine. There were only a handful of times I'd drank from someone. As a child it was always animals. We were taught control from an early age.

It was rare for vampires to bite other beings unless there was a relationship of some sort given the aroused feeling our venom contained. As a teenager, it was once with a warlock I was seeing, and then college with another vampire. But with Flynn?

It was something else. It was different. His blood mixed with his magic gave me a surge of strength that I didn't know I could possess. There was something in his blood that felt right. It was like my body had finally found peace. It also made me hot and bothered.

Stars. Feeling his arms around me, his hands on my body and his groans in my ears *almost* made me cave in on the stupid bet.

But I knew it would happen. A vampire bite had a euphoric feeling meant to cover up the sting and the blood loss. It wasn't just a euphoric feeling in the person being bitten, but in the vampire as well. Mixing that with the fact that we were actually attracted to each other made it feel like the ultimate high.

I hissed beneath my breath. "Lola," Stephanie warned. I glanced at the mirror to look at my cousin. She was shorter than me, with curves for days. She was one of the few people I trusted to do my hair. With the upcoming heat and the fact that I was running back and forth between the garden and clinic I *needed* my hair rebraided, out of my way, and protected.

"What are you thinking about?" she asked, starting another section. My fingers twitched. She must have scented what I was feeling. Kraken's crap. I felt Lily's and Eleanor's eyes on me "Flynn?" she teased. My cheeks warmed.

"No!" I said too quickly. My cousin hummed in disagreement. It was stupid to lie to a vampire. "I was thinking about the fact that I helped a griffin lay two eggs last night," I said in a huff. Lily's eyes widened comically.

"No way! Have the eggs hatched yet?" Lily asked as Babs brushed through her hair. Lily quickly glanced at Babs, eyes narrowing. Lily had very wavy hair and always got nervous when people cut her hair since the length changed depending on whether it was dry or wet. Through the mirror Steph narrowed her eyes. She definitely knew I was lying.

"Not yet. They won't for a few more weeks. But it was tough. The poor mom had trouble pushing them out so Flynn-" I stopped immediately. My cousin paused her braiding and I could see her raised one delicate eyebrow through the mirror. "Stop giving me those looks. He helped me help the griffin give birth. That's all."

ISABEL BARREIRO

"What time?" Eleanor asked.

"Close to midnight," I said. Lily nodded.

"So he left after our meeting," Crystal said with a tiny tilt of her lips.

"Meeting?" I asked. Crystal nodded.

"He has a theory that a piece of the root broke from the Hollow Tree when it was dying. The problem is figuring out where," Crystal recapped. I nodded. That made sense, and honestly it was my hunch as well.

"Why did he come over?" Lily asked. I stared at myself in the mirror as I recounted our late evening. Actually, why *did* he come? He never did say.

"I don't know," I said quietly. Stephanie ran the tail end of the comb through my scalp, creating another section. She slathered some gel along the roots of the section so that the braid would come out smoother. The great thing about having a vampire hair braider is that they typically worked fast.

"You can ask now," she said with a smirk. The door to the salon dinged open. I didn't need to turn my head to see who it was. The comforting smell of sunscreen and Earth filled my nose. But there was something else. My stomach growled.

"Flynn! What a nice surprise. Are you getting a haircut?" Eleanor asked with a cheesy smile.

"Um, no," he said as he rocked back and forth on his heels. His eyes met mine briefly and once again I was reminded of last night.

"Manicure? Your nails must be taking a brutal hit with the garden," Lily teased. The tips of his ears turned pink and I bit my lip to keep from laughing. He lifted a bag in the air.

"I brought food," he said. There was another ding as the door opened.

"For who?" Crystal asked, smiling unabashedly.

"Yeah for who?" Celestino said, slapping a hand on his shoulder. Flynn stuttered for a second.

"Crystal," he said quickly. I raised my eyebrows in surprise. I could tell he was lying. His nose twitched and his eyes were wandering around, avoiding me when he answered. Sailor slapped a hand on his other shoulder.

88

"But I have her lunch," Sailor said. His fingers dug into Flynn's shirt. Flynn's eyes twitched at Sailor's strength and I stifled another laugh.

"You brought me lunch?" Crystal said, leaning up from the pedicure chair. Sailor smiled and began to speak.

"Well, we brought you all lunch. You too Steph," Celestino said, cutting him off. Stephanie clapped her hands.

"Perfect, my fingers needed a break," she said. I rolled my eyes. Stephanie left to go wash her hands and Flynn came to stand behind me. He stared at me through the mirror and it was difficult to maintain eye contact. I was never one to shy away from anything or anyone. But lately Flynn has been making me feel and act in all sorts of ways.

"I brought you food. Your dad suggested you were probably hungry. There's a hamburger, medium rare with swiss cheese and fries," he said quietly. My heart thumped.

"My dad?" I asked. "I'm starting to think you prefer him over me," I joked. Flynn rolled his eyes.

"He was picking up an order," he said as his gaze flickered to the box of charms that sat on the salon's service tray.

"Is that all?" I asked, taking the bag from him. The food smelled divine. From the corner of my eye Eleanor scooted closer to Sailor and Crystal. Sailor was helping feed Crystal since her nails were still drying. Her face was red. Celestino had his hands caressing the back of Lily's neck who was happily munching on fries.

Everyone was distracted and it made me feel like Flynn and I were in our own little world. He pulled out a discreet bottle from the bag and handed it to me. Cracking it open I could smell iron. He brought me blood. I fought back a smile. Looks like Mr. Tin Can Knight was proving to be a teddy bear.

"Actually, no. Did they tell you about my theory?" he asked, glancing at our friends. I nodded and began drinking. Flynn scratched the back of his neck. "Do you think when you're done you could come to the tree with me and Celestino?" he asked. I bit back a smile. Flynn asking *me* for help? That was new.

"Sure, but I need you to pack up some more herbs from Priscilla for the clinic. The griffin needs more nutrients, she was consuming stars' knows what from the forest," I said. I had an unsettling fear that many creatures were dying inside the forest.

First the pegasi, then the unicorn, *then* Nessie and now the griffin. Flynn nodded his head, before picking up one of the hair charms. His eyes were back on me. His gaze slowly traveled down the side of my face and neck before making his way back up to my lips. On instinct, I darted my tongue out to wet them.

"Rider," I said in a singsong voice. His eyes narrowed.

"Lola," he warned. He leaned slightly forward and I felt entranced. His eyes were brighter today. I could see the flecks of gold and green in them that made me weak. "You think because of that one moment that I'll let you get away with calling me that?" he said.

My heart picked up. I leaned back, arching my neck up to look up at him. He bent slightly further down, eyes locked on mine, and the room faded away.

"And what were you feeling in that moment," I whispered. His chest rose sharply.

"We still have a bet in place," he pointed out. I hummed.

"And I still think you'll cave first," I said as my eyes wandered to his neck. I felt my fangs poke my lips. *Fuck.* He tasted delicious last night. I could only imagine what it would be like to bite him while he's inside of me. Flynn's eyes sparkled with mischief as if reading my mind. He reached over to the charm box again.

"I don't know Sunflower. You're the one looking at me like you want another taste," he said, dropping a charm he had picked up in my lap. It wasn't until he said goodbye to everyone that I glanced down to see what it was.

A sunflower.

Excitement coursed through me. He was coming around and I could feel it. And because I could sense it I couldn't stop the stupid smile stretching across my face. My cousin came back to the front, eyeing me through the mirror as she took a bite of a taco. I rolled my eyes. She shrugged her shoulders and went back to eat with Babs.

I glanced over at Sailor, remembering I had the book in my bag. "Hey Sailor, I need your help," I said as I set up my food on the counter in front of me. He looked at Crystal who motioned for him to go.

"What's up Lola?" he asked. I pulled out the book and handed it to him.

"My mom gave me this book. It might have some insight on how to help Nessie with her situation," I said. His eyes widened and his heart-beat picked up. His pores opened up and I could smell sweat. His fingers brushed against the worn leather before sucking in a deep breath.

"Everything okay?" I asked, taking a bite of some fries. Sometimes it was difficult to ignore what I could sense and see. He swallowed and nodded quietly. I glanced over at the girls who all had the same concerned look. We all felt that Sailor had been keeping a secret from us, about his town and family.

"Sorry. I just...I know who wrote this," he said quietly. I reached over to take the book back but he swatted my hand away. "It's fine," he said, cracking it open. He flipped throughout the book and I couldn't help but feel guilty.

"It's so nice to have Nessie around," Crystal said, trying to break the tension. "I remember when she used to tug us around that little boat," she said with a smile. The girls giggled.

"I don't think she can do that this year," Eleanor pointed out. "Which means I need to come up with something else," she said, the wheels in her head already turning. Sailor grunted. We all glanced at him. He scratched the back of his head.

"Alright. Nothing too difficult," he said. I raised an eyebrow. "Some of the writing is written in old Atlantian," he said. Lily held up a hand.

"Explain," she said. Sailor sighed.

"It's in the language of the sirens who are from the Atlantic ocean. But we don't really speak like this anymore," he said, his eyes scanning the pages. "Nessie giving birth would be similar to a dolphin. If you want to make the birth easier, you can fill the swamp with some herbs: laven-der, chamomile, and even some sea salt. Make sure to maintain the temperature of the water," he said, handing me back the book. So basi-cally, I was doing everything correctly already. I sighed in relief. *Thank the stars.*

"That was so much, yet so little information about sirens," Eleanor said, crossing her arms. Sailor winked.

"We love our secrets," he said, shrugging his shoulders.

CHAPTER 14
TANGLED

FLYNN

The sun was relentless against a cloudless sky. The community garden was covered in hydrangeas, dahlias, daffodils, hyacinths and so much more. I sucked in a deep breath, the sweet floral scent setting my body at ease.

I glanced over at Lola's section which was blooming with roses, azaleas and tulips. Despite having to run around saving lives she's been able to keep all of her flowers alive.

"Hey Flynn, we just got a shipment of soil," Mr. Hale said from behind me. Because of the rot happening on our grounds Mr. Hale has made it his company's mission to help provide whatever labor materials we might need, which included dirt. His workers also helped build all of the raised beds. I know Eleanor has had issues with her dad, but I couldn't deny that he's been a really big help.

"Leave it by the greenhouse and I'll separate them by which garden bed needs them," I called out. I lifted my shirt to wipe the sweat from my forehead.

Sure it was spring and there was a mellow breeze but by the stars was the sun was brutal. I had a feeling it was going to be a hot summer. I cracked my neck and began harvesting some of the herbs Lola needed: mint, fennel, lemon balm. From the corner of my eyes I could see ginger. That should help as well.

As I placed the herbs in my basket I couldn't help but frown at the thought of Lola sleeping in that stars forsaken poor excuse of a bed. It was basically cardboard. Trolls had comfier beds.

Considering what her job is, she needs a good place to sleep. I sat back on my feet. I closed my eyes briefly, knowing that I was going to regret this call. But if I didn't do it then Lola and her stupid cot would continue to distract me. I pulled off my glove and reached for my phone.

"Hey, I need you to do me a favor."

✳ ❖ ✳ ❖ ✳ ❖ ✳ ❖ ✳

IT WAS ABOUT four in the afternoon by the time Lola showed up to the garden. She was wearing pink scrub pants and an off the shoulder cropped graphic tee. My eyes followed the gentle sway of her hips as she made her way towards me. It was like she was purposely trying to turn me on. She was effortlessly elegant.

As she got closer I could see that her hair was braided down, gently hitting the curve of her ass. Gold charms reflected in the sunlight. She waved her hand at Mr. Hale who nodded in return.

Standing in front of me I tilted my head back to gaze at her. From this position the sun painted a halo behind her. We were quiet for a moment, our eyes drinking each other in.

Lola took her time as her gaze trailed up and down my body. Her throat bobbed up and down. I stayed kneeling at her feet. I hated to admit that I quite enjoyed this position. She raised an eyebrow, a delicate smirk on her lips as she looked down on me.

"Don't you look good on your knees, Pretty Boy." Her voice was huskier, just like it was at the clinic. My cock twitched in my pants. I shifted slightly so I was directly in front of her now. Her eyes slightly widened as I slowly rose to my feet, careful that our chests did not bump into each other. Her eyes wandered down.

"No shirt?" she said. Was she out of breath? I shook my head. The shirt had been plastered to my skin and so I tossed it somewhere. She hummed in appreciation and my chest swelled with pride.

"You look like you want to touch me," I teased. Her eyes eventually made their way back to my face.

"You're going to be the one to cave first Rider," she said. I shook my head back and forth.

"Sure. Is that why your hand looks like it's about to grab my belt loop?" I teased. Lola fought back a smile and we both watched her pull her hands back to her side.

"I think we're both aware of the fact that we are attracted to each other," she said. My lips twitched and I closed the gap between us. Lola did her best to seem unbothered, but by her rapid breathing and dilated pupils I could see that she was teetering on the edge.

"Come on, *Sunflower*. Have a taste," I said, my voice low. A noise escaped past her lips and it made my body roar to life. I wanted to hear more of her sounds while my hand kneaded her breasts, and my fingers played with her pussy. She was so close to giving in.

Her head tilted slightly up and her lips parted. At the right angle I could make out her fangs. My stomach twisted and my cock strained. I wanted her to bite me again.

"Flynn, be a good boy and give in first," she said. This time I hummed as my eyes fluttered closed. By this point, our chests were pressing against each other and I could taste the mint on her breath. "Almost there," she teased.

There was a giant thump and we sprang apart, breathing heavily. "Sorry, last bag of dirt," Mr. Hale said with a smirk. I groaned inwardly. *Cockblock.* My gaze slid back to Lola. Her hands were tugging at her graphic tee as she took a deep breath. A sliver of her soft, brown skin caught my eye. Fuck. She was so beautiful.

"Let me know if you need anything else," Mr. Hale called out as he walked away.

"So," Lola began.

95

"Damn, who knew Mr. Hale would be a cockblock," a voice teased. Our heads turned to Celestino who was at the gate of the community garden. I was not going to fucking hear the end of this.

"I could give you guys a few minutes in the greenhouse if you-"

"The Hollow Tree. Let's go," I said, cutting him off. Lola let out a giggle and I adjusted my pants. I could practically **hear** the family group chat once Celestino told Caleb what he saw.

❋⬦❋⬦❋⬦❋⬦❋⬦❋

AS WE WANDERED through the forest my chest felt tight. The trees were holding up, though some were shedding their leaves. The sun was high up and the branches scattered the light across our paths. Twigs broke in the distance, the signal that creatures were making their way around.

I could feel the forest softly buzz around with life, but it was weaker than usual. Typically there was a pulsating warmth that began to radiate during the spring. Spring was the season of rebirth, when the forest was waking up after its long winter nap.

We walked in comfortable silence. I glanced over at Lola who was animatedly talking to Celestino about the unicorn. My stomach sank. I liked having her around. I liked the comfort she brought me. I enjoyed our rivalry and endless banter as much as I enjoyed making her smile and laugh.

Her dark gaze collided with mine as she tucked a braid behind her ear. One of her charms sparkled beneath the broken sunlight. My heart skipped. It was the charm I had picked. Slowly Lola was convincing me that I could have more, that I <u>deserved</u> more.

The baby Hollow Tree stood at the center of a small clearing, surrounded by other trees whose branches leaned towards it. The tree was growing steadily. Right now it was getting close to three feet tall and I could spot new branches growing. It was amazing what a little magic and love could do.

"It looks healthy," Lola pointed out. I nodded.

"You guys are doing a good job," Celestino said, crouching down to get a closer look.

"Yeah. Mr. Hale, the pixies, the fairies and I have been monitoring its progress and giving it spellbound fertilizer to keep the rot away," I said.

I knelt down, my knees sinking into the grass and my body slowly relaxed. I leaned over and dug my fingers into the ground.

"I'll place my hand on your shoulder and let my magic flow through you," Celestino said, moving to sit next to me. I nodded silently.

We simultaneously took a breath and I felt his power seep into my body. It flowed beneath my skin, looping around my muscles until it connected with my own magic. While his magic was dark, there was a calmness to it that soothed me.

I propelled our combined magic towards the Earth, intertwining with the liveliness of nature. I closed my eyes, allowing my mind and body to connect. There was a soft rustle next to me and then the smell of citrus. I assumed Lola was sitting next to me now. A mixture of English and Gaelige poured out of me as I searched with my magic for the rotten root.

Like a beam of light my magic was zooming through the Gasping Greenwood, making sharp turns, left, right, and then circling back. Sweat dripped down the side of my head.

I sucked in a lungful of air. I needed to push more. I was getting closer to something dark. It was almost nauseating, and sadness drifted into my body. My hands began trembling. I was almost there. Another left.

The closer I got the more my inner shadows attempted to take over. This was pointless. There was no way I was capable of doing this. I wasn't as strong as Caleb or as confident as Bridget. Stars, I wasn't even as optimistic as Greg.

If I was then I wouldn't be so afraid to– I must be near the rot, waves of negative emotions begin tackling my body. A pain shot up my right arm and I hissed. Celestino's hand tightened on my shoulder while a warm hand braced my arm.

A noise escaped past my lips as my body tensed. A strange new power surged through me. "You can do this," Lola said softly, lips brushing my ear. I dug my fingers deeper.

"*By my will, find what is ill*," I whispered. Celestino repeated my words until we both began to chant them in unison. A blinding light pierced my closed eyes. My magic brushed something, a root, broken off and alone. It was embedded in the earth and…growing.

Wait.

This wasn't just a broken root. It was a sapling. A dead Hollow Tree had been growing. I gasped, yanking my hand out and falling back on my ass. Celestino stared in confusion as I sucked in a long, full breath of air.

I glanced over at Lola whose eyes were wide with worry. She reached for me, one hand caressing my cheek.

"Flynn? Flynn, are you okay?" she asked. I stared at her, mouth agape as I tried to piece together what I had discovered. "Please answer me." Her voice shook at the end of her sentence and it broke the spell I was under. I nodded and she sighed in relief. Her hand dropped back to my shoulder and squeezed.

"Thank the stars. You scared me with the way you were shaking. I don't think I've ever seen you use that kind of magic," she said, her eyes casting between me, Celestino and the tree.

"That was intense," Celestino said, trying to catch his breath as he stretched his fingers. I nodded, silently.

"This might be worse than we thought," I said.

CHAPTER 15
WATER BIRTHS ARE MESSY

LOLA

F lynn was still breathing heavily as we made our way back to the garden. He still hadn't told me what happened when he used his magic but with the way his eyebrows were furrowed and his cheeks were flushed I knew it wasn't good.

"Something is definitely dead," Celestino said, rubbing his hand. When I placed my hand on Flynn's arm I could feel their magic pulsing together. It was powerful, but something was off. I placed my hand on him without thinking and prayed to the stars that my magic could connect to his like I did with the animals. It seemed to have worked.

We were near Flynn's greenhouse when I forced him to stop. Celestino looked between us. My hand wrapped around Flynn's wrist and I pulled him towards me.

"What?" he snapped. His hair had come loose from his headband and now grazed his shoulders. I stared at him in shock. His honey brown eyes were muddled with fear and sorrow. His lips were twisted into a frown of frustration. I had never seen Flynn look so dejected.

"Talk to me Flynn. What happened?" I asked, mindful of my tone. With the way his fingers drummed against his thighs and his feet kept shifting, it was as though he was ready to bolt. "You can tell me," I said as my hand wandered up his arm to cradle his elbow. His eyes tracked the movement.

"I don't even know how to explain it," he said, softly.

"Me either," Celestino said, looking back at the forest.

"Try using an analogy," I offered. My heart hammered in my chest. This was not the Flynn I knew. This was a part of him that he kept hidden, a part that was covered in anxiety and insecurity. His eyes stayed on my hand around his elbow.

"Rider," he muttered. I raised an eyebrow.

"Yes Rider?" I asked. He nodded.

"Did you see the show?" he asked. I bit back a laugh and nodded. "Okay. Remember the moonstone and how it destroys?" he asked. Dread began settling in my bones. I nodded again. "And the sundrop flower?" he continued.

"Flynn," I warned.

"My theory was right. A root broke off from the Hollow Tree and managed to sprout into a sapling," his words rushed out. I dropped my hand, the severity of our situation dawning on me. His fingers brushed the back of my arm, connecting us again.

"Fucking stars Flynn," Celestino said. "*That's* what we felt?"

"Yeah. Maybe we could heal it the same way we did the Hollow Tree," he said. Fucking stars. As the inverse of the Hollow Tree, instead of healing and spreading life it was doing the opposite.

"Why not just…" I trailed off. Flynn glared at me

"No we will not," he said firmly. I scoffed.

"It's causing sickness Flynn. Possibly death," I pointed out.

"What are you two talking about?" Celestino asked. Flynn swallowed, shaking his head.

"There's probably a way to *heal* it Lola. It's a living thing and I will do everything in my power to help it. I think someone like you can understand," Flynn said, taking a step back. My mouth hung open in shock.

"Of course I do. But look at what I've been going through. I'm sleeping at the clinic every night. Every day there's some creature that needs help because the literal *Earth* is making them sick. I have animals ready to give birth at any notice and I can't even trust what we grow or our own damn water!" I said. "Look at how it's affecting the town," I finished. Flynn's nostrils flared and Celestino took a step back.

"Don't you think I know that Lola? I'm working overtime for the festival. I'm making sure you have everything you need so you're not stressed. I have ingredients that I need for work, for you *and* for the town," he spat out. My heart skipped.

"I know that, and-"

"Lola!" A voice yelled. Carrie was running up to us, her red hair slipping out of its bun.

"What's wrong?" I asked, my heart already racing. Carrie pointed towards the swamp.

"Nessie...baby...*now*," she managed in between breaths. My eyes widened. You have got to be fucking kidding me. I stared at her as she trembled. I wasn't prepared yet. I didn't think she would be giving birth now. I thought I had more time to study the siren book with Sailor. From the corner of my eye I saw Flynn motion to Celestino.

Okay, I've done a few water births. I've helped sea creatures give birth during college. Granted, I've never dealt with a creature of Nessie's size, but I could do this. I hesitated when taking a step forward when I realized something.

I was alone. I had never helped a sea creature give birth *alone*. Ms. Heinstein still wasn't back so I was the only vet in town and had no choice. I took a deep breath.

"Let's go," I said.

❋ ❀ ❋ ❀ ❋ ❀ ❋ ❀ ❋

NESSIE WAS SWIMMING BACK and forth. The water of Boogeyman's swamp was swishing towards the shore. A deep rumble shook the swamp. Nessie was in pain.

Of course she was. She was about to give birth. Carrie was by my side, still shaking. I tugged off my shoes and socks and tossed them to the side before stepping into the water. It was warm, which was good. It would soothe her.

Nessie spotted me with her big green eyes. She lowered her body, keeping her head above the waterline so that I could place my hand on her skin. She was hot, her eyes drooping. She groaned. I closed my eyes briefly, feeling my magic swirl deep in my belly.

"I'm here baby girl," I said.

Come soon

"And I'm going to help you," I said, ignoring the small bits of her pain slipping through me. "I want you to try and stay near the shore so I can check periodically if the baby is starting to poke out. You think you can do that?" I asked.

Of course Lola. But so much pain

I knew she was in pain because I could feel it. Unlike other vampires, because of my empathy I could feel a fraction of their pain whenever I connected with them.

I heard footsteps behind me and turned to see Flynn with Dahlia and Daisy. My eyes widened as Flynn chucked off his shoes and came into the water.

"What are you doing?" I asked. He stared at Nessie, hesitating a moment as she pulled her head out of the water.

"I figured you needed some water fairies to monitor the water or something," he said pointing behind him. "I had Celestino run to get Dahlia while I got Daisy," he said. I stared at him in shock. Despite our heated words he didn't hesitate to help me. A bubble of emotions grew within me and threatened to spill out. As much as I felt like breaking down in tears, I had work to do.

"Tell us what to do Lola!" Dahlia shouted. Flynn was here. Not only did he bring help, he was standing in the water with me. His hand brushed my elbow as Nessie bellowed in pain. I bit my lip to hide my wince. The pain shot through my stomach.

"Daisy, keep the water at an even temperature. We need to make sure she stays relaxed," I said, glancing back at Nessie. "Dahlia, is there any way you can use your magic to alleviate pain?" I paused. "Fuck, I think we need Priscilla to bring some herbs or something," I said out loud.

"I'll call her!" Carrie shouted. I nodded.

"What do you want me to do?" Flynn asked.

"Remember how we massaged the griffin? I need you to do that on her lower abdomen. Periodically I'll go underwater to check on where the head is at," I said.

"But you can't breathe underwater," Flynn said, eyes wide, pulling me closer. I don't think he even realized what he just did. A smirk graced my face.

"You're about to learn all about my powers today, Rider."

❋ ❀ ❋ ❀ ❋ ❀ ❋ ❀ ❋

PRISCILLA AND DAHLIA were enchanting the water with some herbs and oil while Daisy monitored the temperature. It was the perfect relaxing bath for a pregnant Loch Ness monster. Flynn was doing his best to massage Nessie. He freaked out the first time he felt the little baby, his eyes wide in awe and confusion.

Had I known that Nessie was going to give birth today I would have waited to get my hair done. But sometimes you can't plan a Loch Ness monster's birth.

My clothes were weighing me down as I ducked under water to check on how far Nessie was dilated. The special thing about my magic was that while I was able to connect to all animals, when it came to supernatural creatures I was able to use some of their magic. Which meant that for a tiny bit I had the ability to breathe underwater.

The small waves that Nessie was making were pushing me back as I swam under, using my vampire strength to muscle through. Under Nessie's tail, a head was beginning to poke out. I placed my hand on her tail and tapped twice.

Okay Ms. Luna.

And then I inwardly lost my collective shit as I stayed underwater to catch Nessie the Loch Ness monster's baby.

＊◦＊◦＊◦＊◦＊◦＊

THE SUN WAS SETTING and there was a gentle breeze as we all watched Nessie happily swim with her mini me. I smiled warmly. I delivered a Loch Ness monster. I glanced around at Carrie, Priscilla, Dahlia and Daisy. Dahlia and Daisy had enchanted the water again to keep it nice and warm for the next few hours and Priscilla promised to come back tomorrow to sprinkle it with some soothing herbs.

Flynn brushed his hair back and my heart squeezed. Despite our disagreement, he got help. Something I didn't think to do. Sure, he'd seemed scared but he had pushed that away to be there for me. My eyes pricked again with unshed tears. There was so much more to Flynn than just a smart elf with the occasional attitude.

"Take a picture, Sunflower. It'll last longer," he said with a smirk. I snorted, shaking my head. He looked at me and the edges of his lips softened, tilting slightly up. The shadows that usually lurked in his eyes seem to have retreated back. He looked relaxed, content. I smiled at him. His chest rose sharply.

"What?" I asked, a giggle erupting.

"Your smile…it's like a shot of sunshine, clearing away the clouds," he said. My cheeks warmed at his tenderness. "There's something I think we deserve," he said. I tried to ignore the sprites that were flying around in my belly. That was the sweetest thing he had ever said to me, that anyone has.

"Can I ask a question?" Flynn said. I raised an eyebrow.

"Consent looks hot on you Flynn," I teased. He rolled his eyes but a faint blush on his cheeks bloomed.

"Why did you become a vet? Is it just because of your inclination?" he asked. I turned to watch Nessie and her baby float around the swamp. A soft smile tugged on my lips.

"Yes," I said. "As beings we can communicate our troubles. But the creatures don't. Human vets have to use deduction to figure out what's wrong. My magic allows me to speak to them directly. It would be a waste if I didn't do this job," I continued.

I lowered my hand to pet the newborn baby who swam up to my feet. My heart thumped at her adorable vibrant green eyes and pale green scales. They would most likely darken as she aged.

"Plus I genuinely love what I do. I love watching them grow, learn, and heal. It's a beautiful thing that I get to witness. It's a privilege that I have a hand in helping a life *live*." Nessie's baby moved onto Flynn, who rubbed the top of her head. I got to witness and participate in a beautiful moment.

"Why do you do what you do?" I asked. Flynn laid back in the grass, the sun turning his eyes into the color of melted gold. He was a work of art. But even now I could see a smidge of sadness lurking in the depths of his solemn gaze.

"At 16 our dad let us try whiskey. I tried it and hated it," he said. I giggled and he cracked a small smile. "Growing up I watched my mom and Greg try different recipes with food. I kept wondering if there was a way to make whiskey that I could enjoy." I laid down on my side, and pushed a lock of hair away from his forehead. He turned his head to the side, his gaze falling to my lips.

"Whiskey making involves a lot of science, which we both know I love. I kept trying to figure out what herbs, fruits and flavors I could blend and make enjoyable," he paused, taking a breath. "My dad didn't push his business on any of us but I knew he was happy that I had taken an interest, and I do love it. I love applying science and my horticulture knowledge to make something that everyone can enjoy and share," he said.

When Flynn met my gaze again my heart stopped. A smile stretched across his face, lighting up his eyes. His love for his job was pouring out of him and I understood it.

"I still can't get Bridget to like whiskey though," he said. My body relaxed into vibrant laughter. He joined me, his carefree laugh pouring out of him. We lay in the grass, pinkies nearly touching as we enjoyed the warm spring afternoon.

I didn't want this moment to end. I didn't want what was beginning to brew between us to end. These moments with Flynn were always fleeting, like flower petals drifting in a breeze. I wanted to collect them all and hold them close to my heart.

He stood up suddenly and offered me a hand. There was a cheeky look in his eyes that told me to follow him. I took his hand, enjoying the feel of his calloused skin against mine.

"Follow me, Sunflower," he said.

✻ ❀ ✻ ❀ ✻ ❀ ✻ ❀ ✻

THE GREENHOUSE WAS warm and welcoming. We were surrounded by different herbs and fruit trees. I spotted a sage plant in the corner and my lips twitched. I watched Flynn as he looked for something under his work table. He pulled out an unmarked bottle and two mugs. I raised an eyebrow.

"I think we both deserve some whiskey after what you just did," he said with a grin. I walked over to him and bumped his shoulder.

"I think you mean what *we* did," I said. His eyes did that thing where they softened and I wanted to melt. He was so relaxed. He poured us each a cup. The greenhouse glittered with the setting sun. Warm orange and pink hues danced around us.

"This place is beautiful," I said. Flynn looked around at the tiny world he'd created.

"It's my quiet place. A place for me to…" he trailed off, struggling to find the words.

"Be you?" I offered. He turned toward me and handed me my cup with a silent nod. I stared at the amber liquid. I could smell honey, hints of sage, and some smokiness.

"Flynn," I said. He swallowed, a storm rolling through his gaze. "Can we talk about the tree?" He turned away from me, a tick in his jaw.

"You're right," I quickly said. He swirled his cup before taking a sip.

"I'm right?" he asked, casting a glance at me.

"We should try to save the tree. Maybe there's a spell that we can use. Would the same potion Eleanor used before work?" He leaned against the table.

"I think it should honestly. But you're also right. We'll try to heal the tree and *if* that doesn't work, we'll have Hale's Lumber destroy it. But properly," he said. I offered a small smile and nodded. I finally took a sip and a noise of delight escaped me. Sweet, smokey and the burn was just right.

"Fuck. This is great, Rider," I said, a smile stretching across my face. Flynn's eyes didn't meet mine.

Instead they stay focused on the corner of my lips. His pupils slightly dilated and I could see a tiny bead of sweat drip down the side of his forehead. My vampire senses heightened as the earthy scent around us began to mingle with the scent of Flynn's arousal.

His thumb came up to swipe softly against my bottom lip, making my face tingle and my body ache for more. He slowly brought his thumb to his mouth. I couldn't stop watching as his tongue peaked out to take a delicate lick.

Fucking stars.

CHAPTER 16
WHISKEY KISSES

FLYNN

L ola was in my greenhouse. My sanctuary away from the world was being filled with her sunshine. Watching her get in the zone and help Nessie deliver her baby unlocked something in me. She was achingly beautiful when she took charge.

I knew she was nervous by the way she kept biting the inside of her cheek but despite all that she did it. It was fucking hot as shit every time she came up for air to update us on Nessie's dilation.

And the fact that she can take on some of their magic? That was impressive. I was ready to say fuck it to the bet and kiss her in the middle of all of the swamp water.

My eyes traveled down her body. Her t-shirt was still drying and her scrub pants were molded against her curves and long legs. That soft little moan she let out when she tried my whiskey nearly made me snap. My control was breaking in half with just the thought of tasting her.

"You taste good," poured out of my mouth. She arched an eyebrow.

"I think you mean *it* as in the whiskey," she said, taking another sip. I shook my head.

"No, I mean *you*," I said firmly. She moved to stand next to me, her hip leaning against the table. Her dark eyes were weakening my defenses and I gripped the table's edge. I could see her brain working for a slick comeback.

"But you haven't tasted me Flynn," she said, eyes narrowing. She was pulling me in with her words, the tilt of her smirk and the mischief behind her dark eyes. My eyes flickered back to her lips before looking away.

"Did Nessie name her baby yet?" I asked, needing a break from our tension. I still had a tiny bit of restraint left. Lola let out a giggle that warmed my soul. Her laugh was an addictive sweet melody that could chase away my darkest days.

"She said I could have the honor of naming her," Lola said. I stared at her. Her eyes were misty and casted downward. She dug her sneaker into the ground. I leaned down, trying to catch her eye.

"What are you going to name her then?" I asked. She dropped her head back and her braids pooled onto my table. My cock twitched as images of taking her on this table flooded my brain.

"Lucky, I think," she said.

"Why?"

"Because I felt lucky today. I'd never delivered a Loch Ness monster's baby. I had a vague idea of what to do. If it wasn't for you getting Celestino to bring Dahlia and Daisy, and Carrie getting Priscilla to help, I don't know what would have happened. Even my mom getting the book was a huge help." My heart rattled against my chest at her words. A tear escaped her eye and I wiped it quickly. She sniffled before turning her face towards me. "I'm lucky to have you, and everyone. And Lucky is too."

"That's a beautiful name," I said, my heart swelling in my chest. She was making it fucking hard as shit to keep this stupid bet.

"Hey Flynn," she said nervously. I took a sip of the whiskey, savoring its flavor.

"Lola," I said, urging her to speak.

"Thanks for…you know…the b-blood," she stuttered. My face flushed at the memory. I could *almost* feel the ghost of her lips soft against my skin, her teeth digging in and eliciting a euphoric sting. Lola made me ache for the sun. She banished away the clouds that constantly consumed me. But I wasn't worthy of walking in her light.

"You said the last time you did that, it was with an ex," I said, a bite at the end of my tone. When Lola was sucking my blood I had to fight every nerve in my body to keep myself from touching her the way that I've been wanting to. At that moment I *needed* her– beyond comprehension.

"Yes. A vampire's bite has a euphoric consequence," she said, sneaking a glance at me as she drained the last bit of her whiskey.

"I wouldn't call it a consequence," I said. She snorted.

"Then what would you call it," she asked. Her dark gaze began pulling me in, like it always did. She settled her cup on the table and crossed her arms, without breaking eye contact.

"A reward," I said. Lola's eyes widened. I stepped in front of her and she leaned back slightly. I grinded my teeth, my control hanging by a thread. My hand came up to cup her cheek. She sucked in a breath, eyes falling softly closed as I leaned in. My lips brushed right below her ear. "I think it's only right that you repay me," I whispered against her neck. She shuddered.

"H-how?" she asked, eyeing me. I reached for her empty cup with my other hand as I tilted her head to the side. I hovered the cup above her neck and watched a tiny drop of whiskey fall and splash across her skin. The delicate drop ran down her neck, and before it could slip beneath her shirt I moved.

Lola's hands flew to my arms, holding me in place as my tongue licked the trail my whiskey left on her skin. She let out a small moan and I pressed against her. Her nails dug into my arms and I couldn't stop myself from sucking on her skin. She yelped as I took a bite but I quickly soothed it with a gentle swipe of my tongue.

I pressed my forehead into the crook of her neck. "Mhmm. The whiskey does taste good," I said with a smirk. I could feel our hearts racing against each other. Lola's hands pressed up against my arms rising higher until they came around my neck. I pulled back slightly, my lips brushing her jaw.

She stared at me with wide eyes filled with need.

"Flynn," she whispered, breathless. I glanced at her lips, slightly parted, tongue poking out. "You want something. I can see it in your eyes," she said. It wasn't that I wanted something. I *needed* something, and that 'something' was her. I needed to taste her.

"You," I said. And then I crashed my lips against hers, not giving a shit about our fucking bet.

CHAPTER 17
WHISKEY TASTE GOOD ON YOU

LOLA

W*arm. Tender. Hesitant. Blissful.*

Words I would have never associated with Flynn. But now? Now that he was *finally* kissing me I was going to have to flip through a dictionary to describe how he felt, and how he made *me* feel.

His lips were soft against mine and his hands trembled against my cheeks. My heart was pounding in my chest, and since my head was tipsy off of his whiskey I tugged him closer by his shirt before he could pull away. There was no way I was letting him go. My tongue peeked out, teasing his bottom lip. He shuddered against me.

"Lola." Even though his voice was barely a whisper it imprinted on my brain, heated my body, and made my fangs ache. I nodded, slipping my hand behind his neck.

"Yes," I said breathlessly. I needed him to know that this was okay. Everything about this was right. I had been working nonstop with many sleepless nights and after a few seconds with Flynn, I felt weightless. The worries of the festival, the town and the creatures melted away.

Right now it was just Flynn and I locked away in his greenhouse, away from the world. I moved to slip my fingers in between his, which were still cupping my face.

"Yes, Flynn," I assured him.

His grip tightened and his confidence bloomed. His hands slid down to grip my shoulders and then my waist, pulling me closer. I parted my legs wider, needing him closer.

"Fuck," he whispered before dragging his lips back to mine.

I tried to nod as he boldly slipped his tongue to tangle with mine. My hands found themselves tugging at him. Our bodies were molded together and it still didn't feel like enough. I hopped onto his table, locked my legs around his waist and pulled him flush against me. Flynn let out a deep groan.

"You like it when I take charge, Pretty Boy?" I whispered against his neck. I took my time sucking, nicking his skin carefully with my fangs. I could tell it drove him wild with the way his hands dug into my thighs; it was a delicious pain.

"Flynn?" I asked. He hummed as his hand came up to toy with my waist. I shuddered as his fingers followed the hem at the top of my pants. I squeezed my legs, needing friction. "I have an idea," I said. He pulled back slightly, face flushed and lips swollen. He was fucking gorgeous. He raised an eyebrow.

I took a quick breath and shrugged off my shirt, revealing a lace bralette. Flynn's eyes darkened and he let out a string of curses, English blending with Gaelige. I reached for the bottle of whiskey and carefully tipped it over my chest.

"Lick," I commanded. Flynn dove in before the whiskey could slip beneath my bra. I moaned loudly as he licked and sucked down my breast. His hands brushed my nipples and I gasped.

"I knew you would taste good," he said against my skin. I whimpered as his fingers rolled my nipples beneath the lace. I started rocking back and forth, enjoying the feel of his erection.

Fuck, was he big? It felt like he was. Flynn slammed a fist into the work desk rattling the pots, sending me closer to the edge.

He lifted his head up and I stared into his eyes. "Lola," he said with warning. My eyes fluttered closed. The hand on my breast lowered until he pressed against my core and I yelped at the pressure. I squeezed my eyes shut and rocked into him. I needed release so badly and I wanted him to give it to me.

"Do you want to come, Sunflower?" he asked, placing a bite on my neck. I mewled as I tried to get him to move but he was still like a garden statue.

"*Please*, Flynn," I pleaded. He let out a dark chuckle that made my stomach tighten.

"What are the chemicals that are released during an orgasm?" he asked. My eyes snapped open as I stared at him. A science question? In the middle of all of *this*? He raised an eyebrow, waiting patiently.

"Flynn. Now is *not* the time t-!" I gasped as he lightly smacked my ass.

"Tell me Sunflower, or I'll walk out," he taunted. I cursed. How could I think when his hand kept playing with my pussy through my panties. He used his teeth to tug my bralette to the side, releasing my breast then taking my nipple in his mouth. My hands flung to his hair, tugging.

"Yes, yes, yes!" I said as he began sucking, his teeth slightly grazing. After a few seconds he pulled away.

"Answer," he demanded.

"Um..oxytocin, dopamine, and…" I trailed off as he moved to peel off my scrub pants.

"And?" He urged me to continue but how could I, when he was taking my clothes off? His eyes widened as he stared at my soaked panties. "You're so fucking wet for me Lola."

I nodded desperately, my hands cupping my breasts, needing the sensations to continue. He reached for the bottle of whiskey before turning his eyes back on me.

"Lay down, and you haven't finished answering the question," he said. *What was the last chemical? Fucking stars.*

I scrambled to lay back on the table, exposed to him. He stared at me, his eyes devouring every inch of my skin. My face flushed, I had never seen that look on his face before. His cheeks were red, his lips swollen and his eyes full of need.

The wooden table bit into my ass and I felt a cool wetness splash against my skin. I hissed as Flynn's mouth licked against my lower stomach. I bucked forward as he began teasing my heated skin. My hand latched onto his hair and I tried shoving him south. I needed his lips on me.

"You keep saying I taste good but you haven't actually tasted me," I said through gritted teeth. My thighs kept clenching at the need for friction. Flynn let out another dark chuckle.

"Answer," he demanded as he nibbled on my inner thigh, pushing me open. I leaned my head back, staring at the greenhouse ceiling that was tangled with vines. His tongue brushed the side of my labia and I placed one of my legs on his shoulder, holding him in place.

"Vasopressin. Now eat me," I demanded. Flynn's face broke out in a wide grin as his mouth descended to the neediest part of me. His tongue teased my hole before licking up and finding my clit. My legs tightened as he changed between flicking and sucking. He moaned deeply, the vibration making me arch my back.

"Keep going," I panted, my hand coming up to play with my nipple. Flynn's eyes caught the movement and his body tensed. My hips jerked faster and my heel dug into his back. I kept trying to press him closer. My stomach tightened and I knew my orgasm was close.

Flynn slipped a finger inside and I bucked up harder, the whiskey bottle rattling. His finger pumped in and out of me, in tempo with the flick of his tongue against my clit. My hand pinched my nipple harder and his name spilled out of my mouth over and over again. Stars teetered at the edge of my vision.

Flynn curled his finger and lightning shot through my body. I cried out his name, needy and spent. Waves of pleasure rippled up and down my body as he continued pumping his finger and keeping his mouth on me until I began to shove him away. He slowly lifted his head up, a smirk on his lips.

He pulled his finger out and I hissed. I watched him suck his finger clean before reaching for a shot of whiskey. His throat bobbed up and down as he swallowed and a swirl of lust began consuming my body again.

"Delicious," he said.

CHAPTER 18
SOLVING MYSTERIES

FLYNN

"Really Flynn?" Caleb pulled me from my thoughts. I looked up at his piercing blue eyes that screamed *I'm annoyed at my younger brother.* I raised an eyebrow and he pointed to my hands.

"Fury fuck," I hissed. I hadn't noticed that I overfilled someone's beer. *Again.* I muttered a few curses as I wiped the bar. My brother snorted next to me as he began refilling the drink for me.

"So are you going to tell me?" he asked. I rolled my eyes.

"I have no idea what you're talking about," I said, tensely. I wrung the towel in the sink and tossed it in a bucket we had underneath. Bridget stood in front of the bar and handed me a new towel.

"You know what he means," Bridget said before sauntering off to grab orders. I moved to reorganize some of the new liquor she brought in from storage.

I sighed. I knew what they wanted from me. *Lola.* They wanted me to spill about her. The last time I did something as stupid as messing up an order it was because I'd gotten distracted by her. And nothing distracts me. *Except* for the beautiful vampire with the enchanting smile who always smells like a spring day, everywhere she goes.

We haven't seen each other yet, it's been a few days since the green-house. She's busy with all the sick creatures and newborn babies popping up, and I've been busy with the garden.

One bed of roses started dying and I quickly noticed the roots from the Dark Hollow Tree were trying to make their way into our raised beds. I had asked some of the earth fairies of Lavender Falls for help. I gripped a tequila bottle tightly. Today we would be telling the group about my little discovery.

My thoughts drifted back to the greenhouse again. I had finally tasted Lola Luna, and fuck was I craving more. My whiskey against her soft skin, her little gasps, her hands in my hair. It was so much sweeter than I could have ever imagined.

And that was unsettling. She was better than any fantasy. She had burst my little bubble of thoughts and dreams about her in the best way possible.

Now that I knew how perfect and right she felt under my hands and mouth there was an even greater possibility of me fucking things up. Lola was like a sunflower, bright and warm. I was a gray cloud and the last thing I wanted to do was dim her light.

"Flynn," Caleb warned me.

"It's working hours," I pointed out. My older brother rolled his eyes, before leaning against the bar.

"It's a slow day," I heard Celestino call from behind me. I briefly closed my eyes.

"Yeah, so out with it," Sailor teased. This was beginning to feel like an intervention. Of course my brother had called them. I bit back a groan and turned around to see all three of them staring at me. I glanced at my watch. It was 3:30 pm.

"Shouldn't you be at work?" I asked, glaring at the warlock and siren. Sailor gave a fetching smile, wide and all teeth.

"Well, Tino and I finished setting up our projects for the day," he said, clapping Celestino's back. Celestino decided after moving back to town and working in events that he would pursue his actual passion which was woodwork. He had a partnership with Hale's Lumber Industry.

"I still have no idea what you guys want from me," I said, casually shrugging my shoulders. I was attempting to play this off nonchalantly. Sailor snorted.

"He's worse than you," Celestino said, pointing at Caleb. Bridget handed me an order and flicked her long blonde hair back.

"Just say it," she demanded. I sent a glare her way and crossed my arms.

"Will you stay out of this?" I said. She huffed and pointed a finger at me.

"You made it my business when you messed up two of my orders. So spill whatever the fuck is on your mind so that you can get back to work," she said. A flush crawled up my face. For a little sister Bridget was stubborn and watchful as fuck. I slid my gaze over to Caleb.

My older brother was stubborn and reclusive. Because of the curse he was under he'd stayed away from relationships, but then Eleanor made him change his mind.

Sure, I could see our similarities. We were both grumps although I definitely had more charisma in one thumb than he did in his whole body.

But Caleb was braver than me. He didn't put up with anyone's bull- shit, while I liked to maintain peace. I was always better at giving advice, at telling someone else what to do rather than applying the advice myself.

Everyone looked at me, waiting. The smart thing would be to just confess my feelings. Tell them how I'd kissed Lola in my special place and it was the best thing ever, and that now I was terrified of screwing up.

But how could I? They looked at me and assumed everything was okay, that I had everything I wanted. That my life wasn't filled with thoughts of insecurity blanketed in clouds of my worry. I was there for everyone and in turn made sure no one had worried about me. As the middle child who yearned for attention I had learned that it was okay to be in the background, hanging on the wall like a frame. It was comforting.

"Flynn, please don't make me," Sailor said. I turned to him and raised an eyebrow. He hesitated a second, looking down. When he looked back up his eyes shone brighter and the air around us cooled. "You know I see energies and I've always noticed yours," he said quietly. I swallowed. I felt like there was a lot that Sailor hid from us. Not just his powers but his past. I felt a prickle in the nape of my neck. Sailor could see the storm that was constantly hanging over me. And yet he's never said anything.

"You can tell us," Celestino said. My hands reached for the towel, twisting it. We've consistently preached to Caleb and Lilianna that they should let us be there for them, and here I was shutting everyone out. I squeezed the towel in my hand. This group was my family. They trusted me and I *should* be able to trust them. I sucked in a deep breath.

"I kissed Lola," I muttered. There was a pregnant pause before everyone erupted with smiles and laughter.

"Dude, congrats!" Celestino said, reaching to snatch the towel from my hands.

"*Finally*. I've been waiting years for this," Caleb said, pulling me into a side hug. I shoved him away quickly.

"No," I said. They looked at me confused. I looked at Sailor again, who had stayed silent, just watching me and my storm.

"Did you not want to kiss her?" Bridget asked.

"I did," I confessed. A flush crawled up my face.

"Then? What's wrong?" Celestino asked. My stomach coiled tighter than a basilisk.

"Lola...I'm not good for Lola," I said, quietly. Caleb stared at me in shock.

"What the *fuck* does that mean?" Caleb asked. I bit the inside of my cheek. *Fuck*. I hated this. I didn't want them to know that I was scared of myself. Sailor was about to say something when the door opened and the girls walked in. "This conversation isn't over," he said, leaning in.

❋ ❋ ❋ ❋ ❋

THE GANG SAT at a table instead of a booth. Celestino had his arm around Lilianna. Eleanor sat in Caleb's lap unabashedly. Lola sat next to Crystal who sat across from Sailor. There was an empty seat on the other side of Lola.

I hesitated before sitting down. She glanced at me, her dark eyes glittered with challenge as she fought back a smirk. She clearly didn't seem rattled to be around me, and if she wasn't then neither was I.

"So why are we gathered here today?" Eleanor said, assuming the leadership role. I looked at Lola again who waved her hand, signaling for me to speak.

"I know what's wrong," I said before launching into my explanation. Curses rattled among our group.

"That show was so good," Lily said, absentmindedly. Crystal's eyes widened and she smiled.

"The music is amazing!" Crystal exclaimed happily.

"I didn't know there was a show," Sailor commented. Celestino let out a laugh.

"Oh, it's *so* good! And Jeremy Jordan voices one of the characters and– I'm sorry. I'm distracting everyone from the conversation." Crystal said, biting down on her bottom lip, face flushed. I couldn't help but chuckle. Lola wrapped an arm around her, giving her a gentle squeeze.

"You'll have to show me the show sometime," Sailor said. Crystal nodded, keeping her eyes down. I glanced at Celestino. He winked at me and Eleanor bit back a smile, watching the exchange.

"What do you need from us?" Lily asked, taking charge.

"Priscilla still has the spellbook that my mom gave her. We're thinking it might contain a healing incantation for the tree that we could test, and then you or Eleanor could cast it. Eleanor was connected with the Hollow Tree last time, so she might make the most sense," Lola said.

When the Hollow Tree was sick, Eleanor had discovered that she held some of its life force within her. She was a sick baby and her mother had pleaded to the Hollow Tree for help. With a special spell from Eleanor and Caleb's magic, they were able to help the tree reincarnate as a sapling. A similar ritual might work now, too. Eleanor nodded.

"I have a feeling it'll be a different spell with different ingredients," I pointed out. It was another theory I had in mind. The last time our Hollow Tree had become sick; this time we were dealing with a reincarnated sapling which was a different situation.

"That makes sense, because this just isn't a rot *on* a tree. That whole tree was born *from* the rot," Lily said. I nodded. "I'll talk to Priscilla, and if she needs anything I'll let you know," Lily offered. Both Lola and I sighed in relief.

"Well based on that reaction I'm happy that we're having this conversation," Eleanor pointed out. I grimaced.

"Sorry you guys, but with all the creatures getting sick and me sleeping at the clinic it's been stressful," Lola said, playing with the straw in her water.

"You're still sleeping on that cot?" I asked. I glanced over at Bridget who discreetly gave me a thumbs up as Lola snorted.

"Of course. It's either that or sleep on some hay next to the unicorn, remember," she said with an eye roll. My jaw tightened. I didn't like the idea of her sleeping on a cot. It grated my nerves. She was running on fumes alone as it was and sleeping on an uncomfortable cot wasn't going to help her, which is why I had instructed Bridget to get her something better to sleep on.

As much as I hated to admit it, I relied on Lola's gardening for the spring festival, so I needed to make sure she was taking care of herself. I couldn't handle the festival alone. At least that's what I told myself. I didn't want to admit that I just needed her– well rested and healthy.

"You need to sleep in a bed. How can you expect to take care of any animals or the flowers if you don't even take care of yourself?" I asked. Our eyes locked in a mutual glare.

"I've been doing just fine," she said, her voice trembling in anger.

"Really? Is that why you nearly passed out the other night and I had to let you drink my blood?" I said. My heart raced against my chest. Lola's eyes widened and she looked at our group of friends. *Fuck.* That wasn't supposed to come out.

I glanced at Caleb who had raised an eyebrow. Sailor was smirking into his beer. Lily and Crystal were blushing as Eleanor tried not to laugh. But Lola looked **pissed**. Her nostrils flared and she was gripping her cup of water.

"The supply closet. Now," she ordered. I briefly closed my eyes. I was screwed. Our chairs scraped as we stood up.

"Should we turn up the music," Eleanor teased as we walked off.

* ● * ● * ● * ● * ● *

I FOLLOWED Lola into the supply closet. I sighed, leaning against the door. "I'm sorry. I shouldn't have blurted that out," I said, eyeing the floor. Lola crossed her arms. I could feel her staring at me. "I don't know why that came out," I mumbled. Lola scoffed.

"Don't lie to yourself," she said. My head snapped up.

"What do you mean?" I asked. Her lips twitched and she stepped forward, causing my heart to skip.

"Why are you upset that I'm sleeping on a cot?" she asked. I bit the inside of my cheek.

"Because that sounds uncomfortable as shit and you're a fucking doctor. You need proper sleep," I pointed out. "Also, I need to make sure you're pulling your weight for the festival," I said. She hummed in disbelief, her hand raising to press against my chest. She was close enough for her honey perfumed to engulf my senses, short circuiting my synapses.

"Is that really the reason?" she pressed. I swallowed. Her eyes searched for the truth but I wanted to stay behind my wall for just a little longer.

"You need to sleep properly," I said, redirecting the conversation.

"That last time I slept well was after our moment in the greenhouse," she whispered. Her lips hovered slightly below mine, taunting me. "And you know what?" she asked.

For a split second my brain quieted. All I could focus on was her lips hovering slightly below mine. I nodded for her to continue, not trusting my voice. Her hand seared a path up my neck and into my hair. She tightened her grip and my eyes fluttered closed, a tiny moan escaping.

"I won our bet," she said, pressing a kiss against my neck. *Fury fuck.* She was right. I did give in first. She had won our ridiculous bet.

"That may be so, but I also won a bet," I pointed out. She pulled her head back.

"You figured out the tree," she said. I wasn't going to admit that I overlooked that bet with how busy I've been. I nodded. I quickly turned us around and pressed her against the door. Lola let out a soft gasp.

"So what do you want, Sunflower?" I asked. She wrapped her arms around my neck.

"You. At the time of my choosing. Is that acceptable?" she asked, tilting her head to the side in challenge. As if I would disagree with that.

"Accepted," I said with a smirk, ignoring the clouds gathering in my mind. My hands trailed down her hips before grabbing a handful of her ass. Lola tilted her head back and moaned. Her hands dug into my hair.

"W-what do you want?" she asked, breathlessly. There were many things I wanted. Some stayed in my dreams just out of reach, and some I turned into reality. I dreamt of having Lola, the fantasy of tasting her had become a reality and I was quickly becoming addicted.

"Bridget is going to be bringing you a mattress pad, a better pillow and blanket. I need you to accept them," I said. The original plan was for Lola to not know they were from me, a simple gift that she would assume came from her friends.

Now though? Now I wanted her to know that it was from me. That the elf she was so consumed with having, was taking care of her. I knew this was going against my need to keep my feelings compartmentalized but Lola had a natural way of making me want to toss my carefully crafted boxes into a fire.

Her eyes widened as I cupped her breast possessively. She was wearing a sports bra beneath her scrub top but I could still feel her tantalizing nipple tighten under my touch.

"You don't hav-" I squeezed her breast, cutting her off. "Fine. *Fine.* I accept the gift," she said. I pulled away from her, not wanting to spend too much time away from our friends.

"Good girl."

CHAPTER 19

GIRLS NIGHT

LOLA

W e were all hanging out in Lily's apartment. Crystal and Lily were in the kitchen making *cantaritos,* which I knew involved tequila and grapefruit. Apparently it was a drink Crystal had tried on a business trip to Miami, one of the very few drinks she enjoyed. She'd ended up having dinner at a restaurant that the Miami futsal team, The Falling Iguanas, attended and they had ordered the drink for everyone.

I passed Eleanor one of my mother's Nigerian *puff-puffs,* a delicious, slightly sweet fried dough ball. In turn Eleanor handed me Lily's mom's *rissois's* which I knew as 'Portuguese empanadas'.

"Hey, do you know if our moms are going to be cooking for the spring festival?" I asked Lily.

The spring and summer festivals were the times that the town moms usually offered to do a cookout. It was a giant cultural feast that we all looked forward to.

"Yeah! I think the moms are having their menu meeting this week," Lily said, handing the cups to Crystal.

"Oh, I've missed that!" Crystal said. Eleanor glanced at her sister, eyes filled with regret. I patted her knee and offered a smile. Eleanor nodded. While Eleanor and Crystal missed out on years with each other, Crystal was back in all of our lives.

Eleanor took a bite of the puff-puff before her eyes lit up with mischief. I ignored her look and continued munching. I knew Eleanor was biding her time until she could corner me with questions about Flynn. They all were. I could feel it through their watchful glances. Eleanor moved to settle into the chair across from the couch when Lily and Crystal handed us our drinks.

"I think you guys will like it. When we had margaritas that one time I remembered them. I like drinks that are sour but if it's too sour you can sweeten it," she said, nervously. I smiled at her.

Crystal was quiet and shy, but when she talked about the things she enjoyed she opened up like a flower. She also had a bit of a bite when crossed, though that wasn't a part of herself she felt comfortable showing all the time. It almost felt as if there were times where she held back from fully expressing herself.

"They look amazing!" Eleanor said, beaming at her younger sister.

"It's so yummy!" Lily said. I took a sip and enjoyed the bite of sour mixed with a subtle sweetness. Add in the tequila and it was *just* what I needed, along with the girls of course.

"Now that you've taken a sip, *spill* Lola," Eleanor ordered. I scoffed.

"Not going to ease into it?" I joked. Eleanor smiled, settling further into her chair. Small taps echoed in the apartment and Fabian, Lily's familiar, hopped into my lap.

"Please tell them," Fabian said. I raised an eyebrow at the tiny fox.

"Tell them what, Fabian?" I asked. Fabian's eyes sparkled.

"I've heard quite a bit from the animals that were around a certain garden at a certain time of night," he teased. My eyes widened and my cheeks flushed.

"Wait, *what*?" I said.

"Pause. You and the animals have your own version of Sip n' Spill?" Lily asked, leaning forward. Fabian rolled his eyes, at least it looked like he had.

"Small town. Everyone and *everything* talks," he said. Eleanor took a gulp of her drink, nodding her head.

"I knew those cats were looking at us in the alley way," Eleanor muttered.

"The alley way? Isn't that gross?" Crystal said. Eleanor rolled her eyes.

"It's hot, Crystal. Have you ever been overcome with a visceral urge to just makeout, regardless of the location?" Eleanor asked. Lily and I tried not to laugh.

"No. That would require a guy being interested **and** interesting," Crystal said, her eyebrows dipping in annoyance. I watched her closely. I had a tiny speculation that the shy pixie didn't have much experience, which honestly I understood. It was tough finding someone. I went on enough disaster dates to know that she wasn't missing much.

"Have you kissed anyone? It's okay if you haven't," Lily said. Crystal sighed, staring into a drink.

"I kissed a guy at a college party and it took me five seconds to realize that one: I don't do frat parties and two: he had fish breath," she said. Eleanor smiled at her sister.

"Is it something you're interested in trying again?" Eleanor asked. Crystal rolled her eyes.

"I read enough romance books and watch enough movies to know what I might want. It's just a matter of finding the right person. I'm not exactly outgoing and I don't trust–," she sighed, sounding defeated. "I don't want someone taking advantage of my curiosity. You know? I want respect and understanding," she continued. "Someone cute, funny, and with a great smile. Normal stuff you know?" she said. Lily smiled.

"Trust me Crystal, I know exactly what you mean," Lily said. Crystal looked at Lily curiously. "Because of my anxiety and need for control, sometimes it's hard to…do things. I'm fortunate to have someone who is patient and understanding," Lily said, her cheeks red. I leaned on Crystal's shoulder and she relaxed.

"You don't want someone who will make you feel like you grew a third hydra head when you ask them if they can tie you up and blindfold you," Eleanor said with a grin. I choked back on a laugh and Crystal covered her face as she giggled.

"You'll find the right person and if you don't, vibrators work great," I said. Crystal blushed heavily.

"Have you ever used a vibrator?" Eleanor asked. Crystal shook her head. "Your big sister has your back. Don't worry," she said with a grin. Then Eleanor focused on me which was the last thing I wanted though I did expect it. "Anyway, Lola…" Eleanor trailed off.

There was no point in putting this off. I had shared so many things with these girls and in turn they had done the same. I knew I could trust them…but I also knew what they were going to say. And I wasn't ready for the truth. I glanced at each of my friends.

"Fine. Flynn and I kissed. It was magical. Whiskey and fingers were involved," I blurted out. They all blinked at me. Lily slapped Eleanor's arm.

"I fucking told you!" Lily yelled.

"Bitch tell us more!!" Eleanor said, grinning like a fool. Fabian snickered and I groaned into my drink.

"We had a bet. Well, multiple bets. He won one of them and is now fixing up my cot at the clinic. The other one I won," I started off.

"Was that what the supply closet was about?" Eleanor asked. I nodded.

"To back track really quickly, he'd come to the clinic to check on me. The night with the griffin eggs. I didn't have enough blood and he'd offered. So I bit him. Which…wow. Anyway, he found out about me sleeping at the clinic," I said, taking a breath. "And saw the cot. He knew I would keep sleeping at the clinic so he's making it more comfortable for me," I said. The girls nodded for me to continue. I took another sip for some courage.

"After helping Nessie we went back to his greenhouse, had whiskey and things got really hot. Now like I said, I won one of our bets which means I get to have him whenever I want next. But…" I trailed off. This time Crystal leaned on my shoulder.

"But what?" she asked.

"I think there's more to Flynn than I thought," I said, quietly. "You know how he is. He's a little grumpy like Caleb, and a beautiful flirt but lately I've noticed this shadow around him. I think it was always there," I said. I reached for a *rissois*, taking a bite of the flaky fried dough that held shredded chicken inside.

"I think I know what you mean," Lily said. Eleanor raised an eyebrow. "Maybe it's because I people watch a lot but Flynn sort of hangs back. He doesn't really talk about himself or his feelings. He's busy working his ass off and helping everyone else," Lily said.

"He's also the middle child and his siblings are pretty successful," Crystal pointed out.

"Bridget isn't. At least not yet," I added. The girls nodded in agreement.

"Not yet though. But we know Bridget has a more commanding presence than Flynn," Eleanor commented. I drank another sip, my thoughts racing back to my memories with Flynn.

I spent so many years dealing with the cocky, know-it-all Flynn that I had been blind to so many things. There was so much more to him than he let the world see. I found myself wanting to see more of the sides he kept hidden away.

I wondered if he could let me in. That thought made me pause. *Since when did I want that? Since when did I want a glimpse into this world?*

"Lola," Fabian said, head tilted up adorably. I continued drinking my drink to mask my thoughts.

"What are the other bets?" Crystal asked.

"Our last one is who can grow the most flowers," I said.

"Now you're working together," Crystal pointed out. I nodded.

"It just ended up that way," I said.

"The way you ended up on his work table screaming his name," Eleanor said with a smirk.

"One: how did you know I was on his work table? Two: I did not scream his name," I said, blushing. Eleanor shrugged her shoulders.

"I had a feeling, since I ended up on Caleb's bar. The Kiernan's must really love mixing business with pleasure," she said, smirking.

"We *sit* at that bar!" Lily and Crystal said at the same time. We laughed again.

"There are cleaning supplies. You are perfectly safe," Eleanor said, defending herself. I shook my head, still laughing.

"I know a few animals who can testify on the screaming," Fabian interrupted. I gently flicked his ear and he swiped my hand with his paw.

"So can we talk about another guy in our friend group?" Eleanor said. I rolled my eyes.

"Is this where you tell us yet again how great Caleb is in bed," I said. Eleanor scoffed.

"No, and if I did it would be the truth," she said. There was a quiet pause, all of us waiting to see what could possibly come out of Eleanor's mouth.

"Crystal!" Eleanor said a little too happy. *Oh no*. Crystal stared at her sister confused.

"Yeah?" she said. Eleanor resettled in her seat.

"So Sailor…" Eleanor trailed off. Crystal rolled her eyes.

"We're friends. Stop that," Crystal said, hiding behind her drink.

"*Just* friends?" Lily said. Crystal's eyes widened.

"Yes! Just friends," she emphasized.

"It feels like you guys hang out a lot," Eleanor said. I grinned. I caught them on more than one occasion at Coffin's Coffee Shop "hanging out".

"Is that why I always spot you together at a certain coffee shop?" I teased. Eleanor's eyes widened comically. A faint blush bloomed on Crystal's cheeks.

"Listen, we hang out. I have a lot of work and he enjoys keeping me company. It seriously isn't a big deal. Please you guys," she said quietly. I could tell Eleanor wanted to keep talking by the way she pursed her lips.

We all suspected that there was something between Crystal and Sailor, but if they were just friends that was fine. Sailor was a friendly guy and in the beginning we said the same thing about Lily and Sailor. They always used to hang out. Eleanor and I quickly realized they were just friends and that Sailor had this quality about him that made everyone feel at ease.

"Hey, how do you think he is?" I asked our group. We all got quiet. During the winter, Caleb, Eleanor and Sailor had to go to Coralia Coast. It was Sailor's hometown that he never really talked about. Any topic involving his town or family was quickly skirted around. He mentioned one day he would tell us why and we've been patiently waiting for it ever since.

"He hasn't brought it up and I don't want to push him. But I think there's way more to Sailor and that town than we know. You guys should have seen how quiet he was," Eleanor said. She talked about how beautiful the town was, a coastal town with tiny shops. The people weren't the warmest bunch. "The town wasn't bad but…" Eleanor started.

"It's almost like they were missing something," Lily pointed out.

"It's awkward. Sailor doesn't really know yet, but Hale's Lumber is trying to partner up with Coralia for a massive project," Crystal said.

"That's amazing, Crys!" Eleanor said, beaming. Something sparked in my mind and I glanced at sweet Lily.

"Wait Lily," I said, getting her attention. She eyed me suspiciously. She and Celestino had taken a weekend trip to the town after the fall festival. They had confessed their feelings and wanted some time away from everyone to get a feel for their new relationship. They had been friends for so long that they needed space to process their new level of intimacy.

"Have you told Celestino the big three words yet?" I asked. Her cheeks looked like they'd gotten singed by dragon's fire. We all giggled. Lily, while having big emotions, always needed to take her time to dissect, process and accept them.

"Guys," she whined. Eleanor bumped her shoulder.

"Just tell him you love him! You did when we were kids," Eleanor said.

" 'I love you' is very big," Lily exclaimed, adjusting the bun on her head.

"You tell us that you love us all the time," I countered. She gave me a look.

"Do I, though?" Lily said. We all stared at each other. Eleanor faked a gasp.

"Do you even love us?" Eleanor said. Lily fought back a laugh.

"Yes, yes. I love you guys," Lily confessed. I sighed dramatically.

"Thank the stars. I was going to have to rethink our entire friendship," I said. More giggles went around the group before Lily spoke up. She stared at the inside of her cup, her brows furrowed.

"I want to. I've always loved him but this feeling is so much bigger than what it was. I want the first time to be special because he makes me feel special," Lily said quietly. I placed a hand on her knee.

"Well if you need help we're here. We can make it as dramatic or dreamy as possible," I said. Lily smiled softly, eyes glistening. My throat felt choked up with emotion. Lily was usually so terrified of her emotions, but since dating Celestino she has come out of her shell quite a bit. We've all been able to have a deeper friendship with her.

"I can help too!" Crystal offered, taking a sip of her drink. Lily reached for her hand.

"Of course. You're a part of our group now," Lily said. I stared at the girls. I was so grateful to have them in my corner. We all nestled into our seats with good conversation, an abundance of food and delectable drinks.

We were watching the third episode of our annual cozy fall show when my phone beeped. I took a deep breath as I watched the unicorn walk around its pen trying to settle.

"Everything okay?" Eleanor asked. I nodded.

"Just waiting for the unicorn to give birth," I said, sighing. It was exhausting. I had no idea what the timeline was. Of course I had a general idea. Unicorns were similar to Pegasi and in turn, similar to horses. The big difference was that unicorns had a giant horn on their head. They also never ever hung around people.

The baby unicorn was going to be born with either a full horn or a nub– I had no idea. The sac was impenetrable; I couldn't get a clear look with my sonogram machine. I even tried asking her multiple times how it works but she kept saying everything will be fine. I guess that, like sirens, unicorns liked keeping secrets.

"Do you have a general idea?" Crystal asked. I drained the second glass of my drink.

"By the spring festival," I said, wincing. "Heal the Dark Hollow Tree, gather enough flowers for the spring festival, help a unicorn give birth and make sure that no creatures are dying," I said, listing off my to-do list.

"So just another festival season in Lavender Falls," Lily said grinning. We stared at each for a second before laughing. It seems we aren't getting off easy with any festival. I wonder what the Fates have planned.

"Alright ladies, it's time to get down to business," Fabian said, getting our attention.

"What's that?" Lily said, opening her arms. Fabian crawled into her lap.

"I'm thinking of dating. How does one find a foxy fox?"

CHAPTER 20
GET IN WE'RE GOING CAMPING

FLYNN

"So I hope you have a tent," Priscilla said early Saturday morning as soon as I walked into her store. I was dropping off a few herbs that she needed for her store and for Lola. Lily had texted me last night that Priscilla might have found the perfect potion to use on the Dark Hollow Tree. Relief ran through me, I was worried we were going to hit complications like we did during the winter season.

But thankfully Priscilla had established a relationship with Meryl who owns the apothecary of Coralia Coast. Because of that connection she's been able to stock certain products only found in Coralia Coast.

"I do have a tent. Why?" I asked nervously. Priscilla twirled around her table and flipped through a few books. She hummed lightly under her breath when she found what she was looking for. I began separating the herbs on her table.

"So honestly we're very lucky this spring. You see we need to heal the...what did you call it?" she began.

"Dark Hollow Tree? We haven't exactly given it a name," I grimaced. She nodded.

"We'll be using a similar potion to heal DHT but we do need one special ingredient. There should be a few falling stars this weekend, and by this weekend I mean tonight," she said. It took a second for her words to register.

"We need a falling star?" I asked, eyes widening. She shook her head.

"Oh no! We don't need that kind of power! But near Cosmic Campground there's a patch of moonflowers. When the falling stars pass over their star dust will sprinkle over the moonflowers making their petals glow and enhancing their medicinal properties," she explained. I nodded along. Great. That sounded simple enough.

"Alright. I'll be back tomorrow with the flowers then," I said. Priscilla nodded, a light smirk tugging at her lips. My stomach sank. There was more.

"Anything else you need to tell me?" I asked, suspiciously. She shook her head before handing me a sack that smelled like lavender.

"Lily enchanted this sack to keep your flowers protected and alive," she said, dropping it in my hand. I nodded but I still felt like Priscilla wasn't telling me everything.

✳ ❀ ✳ ❀ ✳ ❀ ✳ ❀ ✳

MY GREENHOUSE WAS BECOMING PACKED with flowers. There were buckets of hydrangeas, peonies and daisies. I had a few sunflowers, but I needed more. I scratched the back of my neck. I spent most of the afternoon pulling out the flowers that reached their peak so that we could cast a frozen enchantment on them.

Afterward they would be moved to a warehouse that Griffin used to house his frozen goods for the store.

Right now we had a little more than half of the flowers we needed. Half of the floats were already done. It was in these moments I was grateful we were a magical town. While I had faith in everyone being able to execute their roles without magic it didn't hurt that we had a little help.

I checked on Lola's section. I wasn't sure how she was doing it. She somehow managed to find time between taking care of the clinic *and* her garden. She was amazing, honestly. I clenched my fists. She was too good for someone like me. I felt like I was scrambling to get everything done and yet every time I got glimpses of her around town she was smiling.

I was worried about the garden, DHT and I still needed to approve the latest batch of whiskey so it could go into production. I was also struggling to come up with new whiskey recipes. I closed my eyes. I couldn't go down this spiral. Now was not the time.

When I looked around again a garden bed caught my eye. My heart sank.

"Dragon's piss," I whispered. *Fuck.* It was rotten. Staring into the bed of sage a knot formed in my stomach. I had been growing this sage for a few months. It was what I was using for my new whiskey and now the leaves were curled, black spots speckled everywhere. This particular whiskey I wanted to be perfect, I *needed* it to be. My lips twisted in a frown.

Sage reminded me of *her.* And if I couldn't even keep this damn herb alive how could I even have a chance with her? I sighed, aware of my inner turmoil. These thoughts were stupid, my stress feeding my fears more than ever.

I couldn't let this tormenting ideation take over. I just needed to pull out weeds, use the enchanted spring water from the water fairies on my flower beds, and add some manure to replenish the dirt. I eyed the bag of manure near my greenhouse.

I wonder what would happen if I used unicorn manure.

Animal manure was a great way to help fertilize soil. Now, mythical creature manure? It was like giving an excited sprite a sugar cookie covered in frosting.

My phone was heavy in my pocket. Lola's number was there. I just needed to dial it, or at least text her. Texting. That would provide the least amount of interaction with her. I headed to my greenhouse to wash my hands before pulling out my phone.

Hey, it's Flynn. This might be a weird request but do you think I could use the unicorn's feces as manure for the garden?

SUNFLOWER

1. Can't you just say poop or shit? 2. This is the first text I get from Flynn No Middle Name Kiernan and it's about poop? I can't help but feel slightly offended.

Don't roll your eyes

I won't ask how you knew I rolled my eyes. But, can I?

SUNFLOWER

I guess. Sure. I can't promise you that it'll help the garden. We don't know the effects of using unicorn shit.

That's why we have the scientific method. I hypothesize that the unicorn manure might have some fast healing properties. And now I shall conduct an experiment with a potted plant.

SUNFLOWER

I know what the scientific method is. Fine. I'll drop some off later. But let it be known that I warned you Rider.

I do have a middle name

SUNFLOWER

gasp by the stars, do tell me

You're going to have to beg a little more

SUNFLOWER

oh yes Flynn Possible Middle Name Kiernan. I like it when you talk dirty

Unicorn shit please

❋⬦❋⬦❋⬦❋⬦❋

"Here's your shit," a soft voice said from behind me. It was about 5pm and I had just finished tending to all the gardens, repotting and harvesting most of the flowers and herbs. When I turned around Lola had her braids pulled into a low ponytail. She was wearing leggings with a white tank and flannel, with a backpack over her shoulder. She was holding up a wheelbarrow. My eyes widened.

"Did you bring that all the way over here?" I asked. Her lips twitched and I moved to grab it from her.

"I didn't know how much you needed so I brought you everything," she said sheepishly. I glared at her.

"You could have texted me. If I'd known it was this much I would have come and gotten it. I just needed a small sample to test it out," I said. She adjusted her bag.

"Yes but I have a feeling it's going to work so I decided to bring it all," she countered. "Also you seem to forget I'm a vampire. I am technically stronger than you," she said. I sighed.

"Fine," I said as I pushed it towards my greenhouse. Lola trailed behind me. I had a dead rosemary plant inside of a small pot that I could test this theory with. She watched me in silence as I pulled out the rosemary and chucked half of the dirt in the trash can. I added fresh soil and then went back out to scoop in some of the unicorn manure.

The poor rosemary plant hardly had any leaves. The stems were dull and cracked and most of the roots were shriveled up. I placed her in the pot and gave her some water. I pulled off my glove and placed my fingers in the dirt. I closed my eyes, focusing on the magic swirling in my lower belly. A buzzing feeling ripped down my arm and into the pot.

"Wow," Lola said, eyes wide. I bit back a grin and my chest swelled with pride. She hadn't seen me use my magic often as I technically used it when dealing with plants.

"I whisper sweet encouraging words laced with magic. My magic reaches the plant faster when I'm touching it," I explained. She nodded and stayed silent as I placed the plant on the corner of my work table.

"I always knew you were secretly a sweetheart," she teased. I huffed out a hollow chuckle. My hand brushed over the wooden surface. I breathed through my nose, my hands tightening into fists.

This was where I'd made her come, on my desk, in my greenhouse. I glanced at her and her eyes were staring at the table. I wondered what she was thinking. Did she want to go another round? Did she think about our kiss as much as I did?

"So when do we go?" she asked, meeting my eyes. My focus snapped back to reality.

"Go?" I asked. Her lips stretched into a warm, inviting smile.

"The flower? We have to go camping, right?" she asked. My head tilted. Was I hearing her right? Camping with *me*?

"Wait, how did you know?" I asked. Lola's smile widened and turned mischievous.

"Priscilla told me before telling you," she said, confidently. I bit the inside of my cheek. That's why Priscilla was smiling like a damn Cheshire cat. She had told Lola.

"You're not coming with me," I said, turning to wash my hands in the corner. I took some of the organic bar soap from Priscilla's shop and ignored Lola as best as I could. I could hear her shift on her feet.

"I am," she said, firmly. I snorted.

"Lola, I don't need you to come. I'll be fine on my own. I can harvest a damn flower," I said, with a bit more bite than intended. There was a tap on my shoulder and I stiffened. The smell of honey, citrus and a soft hint of sage pulled at me.

I slowly turned around and her dark eyes had softened. My throat closed. She had the tiniest mole on her lower bottom lip. I hadn't noticed it when we were making out. I also had never noticed the way her lashes were short but curled up at the ends, making her eyes seem more alluring.

"I'm going to explain to you why it makes sense for me to come," she said, taking a tiny step forward. I stepped back, my hip bumping into the bin that I'd transformed into a sink. "I'm a vampire which makes me a predator and one of the most dangerous beings in the forest. I also know the majority of creatures and how to handle them. Who knows *what* in that forest is hurt or dying. Those creatures will try to defend themselves against you," she said, taking another step forward until I was pressing against my sink.

"I'm coming with you because logically it makes sense to have someone with my power and skill set at your side," she said, firmly.

We stared at each other in a silent battle with her chest pressed against mine. She wasn't making this easy. Her scent was winding around me, her words settling against my skin and her eyes tempting me to say yes. My nostrils flared.

"Logically you're correct. So fine. We need to head out before the sun is already gone," I said, giving in.

CHAPTER 21
ONE TENT ONLY

LOLA

Flynn had a nice ass. Said ass was currently in front of me in athletic sweatpants that fitted snugly across his ass and thighs. He wore a hoodie that hid the body I knew he had. He was delicious. His hair was pulled back by a thicker headband this time and he had a backpack, much bigger than mine, over his shoulders.

I hadn't expected to be camping tonight. It was the last thing I wanted to do. When Priscilla called me I knew I needed to go with Flynn. It's not that I didn't trust him to take care of himself– I knew he could. Both Flynn and I went on numerous excursions for our science classes growing up.

What worried me was the possibility that one of the creatures in the forest could be sick because of the Dark Hollow Tree and attacked him. Sure the unicorn and pegasi were nice, but it could be worse. I wouldn't be able to sleep if I had let Flynn come in here all alone.

Lily assured me that her and Celestino would monitor the cameras and that if anything were to happen they would send Fabian to fetch me. Being Lily's familiar she could call upon him easily as the fox had the magical ability to teleport. If it wasn't for them I would have stayed back pacing back and forth at the clinic all night.

We took a trail from the back of Siren's Saloon which led to Cosmic Campground. While many people traveled to Lavender Falls just to enjoy our festivals, our campgrounds were pretty awesome too. We had zip lines, spacious areas for camps, fire pits, picnic tables, restrooms with showers, and amazing trails. A lot of stargazers came out to take beautiful pictures.

The trail began opening up as we passed the welcome sign. I smiled. I hadn't been camping in years. The camp was empty which was surprising. If Priscilla knew about the shooting stars, others must as well.

"How come it's empty?" I said, speaking up. Flynn glanced at me over his shoulder.

"Either some of the town folks are afraid to be here with everything going on, or Mayor Kiana put out some kind of restriction," he said. I bit my lip. That made sense.

She probably called this area off limits. My stomach twisted. I looked around taking in the trees that were fighting to keep their budding leaves and branches alive.

It hurt to think that the forest was empty. Even now I could barely hear any creatures running around. Either they scattered out of the Gasping Greenwood, were hiding, or worse…dead. I swallowed.

I needed to focus on the task at hand. We needed to find these flowers and set up camp. Flynn stopped at one of the fire pits that hung around the edge of the campsite. The bathrooms were on the opposite side.

"We'll make camp here. The flowers are just beyond those two trees if you bend down and look. I don't want to be too close in case the Dark Hollow Tree figures out what we're trying to do," he said, setting his bag down. I waved my hands.

"Wait…what does *that* mean," I asked. Flynn looked up at me and my cheeks flushed. He really did look good on his knees.

"Plants are smart, Lola. And we know the Hollow Tree communicated with Eleanor. Who's to say the Dark Hollow Tree can't communicate with witch folk too," he said. "Top that with the way it kept avoiding my magic and I wouldn't doubt the possibility."

I blew out a breath. He was right. I set my bag down and sat across from Flynn who pulled out his tent. His honey eyes stared at my bag and then at me, waiting.

"We should probably set up the tents," he said. I nodded and motioned for him to continue. He sighed. "You don't have a tent do you?" he asked. I smiled wide, fangs and all.

"I packed what I kept at the clinic so no tent and no sleeping bag," I said.

"You had all day," he pointed out. I nodded again.

"Absolutely. But you know I'm the only vet in town and therefore didn't have much time," I stated. He breathed in sharply through his nose before beginning to set up the tent. I asked if he needed help but he pushed me away. I couldn't help but laugh.

The tent was dark green and pinned to the ground after a few minutes of me watching Flynn fight with the flap of the door. Inside he opened up the sleeping bag to cover the floor. He also placed a blanket and pillow on one side of the tent. I tossed my bag inside and fished out my toiletries and a new shirt. When I came back out the sun was setting faster.

"I'm going to take a quick shower. Do you need help with the fire?" I asked. Flynn had filled the fire pit with twigs and leaves. He smirked, before snapping his fingers.

A spark from his fingertips flickered and the fire lit up. I stifled a giggle and rolled my eyes. *Show off.* Could I use magic to light fires? No, but could I read the minds of animals? Yes. And that was a handy ability to have when one was sleeping in the forest.

❋ ❀ ❋ ❀ ❋ ❀ ❋ ❀ ❋ ❀ ❋

I was forever grateful when Mayor Kiana thought to refurbish the campsite bathrooms. The restroom was split between toilets on one side and showers on the other side of the wall. The shower itself was roughly around 4x5 with a shower head that used rain water.

Lavender Falls collected the rain water and then the water fairies purified it to be used in certain parts of the town, especially at Cosmic Campground. Thankfully there was a shower caddy to hold all my things.

Even though the water was cold I welcomed it. I spent the entire day working with the pegasi on their exercises. They had been sick for so long that they needed to ease their way back into flying.

Then I had to give Fabian his annual shots, and check on the unicorn. The griffin's eggs still haven't hatched but I made sure she had everything she needs.

I scrubbed under my nails with the soap, getting rid of all the dirt and grime. I hoped the unicorn poop, or rather, unicorn "feces" had helped Flynn. I knew he was stressed over the festival. I also hadn't forgotten about how he confessed to making sure my part of the garden was safe. I hadn't even realized he had been doing that. I wonder if he even realized what he was doing.

Did he notice that he cared about me sleeping? That he kept making sure I had enough of a blood supply? Flynn kept showing me two different sides of him. One side was kind and thoughtful. It was the side that made me melt and blush. But the other side of him loved pushing me away. He had some walls up and I didn't quite understand why.

I maneuvered myself so that the shower head could pound against my shoulders, releasing the tension I held there. The girls were right, Flynn had a tendency to linger on the outskirts of our friend group, watching.

I caught glimpses of his insecurities and because of them I was confused on where I stood with him. I couldn't quite understand why someone as successful and confident as him seemed hesitant with his heart. Was I fueling his storm, or casting it away? I knew what *I* wanted.

And now we were here, alone and about to share a tent for the night. He reminded me of the Tin-Can man from Wizard of Oz. He walked around acting as if he had no heart yet his actions spoke otherwise. This was my chance to see inside the tin-can heart of Flynn Kiernan.

A scratching noise made my ears twitch. I slightly jumped. Before placing my wash net on the caddy I willed my body to relax. "Flynn?" I called out.

The scratching got closer. I closed my eyes and concentrated on what I could hear. The water from the shower was rushing down and it continued to drizzle into the drain. There was a soft breeze and the air was turning crisp as the sun was setting.

I heard tiny footsteps pattering outside. The creature had to be small, with four legs. My nose twitched as I tried to figure out its scent. Woodland, a little musky and smokey. But maybe the smoke was from the fire pit.

A soft growl rang out and my heart skipped. *Okay, Lola. Play it cool. You are a badass vampire. Creatures are afraid of you.* I peaked my head out from behind the curtain and a yelp jumped out of me. Bloodshot eyes stared into mine.

"Lola!" Flynn yelled. His footsteps slapped against the dirt outside. The door was thrown open and he quickly came into the view. "What the fuck are you?"

Another yell rang out but this time from the animal. The animal's eyes widened and it flicked its tail at Flynn sending a spray. *This idiot.*

"Flynn! Why would you yell at an animal like that?" I asked, slightly stepping forward. He waved a hand out, stopping me. Flynn wiped his eyes with his shirt, giving me a glimpse of the skin beneath.

"*Yell*? You yelled first. I thought something was wrong!" he spurted out. The animal continued to look at one of us, then the other. I sighed and looked down at the creature. My magic flowed easily as I connected with it.

"Are you okay?" I asked. Their eyes watered and my heart cracked. The creature shook its head. I went out to reach my hand.

"You need a towel," Flynn said, tossing me one. The tips of his ears were red and his eyes glued to the ceiling. Ah, the gentle tin-can knight has returned. I shut off the water and wrapped myself in the towel. Kneeling down I scratched behind its ear.

"Give me a minute and I'll help you," I said, softly. The creature nodded and sat down.

"And me?" Flynn asked, glaring at the creature. His shirt was soaked from the creature's spray and by the smell it was emitting, whatever this creature is must be similar to a skunk. He looked at me and his pupils dilated as he took in the scene before him. He cleared his throat and quickly looked away.

"Over where the sink is, there's some mint and rosemary body wash to help with…smells that won't come out easily," I said. Flynn nodded and rushed out the bathroom.

✳ ❀ ✳ ❀ ✳ ❀ ✳ ❀ ✳

TRIXIE WAS LIKE FABIAN– A magical fox that resembled a fennec fox. She kept wincing every time she spoke to me. I placed my fingers, gingerly on the sides of her throat. There was a slight swelling.

"I'm thinking you might have eaten something?" I asked. She nodded. "Something you usually eat but this time it made you feel bad?" I continued. Her dark eyes widened and she nodded furiously. I sighed.

It had to have been the Dark Hollow Tree. It was slowly poisoning everyone. I looked around our campsite. To heal her throat, I would need ginger, lemon balm, licorice and a bit of magic. But I didn't have any of that.

"Can you teleport?" I asked. Trixie tilted her head back and forth.

Kinda. But I would need some help, with how I feel I don't fully trust my magic.

Her voice was rough against the inside of my head. I reached for my phone and called Lily.

"Everything is fine I swear. Crystal's brushing the unicorn," Lily said, teasingly. My eyebrows shot up.

"She's letting her?" I asked. "Crystal is there?"

"Yeah. Caleb needed Celestino to fix something at the tavern and you know the animals really like Crystal. The pegasi are such gossipers by the way," she said. I giggled. Both Crystal and Lily had calming auras about them so I shouldn't be surprised. "Before you ask, I casted a magical spell to be able to communicate with them. You know, just in case," she said. I knew I could trust my friends.

"Anyway, what do you need?" she asked.

"I found another magical fox, her name is Trixie. In my cabinet there should be some medicine labeled "for sore throats". I'm going to need Fabian to teleport to my location and help Trixie teleport to the clinic," I said. Lily gasped.

"No way," she said.

"Yeah. I need you to give her that medicine tonight and tomorrow morning. She can't really speak. Do you think she could stay at your place? The clinic might be overwhelming for her," I said. Her big dark eyes blinked at me. She was obviously in pain with the way she was softly shaking on the ground. Her pupils were dilated and her tongue was hanging out. "Make sure she stays hydrated too."

"No worries Lola. Hey Fabian could you—" A puff of fog appeared by my side and Fabian stood with his head tilted up, one paw perfectly crossed over the other, and the tiniest hint of a smirk.

"You rang, oh beautiful vampire vet?" he said, *oh so* dramatically. I did my best to hide my snort. Trixie's face fell as she stared at Fabian. Then she looked at me and raised an eyebrow.

*Really? **Him**?*

I shrugged my shoulders and Flynn came into view. Fabian's nose twitched. "By the stars, that's a lot of scented body wash. What happened? Did you think Lola won't makeout with you unless you smell like a candy cane?" Fabian said, covering his nose with his paw. Both of our faces burned against the fire light.

"What do you mean makeout?" Flynn asked, raising an eyebrow. My heart rattled in my chest. Fabian snorted.

"We all heard you outside the greenhouse," Fabian said. Flynn's eyebrows furrowed.

"What do you mean?" Flynn hissed. I did my best to not feel hurt by his reaction.

"The creatures overheard you. Do you think you are the only beings around?" Fabian said before turning to Trixie. His eyes softened at her and Trixie scrunched her nose. "Ready Madame Trixie?"

I bit back a snort. I could already see what was going to transpire between these two magical foxes. Trixie looked at me and I nodded for her to go with him. They had disappeared in a puff of fog. My phone beeped with a text from Lily saying they had arrived safely. I sighed happily. *That was one problem solved.*

When I looked back up, Flynn was staring into the fire. His eyes followed the flames, tormented.

"Flynn?" I called, attempting to get his attention. I had a feeling that he was lost in his head again. He looked up in surprise.

"I'm just going to check on the flowers," he said, moving away. I watched him glide in between the trees and into the forest. My heart sank. He was running away. Was he that embarrassed that he kissed me? Did he want to hide from what we did? I walked after him, needing answers.

✳ ❖ ✳ ❖ ✳ ❖ ✳ ❖ ✳ ❖ ✳

FLYNN WAS STANDING near the outskirts of a cluster of moonflowers. They were pure white and nearly glowed. His eyes softened in their presence and I felt a tinge of jealousy. His fingers stroked the grass below as I stood, watching quietly.

I had never seen Flynn this peaceful. He usually wore a scowl or a flirty smile, but at this moment his face was relaxed and he looked vulnerable.

His shoulders dropped beneath his hoodie and his hair came down, barely brushing his shoulders in small waves. His ears gently curved into points at the tip and his pale skin seemed to shimmer in the moonlight. He was breathtaking. For the first time I was getting a glimpse of the real him, beneath his mask.

I gently walked towards him and sat down, our knees brushing. He pulled away slightly and I ignored the pain that sprung in my stomach from that reaction. His fingers froze against the blades of grass and he glanced at me quickly.

"Did the news of the town's critters hearing me come undone over you make you upset?" I asked. His lips twitched.

"You couldn't ease into this conversation, could you?" he said, dropping his head. I rolled my eyes.

"You sure did use a lot of that shower gel," I teased. Despite the fact that he did mostly smell like a walking candy cane, I could make out the hint of sunscreen that always clung to him. His head snapped up.

"She *sprayed* me!" he said, defensively. I shook my head, giggling.

"You didn't need to come running. I'm a vampire, I can handle pretty much anything in this forest," I said, bumping his shoulder. He tensed slightly before staring back at the flowers.

"Of course I came running Lola," he said. I kept my eyes on him, wanting to take in any small reaction that would help me understand him.

"Okay, what if it *had* been a dangerous creature? I'm a **vampire**. I can handle it," I assured him. There was a tick in his jaw. He was biting back his reaction.

"That's the thanks I get?" he mumbled. I rolled my eyes.

"Thank you, but I'm serious. You could have gotten hurt," I said. After seeing him lash out in pain because of the Dark Hollow Tree, I didn't want to risk seeing him like that again. Flynn scoffed.

"It was instinctual, Sunflower. I just did it," he spat.

"Is it your instinct to protect me?" I asked softly. Flynn refused to meet my gaze. He was hiding. I could recognize it now. He was afraid of our connection.

There had always been a cord that connected us growing up. I thought it was due to our rivalry. I assumed that was our fate. We always ended up intertwined, but now I sensed that it was because of something deeper. My heart swelled and my fangs ached.

Him.

My blood, my soul called for him and him *only*.

I placed a hand gingerly on his fidgeting fingers and he seemed to relax for a second. A small puff of air escaped him. Flynn was like the creatures I worked with: hesitant, but longing for love. It was a good thing vampires were incredibly patient due to our long life span. I could wait for Flynn to accept what's hiding in his heart. I would be there to tug on that cord until it wrapped around the both of us.

"Flynn," I said.

"Yes," he bit out. He flipped his hand and we sat with our palms against each other. I held my breath as his fingers slowly intertwined with mine. My heart skipped a beat, and I could feel his racing.

The world seemed to fade into the background until all I could hear and feel was Flynn. His eyes stared at our interlock hands with a mixture of emotions. My soul felt like it was breaking.

How had I never noticed the walls that surrounded him? In his eyes I saw fear, pain, and most importantly: longing. There was a longing for something more.

"And what is it telling you to do now?" I asked. Flynn slowly turned to face me. He wore a broken expression that gutted me. The man before me was the smartest, kindest and bravest person that I knew and yet his biggest fear was opening his heart to others.

I wondered now if this was how Celestino felt with Lily, or Caleb with Eleanor. I gripped his hand tightly, hoping that he could see in my eyes that I was here with him, that I always have been. His gaze traveled from my eyes, down my cheek and across to my lips, drinking me in.

"To kiss you," he whispered, coming out as a cross between a plea and a prayer.

"Then do it. Kiss me, Flynn."

CHAPTER 22
ONE SLEEPING BAG ONLY

LOLA

I cupped Flynn's cheek, his stubble scratching my skin. He leaned forward and my body buzzed in anticipation. The night quieted and the air around us stilled. Flynn hesitated, his eyes watching me. I gave him a slight nod, encouraging him to do what we both wanted.

Just as his lips had barely brushed against mine, a snap of a branch sprung us apart. Flynn wrapped his arm around me to shield me from whatever creature lurked in the shadows. I pried it off and shoved him behind me.

"*Lola*," Flynn hissed, but I ignored him. There was something just beyond the trees watching us. Another heartbeat rattled erratically, its blood rushing way too fast.

Something was wrong. I moved into a crouching position as Flynn reached for my hand. I turned to look at him and signaled for him to be quiet. I made my way toward the tree. The rustling was somewhere in that direction. Peeking behind the tree I froze.

"Oh, fury fucking dragon's piss," I whispered. There was a rustle behind me and I felt Flynn's warmth against my back. From the corner of my eye I could see that his hand was hovering above my elbow, as if afraid to touch me.

"What is it?" he asked, trying to peek over my shoulder. There was a twitch in the distance. This was *not* fucking good at all. "Are those... eggs?" he asked, bewildered. I quickly turned around and pushed him a step back. His eyes widened in surprise. I tilted my head slightly back, my ears on high alert. I slid my hands up Flynn's chest.

"W-what are you doing?" he stuttered. I offered him a flirty grin.

"I need you to wrap your arms around me," I said. He stared at me in confusion.

"Lola what in the fury fuck is happening?" he hissed. I gripped his hips and pushed him towards me until we were flushed against each other. I slid one hand into his hair and the other around his waist, holding him in place.

"I need you to act like we are just two horny adults, alone in the middle of the forest," I said, my lips skimming the side of his neck. His hands clutched my hips and I could feel how his heart pounded against his chest. More branches began snapping behind me.

"Why?" he asked. I fought back a groan. I wished he wasn't being so stubborn right now. He kissed me right below my ear and I shuddered. It was a delicate brush that ignited my body. His hands slipped under my shirt, grazing my skin and leaving behind a trail of desire. *Now* he was listening. "Answer me, Lola," he said, looking at me from beneath his pretty lashes. I kissed his jaw and then his cheek. My lips hovered in front of his, our breaths mingling.

"Those are dragon eggs behind us. Dragon mothers are extremely protective of their young. So, let's look like we want to rip each other's clothes off so that she doesn't think we are trying to steal her eggs," I whispered. Flynn managed to keep his cool for the most part.

His cheeks were flushed and his fingers twitched against me. While he looked exactly how I wanted him too, his scent was giving him away. Fear was mixing in with his arousal. And while it made me want him more, I didn't need the dragon questioning why he felt scared. I cupped his face with both of my hands and gingerly kissed him.

"Don't be afraid. I'm here," I promised. Flynn's shoulders relaxed and he reached for another kiss. His lips were soft against mine and it made me want to melt. He nipped my bottom lip and I opened for him. His tongue swept in, coaxing sweet whimpers from me. His arms kept me crushed against him and my hands sank into his soft hair.

We stayed like that. Two beings, kissing in the middle of the forest while the moon rose to shed light across the night sky. The rustling I'd heard earlier began to fade away. The dragon must have carried her eggs somewhere else.

Our kiss quickly heated up as Flynn's arousal knocked into my nose, sending my blood racing. My fangs began elongating and his tongue gently swept under them. A small bead of blood fell on my tongue and I pulled back rapidly. Flynn stared at me, his lips swollen.

"Sorry Lola. I just-" I didn't let him finish that sentence. I slammed my mouth against his, taking control. One of his hands cupped my ass and I moaned again. I nipped at his bottom lip with my fangs.

"*Fuck*," Flynn said, pulling back quickly before trailing kisses down my neck. I titled my head to the side, giving him more access as my hands tugged at his arms, his hair, his waist. His hand slipped underneath my sweatpants, brushing the skin just above my panties and I moaned loudly.

This was Flynn untethered by the thoughts he kept hidden, or the worries that covered him like shadows. This was him following his desires, his needs, and I could taste it all on my tongue. His teeth dug into my neck and my knees buckled.

My panties were dripping for this grumpy elf. His hardened cock was pressed against my lower stomach and all I wanted was for him to take me against a tree. I had never felt such an intense passion for someone. There were more rustles behind me, reminding me of where we were.

I pulled back, taking a breath before looking at Flynn. He was breathing heavily, eyes filled with lust. He pushed a braid behind my ear and cupped my cheek. His eyes flickered over my shoulder and I nodded.

We silently made our way back to camp as if nothing had happened. The fire Flynn had made had died by this point. I handed him a piece of wood and watched him bring it back to life with a spark of his magic.

Silently he pulled food out from a lunch bag that I hadn't noticed. I couldn't get a read on him, his eyes gave nothing away. His mask back on. It was like there was a brick wall between us. *Did we always have a wall between us?* He tossed me a thermos as he began grilling some hot dogs. I took a quick whiff.

"Venison?" I asked. He nodded.

"In case the hot dogs aren't enough," he said. "I don't need you passing out in the middle of the forest," he snickered. His eyes sparked with mischief for a second before focusing back on the fire. I glanced off to the side.

Our impromptu makeout session had been more than just us convincing the dragon we weren't stealing her eggs. There was more between us. I could feel it in the way his heart fluttered, in the way his fingers trembled against my skin, and how he'd whispered my name over and over again. Flynn's scent was still all over my skin and I wanted to drown in it. My panties were still wet when I got comfortable on the ground.

"I believe we won't have to worry about the dragon anymore," I said, after taking a sip of blood, trying to gauge his reaction. Flynn nodded.

"No more making out," he said, flipping the hot dogs.

"Why not?" I asked, watching him. His hand tightened on the tongs. "I still have that bet to cash in on," I pointed out. He stared at me. His eyes glowed gold against the fire.

"That didn't count?" he asked. I shook my head.

"While that was the hottest kiss I've ever had, that was for our safety," I said. He took a deep breath before pulling out the hot dogs and placing them on a paper plate. Flynn arranged my plate for me. A hot dog with ketchup, mayo and crushed chips on top.

My heart flipped. He handed me my plate before making his. I fought back a smile. For someone who was such a grump he sure did notice how I liked things.

He knew which animal blood I preferred. He knew what foods I liked, and he's also been helping take care of my flowers while I've been busy. He was completely oblivious to what he was doing. I felt sorry for this elf. He still had no idea that he was mine.

We ate in silence. The moon looked like it was hanging perfectly in the sky and there were stars scattered everywhere. The leaves rustled slightly against the wind. There were a few crickets out and about. It was relaxing. I glanced at Flynn who once again seemed entranced by the fire. *I wonder what is going on in that beautiful brain of his.*

"How long do we have to wait for the shooting star?" I asked, hoping to steer him into a conversation. Flynn glanced at his watch.

"Probably an hour or so. I think there's going to be a few," he said. I nodded and tossed my plate into the fire. I could feel his eyes following my movements as I settled back at my seat.

"What shall we do until then?" I asked.

"Sit in silence," Flynn said, deadpan. I glared at him.

"We are not doing that," I said. The corner of his lips twitched.

"Then what do you suggest, Sunflower?" he asked. I tilted my head back and forth in contemplation. What could we do for an hour? I know what *I* wanted to do but as I glanced at Flynn I wasn't sure if I could just blurt out that I wanted him to make me come again. He'd seemed apprehensive when Fabian had mentioned that the creatures had heard what we did. Then, after our encounter with the dragon eggs, he'd seemed to shut down.

"Trivia. Science trivia," I suggested. Flynn smirked from across the fire. He moved to sit on the grass, his back against the log. He crossed his arms against his chest.

"What does the winner get?" he asked.

"Winner gets to name the griffin's babies," I said. Flynn huffed out a chuckle and it warmed my body. His shoulders eased and the wrinkle between his brows faded. He nodded and motioned for me to start. I sat up straighter, a grin on my face.

"Are electrons smaller than atoms?" I asked. Flynn nodded.

"What is the name of the tallest kind of grass on Earth?" he asked.

"Bamboo," I said. He nodded. I bit the inside of my cheek. The thing about science trivia is that we were both very knowledgeable, and I needed to make this interesting. An idea formed. I bit back a smirk.

"What type of fish mate for life?" I asked. Flynn stared into the fire before looking at me.

"Angelfish," he said. I nodded and took off my sneakers, stretching my feet. I didn't want him to realize what I had planned yet.

"What's the term for the kind of body of water made up of both freshwater and saltwater mixed together?" he asked. I smirked.

"Estuary," I said. He nodded. "What is the hardest natural substance on Earth?" I asked. He rolled his eyes.

"A diamond," he answered. I moved to take off my cardigan. Flynn eyed me curiously.

"Lola, what are you doing?" Flynn asked. He must have an inkling of what I was up to.

"For every question that one of us gets right, something has to come off of the other person," I said. His nostrils flared and I grinned. I was going to enjoy this little game.

"You know this is going to end quickly, right?" he said, fists clenching.

"Hopefully that's the only thing that does," I teased. His cheeks flushed against the fire's glow. He shifted to uncross his outstretched legs and placed his hands on his knees.

"Fine. Do flying ants exist?" he demanded. I shuddered. One time I was on a field trip for my college course and I'd run into a swarm of them.

"They do," I said with a sigh. He gripped his hoodie, pulling it off swiftly. My eyes wandered shamelessly, drinking him in. He wasn't wearing a shirt underneath. Farmer's tan, a few scars, a light dusting of dark blonde chest hair. He was gorgeous. My fangs ached to stretch.

"What shape do the tails of mating dragonflies make?" I asked, nerves slowly traveling through me.

"A heart," he said. I nodded and tugged off my shirt, revealing a thin tank top.

"What are some of the healing properties of plantain leaves?" he asked. I glanced down at my wrist where the unicorn had bit me. Flynn had noticed it, and made me a special ointment. My fingers ran over my wrist. Now there was nothing but smooth dark skin, thanks to Flynn and my vampiric healing abilities.

"Inflammation, and it has vitamin K which helps with blood clotting," I said. Flynn pulled off his shoes and tossed them behind him.

"What is the difference between dragons and wyverns?" I asked. Flynn forced himself to meet my gaze and I raised an eyebrow. His nostrils flared.

"A wyvern has two legs and a dragon has four," he said, voice rough. Flynn's eyes flickered to my top before nodding. I took a deep breath before sitting up straight and removing my shirt. Flynn sucked in a sharp breath. His scent shifted again and my body buzzed in response.

While I wore a simple bralette, Flynn stared at me as if I was a painting hung in the Louvre. His eyes caressed my breasts. I wished it were his hands. His tongue poke out to lick his lips.

"I'm cashing in on that bet now," I said, out of breath. His lips twitched.

"Are we not going to finish?" he asked slowly.

"Oh, I will Pretty Boy," I said, standing up. I watched Flynn's throat bob up and down. My fangs pushed against my lips. I wanted to taste him again. "Now, are you going to join me inside or am I doing this alone?"

I turned my back on him and unzipped the tent. Whether or not he was going to meet me inside was on him.

The pillow and blanket he'd brought were by the side that had my bag. I melted at the consideration. There was a rustling behind me. Flynn's fingers grazed down my spine and I shivered at his touch. I looked at him from over my shoulder.

"Face forward," he whispered, turning around to zip the tent halfway down. I sucked in a breath, staring at the tent wall in front of me. My fingers twitched at my sides. "You want to finish?" he asked, his breath on my neck. A whimper escaped me as I tilted my head to the side. I wanted to feel his lips on my skin. I nodded.

"How, Sunflower?" he said as his hands lightly ran up and down on my waist. He shuffled forward and I could feel his erection against my ass. Instinctively I arched my back, needing more. His hands slid up to cup my breasts through my bralette. I reached back for him and he pushed my hands away.

"Ah, you want to feel me don't you?" he teased. I let out a moan as his lips ghosted up my neck again.

"Flynn," I gasped as his teeth sunk into my neck. He squeezed my breasts, his thumbs rough against my lace covered nipples.

"Don't think that I don't know that you've thought about it. You won the bet. So, how do you want this to play out?" he said. I wrapped my arms around his neck, keeping him close.

"I would like you to make me scream your name, but judging by your reaction to what Fabian had to say earlier I take it you don't want that," I said. Flynn grunted. "Why don't you?" I asked. Flynn's hands slipped under my bralette kneading my breasts.

"Because your screams are only for me, Lola," he said. My eyes widened and there was a rush of adrenaline through my body. I quickly turned around and pushed him to the ground. His knees were still bent as I positioned myself over his lap and pulled off my bralette.

"That was the right thing to say Flynn," I said, before my mouth crashed onto his. Flynn's hand gripped the back of my neck while the other slipped under my sweats to grip my ass. I moaned into his mouth as his tongue played with mine.

My hips rocked, needing more friction. He pushed my ass, controlling the rhythm. He tasted like mint. The more I pushed the more he gave. I bit his bottom lip, pulling back lightly as Flynn hissed.

His eyes sharpened and he bucked his hips against me. I gasped loudly. My panties were soaking wet and there was a deep ache within me. I grinded harder against him as his fingers brushed my nipples before pinching them.

"Flynn," I mewled. I shook my head. This wasn't enough for me.

"Let me take control," he asked. I nodded frantically, my thighs burning. Flynn sat up and pushed me off of him. He gripped my chin and placed a chaste kiss on my lips before making his way down my neck. His hands moved to pull down my sweats and underwear. He slipped off his own pants, leaving him in his boxer briefs. My eyes widened at his bulge. Flynn smirked.

"Soon," he promised. I raised an eyebrow. I would make sure he kept that promise. He motioned for me to lay on my side and he settled in behind me, his erection against my ass. He slid one arm under mine and began massaging my breast. His other hand trailed over my hip and towards my pussy.

I leaned my head back against his chest, moaning as his fingers slid between my wet folds. Flynn placed a tender kiss on my temple. I pressed back against his cock.

Soon we were rocking together in a slow, steady rhythm. His finger played with me, making lazy circles around my clit. My whole body tensed, wanting him to speed up. He trailed kisses up and down my neck, taking the time to nip and suck.

"Moan my name," he whispered against my hot skin as he slipped two fingers inside of me.

"F-Flynn," I said, eyes squeezing shut. Flynn began pumping in and out faster and faster as I rocked with him. His cock thrusted against my ass in the same motion. His fingers curled slightly and I gasped his name.

I tried nodding but I was trapped against his body. His hand flicked my nipple to the tempo of his thrusts. There was a familiar warm feeling in my lower belly. I shifted my top leg to lay on top of his, spreading myself wider.

"Fucking stars, Lola," Flynn hissed. I rocked faster, squeezing against Flynn's fingers. He moaned my name in my ear and I gasped. And just like last time I fell apart easily for Flynn "Mysterious Middle Name" Kiernan.

"Yes Flynn!" I cried out as he slowed his thrusts. My whole body burned as Flynn continued to stroke every last tremor out of me. My leg slumped onto his, feeling spent. "Is my ass wet?" I asked with a lazy smile. Flynn groaned into my neck, his hips rocking with the last bit of his orgasm.

"Guess I'm going commando," he mumbled.

FLYNN

I left Lola to get dressed and rinse out my underwear in the sink. I stared at my reflection. Despite my hair being a mess and the bags under my eyes, my face was red from our time together. I swallowed, my hands gripping the sink.

Being with Lola felt...right. With her my clouds of doubt faded away. She felt like a sanctuary, like my home. But I didn't trust myself enough to be that for her.

Lola was someone who was kind, giving and thoughtful in everything she did. People gravitated towards her. She has the wonderful ability to pull everyone into her orbit. But I was a wallflower; I was meant to hang in the background and keep a watchful eye.

My eyes fluttered closed as I thought about our moment in the tent. The way her eyes shone brightly with unwavering trust. The sound of my name, breathless on her lips played on repeat in my head. This was just a bet. No real feelings were involved.

So why did I keep worrying about mine? I splashed cold water onto my face before heading back to camp.

Lola had rekindled the fire and put my hoodie on. I bit down on my cheek. Of course she looked irresistible in my clothes. A wave of possessiveness pushed through me as I walked closer. She had her braids up in a bonnet with tiny baby dragons printed on it. I laid my boxers on the log to dry by the fire.

"It's almost time," Lola whispered softly, her eyes trained on the fire. Her skin glittered in the fire's vibrant hues of orange and gold. She had a fang tugging on her bottom lip and her eyebrows were scrunched. Her shoulders were curved inward as her arms wrapped around her legs.

She looked...lonely. I swallowed. Something was wrong. Despite every cell in my body wanting me to stay away from Lola and what she was making me feel, I needed to comfort her.

I sat next to her and pulled her into my lap. Her body practically collapsed against mine in a deep sigh. My heart rattled in my chest. She leaned her head against my chest, the satin bonnet tickling my chin. We stayed like that in comfortable silence. Slowly her body relaxed against me, and joy burst through me.

"I guess the only bet we have left is over who will grow the most flowers," she said, softly. I nodded, squeezing her tighter. I didn't want our bets to end, despite my doubts. I wanted more time with Lola.

"Let's make another," I said. She pulled away and I wrapped my arm around her waist, keeping her close. Her eyes sparked with mischief.

"Tell me more, Rider," she said. I shook my head, chuckling at the nickname.

"Let's see..." I trailed off. "Well, we never really finished the trivia match," I pointed out. Lola beamed excitedly and wrapped her arms around my neck. She wiggled slightly in my lap and I raised an eyebrow.

"Just getting comfy," she teased. I rolled my eyes. I pulled up my knees so she could lean back. Her hands played with the ends of my hair. "What do I get if I win this time," she asked.

"I'll finally tell you my middle name," I said sheepishly. She beamed at me. "Now what do I get if I win?" I asked.

"I might as well tell you my middle name too," she said.

"Lola Luna has a middle name, does she?" I asked. She rolled her eyes and shoved my shoulder playfully. "What can a shark sense that humans can't?" I asked, starting our game. She smiled, smugly.

"Electricity," she stated. She tapped her chin in thought. "How many seeds does a strawberry have?" she asked.

"200," I said confidently. Lola nodded happily. My hands slipped under the hoodie and went up to her waist, my thumbs below the underside of her breasts. Her nostrils flared and her body tensed.

"What are shooting stars composed of?" I asked. She stretched back, staring up at the sky and exposing her neck to me. My thumbs brushed back and forth against her sides.

"Iron and nickel alloy…and silicate minerals," she said confidently. I pulled her towards me, my lips inches from her mouth. She moved in my lap, getting comfortable again. I took one hand and brought it behind her neck. I kissed her lips, roughly. She opened up to me and my tongue swept to dance against hers. When I pulled back her eyes were wide, her breath coming in fast and her lips swollen.

This time she leaned over, giving me a kiss that was as sweet as honey. I was melting beneath her, *for* her. A sound caught my ears and when I pulled away I looked up at the sky and smiled.

"You forgot one thing," I said.

"What?" she said in confusion. I brushed my fingers across her cheek before tipping her chin slightly back.

"Magic," I said as we stared at the night sky.

"Wow," Lola whispered. *Wow indeed.* Shooting stars were zooming across the sky, their magical dust blanketing us below. Lola tugged me closer and I wrapped my arms around her. "This is beautiful," she said, eyes trained on the sky. A pang rang through my chest. Not only was the sky beautiful, Lola was too. This whole moment was achingly beautiful and I felt undeserving.

"So what's your middle name Lola Luna?" I asked. She kept her eyes on the stars, a smile on her lips. Her dark eyes met my gaze after a moment and she held out her hand.

"Hi. I'm Lola Sade Luna," she said. I gripped her hand.

"I'm Flynn Niall Kiernan," I said, shaking her hand. She giggled. Since I'd won I didn't technically need to tell her my middle name, but I wanted to share this moment with her.

"You know, in Yoruba Sade means 'honor earns a crown' while in other languages it means 'rain'," she said, wrapping her arms around my neck, head tilted once more to the sky. My heart swelled.

"Niall can mean 'hero' or 'cloud'," I said softly. Lola hummed.

"Well, seems fitting don't you think?" she whispered as we stared at the shooting stars.

CHAPTER 23
TENT SHENANIGANS

LOLA

A warm hand was clutching my lower stomach and my back was pressed against Flynn's chest. I could feel his breath lightly against my neck. I smiled, my eyes still closed.

After we watched the shooting stars I helped him collect some flowers for Priscilla. Then we crawled into the tent with Flynn pulling me flushed against him.

I opened my eyes and looked down at where my hand was wrapped around his arm, as if to make sure he wouldn't escape me in the middle of the night. I could hear the faint whistling of birds outside of our tent. I sniffed at the fresh dewfall. There was some light coming into the tent which meant the sun was rising.

Flynn's hip shifted and I bit back a moan. His morning wood was on my ass again. On instinct I pushed back. His hand on my stomach tightened and there was a deep rumble from his chest. His lips brushed my neck, his breath hot on my ear.

"Are you awake?" he asked, voice groggy with sleep.

"Yes," I said, my voice barely audible as I rocked back. Flynn's pinky slipped under my waistband.

"Lola, are you awake enough for this?" he clarified. His other arm slid from under my pillow and settled in the middle of my chest, pushing me closer. My body was sluggish but slowly waking up. I nodded. "I need words," he said, his voice low.

I closed my eyes and pushed him until I was lying on my back. Then I tugged him on top. I widened my legs as he settled himself in between them.

"I'm awake enough to know that I want your mouth on my clit and your fingers stroking me," I said, my eyes half closed. Flynn hummed in approval as he kissed my neck, his hands already pulling off his hoodie that I was wearing.

"If only there was enough space for us both to get what we want," he teased. His hands tugged my sweatpants and underwear down.

"I bet we can," I said, as his finger brushed my clit. He placed an open mouth kiss on the center of my chest before lifting his head to meet my gaze. He was still sleepy, I could tell by the way his eyes kept fluttering closed.

"A bet?" he mumbled against my neck, pressing his body weight against mine. I yawned with a nod, stretching out. My feet brushed the end of the tent.

"I bet we can 69 in this tent," I said, running my hands through his hair. He chuckled, rubbing his cheek against my chest. His hands gripped my hips.

"And I bet I'll get you to finish before we both get a cramp," he said, sitting back on his heels. I watched him through my lashes as he pulled his shirt over his head. This was the Flynn I had grown up with, stubborn and demanding.

But now he was a man and those traits had an enticing quality that made my hips rock and my panties wet.

"One condition," I said. He placed our clothes in a pile before adjusting the sleeping bag so that it covered every inch of the tent again. "I stay lying down," I said, sheepishly. Flynn threw his head back in a laugh and my cheeks heated. He was so beautiful when he was carefree. He removed his boxers and his cock stood at attention. My tongue felt thick in my mouth.

"Sure thing, Princess. Lay there and enjoy my mouth and fingers fucking you," he said with a smug grin. My hips lifted, his words making me needy.

Flynn turned around and settled his thighs on either side of my face. I licked my lips in anticipation. I needed to be careful with my fangs. Flynn rested his forearms on the inside of my thighs, pushing me apart.

First he bit the inside of my thigh. I hissed and he soothed it with a gentle kiss. I pulled his hips down before swiping my tongue against the head of his cock.

Flynn groaned, dropping further down as I took him in my mouth. With one hand on the base of his cock I sucked slowly, enjoying how full he felt. My shoulders twitched as his tongue ran from my clit to my entrance. My eyes closed briefly, enjoying the sensation of giving and receiving.

It was almost too much. I rocked my hips in time with his thrusts. My thighs pressed against his arms. I needed to be filled.

I swirled my tongue around his head as I reached out to cup his balls with a squeeze. Flynn pulled away from me for a second. A string of curse words flew out of his mouth. I met his eyes briefly and I saw a flash of competitiveness.

I tilted my hips up before raising an eyebrow. He brought his tongue back on my clit, flicking up and down as I felt a finger tease my hole. I moaned, my mouth full of his cock.

I arched again as he sucked my clit, slipping inside. We began moving in the same rhythm but at some point I couldn't focus anymore and I think Flynn could tell.

He pulled away from my mouth and turned around, throwing my legs over his shoulders, his mouth diving back in. I moaned loudly as he slipped two fingers inside, stretching me. He curled them slightly. My heels dug into his back and my fangs stretched, poking my bottom lip.

"Play with your nipples," he murmured. I rocked shamelessly against his mouth, his tongue circling my clit, easing the pressure at the right times.

"Flynn," I chanted over and over again as I flicked my nipples to his tempo. Then, it happened. The spark in my lower belly, the build up to an explosion of ecstasy that Flynn created. I threw my head back, body bowed, and yelled his name to whoever and whatever the fuck was out there.

Flynn continued to pump in and out of me until all my tremors stopped. I felt like a lily pad floating in a pond. I took a deep breath and stared at him.

"Switch now," I demanded. Flynn licked his lips and shook his head. I glared at him and tugged him up. "Yes."

"I'm fine," he said, reaching for his shirt. I rarely used my vampire strength, but in this moment I grabbed Flynn and pushed him until I was straddling him. His eyes closed briefly before opening to roam all over my body, drinking me in. He sighed deeply.

"I can't say no to you, can I?" he muttered. I grinned before sliding down and wrapping my hand around his cock once more. I met his gaze again as I licked a bead of pre-cum off of him. Flynn groaned, his hands digging into the sleeping bag.

I took him in my mouth, sucking slowly up and down as my hand twisted. Soon Flynn was pumping his hips and I desperately tried to keep up. His cock hit the back of my throat and tears sprung in my eyes.

"Come on Lola," he pausing to meet my gaze. "I know you can make me come. Can't you, Sunflower?" he said through gritted teeth. I moaned at the encouragement and the sound made his whole body tighten. I was already aching for him again.

"Harder baby. Make me come in that hot slick mouth," he said. I squeezed my eyes shut. I never thought I would hear words like that out of his mouth but *fuck*. I squeezed my thighs together, feeling wetness drip down, needing fiction. I scraped my fangs lightly against his cock and he shivered uncontrollably, panting hard.

After a few more pumps Flynn's entire body froze and he moaned my name loudly as his release came down my throat. I swallow every drop before pulling away. I place my hand on my lower stomach before slipping my fingers down to touch my clit.

Flynn watched me through hooded eyes before sitting up to take my nipple in his mouth. His tongue ran over its sensitive peak and with a few swipes and his tongue I came again.

I collapsed against him and he held me close. We both stayed like that for a few minutes, catching our breath. That was a firework show. That was a thunderstorm of passion. It was more than I'd thought it could be.

"I guess you won the bet," I said. He huffed out a laugh before shaking his head.

"I guess–" a ringing cut off whatever Flynn was about to say. I reached toward my corner and pulled out my phone. Crystal was calling me.

"Hey-"

"So I came to check on the creatures because Lily and Eleanor are busy with the festival and there's a dragon in the middle of the pegasi pen with four eggs. She doesn't look like she's going to eat me, but she does look annoyed," Crystal said, cutting me off when I attempted to interrupt her. I slapped Flynn's shoulder, my heart hammering. Flynn took this as a sign to help me get dressed as I put the call on speaker.

"Are you alone?" I asked her. *Kraken's crap.* I wonder if it was the same one we'd distracted last night.

"Y-yes. I texted Sailor since everyone's at work but…" she trailed off. Her breathing was slightly off. No doubt that she was trying to remain calm.

"I'm heading over there right now. Slowly avert your gaze and sit down with your head bowed," I instructed. Flynn had finished getting dressed and was handing me my bag, urging me to go. I crawled out the tent. "Just stay calm. I'm sure Sailor is almost there," I said, glancing back at Flynn.

I'll see you later, he mouthed. I swallowed a lump in my throat. I heard Sailor's voice in the background and sighed in relief.

✼ ❖ ✼ ❖ ✼ ❖ ✼ ❖ ✼

It took less than two minutes to get to the clinic with my vampire speed. By the time I got there Sailor was already sitting down next to

Crystal. The dragon was staring intently at them, her tail wrapped around her eggs to keep them warm. She lifted her head when I came into view. Her pupils widened with recognition. I took a seat next to Crystal.

"Sorry to have interrupted your morning," she said blushing. My cheeks warmed.

"I had just woken up," I said, hoping my voice and face didn't give anything away.

"The dragon has just been sitting there," he said, softly. I noticed his hands kept pulling at the grass by Crystal's foot.

"Was she here before or after you got here," I asked.

"Before," she said. "I didn't know what to do and I knew you were probably busy with trying to get that ingredient for the spell, but she just seemed worried," Crystal said. I snuck a glance at the dragon. She was big with deep purple scales that glittered violet, gold and blue. Her eyes were bright green. She was a magnificent creature.

"You were very brave Crystal," I assured her. Honestly, I was surprised by how calm she was on the phone, and even now. Most people would shiver and run when confronted with a dragon. But Crystal's face looked like a stoic doll.

"I texted Sailor in case we needed his siren abilities to calm her down," she said. My eyebrows raised. That was a brilliant idea. I had never thought of that. But now I remembered that we did have a few sirens in my class to help out during surgeries.

"That is so smart Crystal, I don't know why I hadn't thought of asking Sailor for help before," I said. Crystal's cheeks flushed and she smiled, her freckles stretching across her face. Sailor kept his eyes on her and smiled softly before looking at me.

"Any time Lola," he said, earnestly. I nodded.

"Here is what is going to happen. I'm going to connect with the dragon and see what's up. Sailor can you stay just in case? Crystal you can go if you want," I said.

"Can I stay in case there's a way for me to help?" she asked, her hazel eyes filled with worry. I sighed.

"Actually I would really appreciate that," I said. Crystal and Lily both shared a calming aura that seemed to always put me at ease.

My eyes connected with the dragon and I took a deep breath. I searched for my magic and felt it zooming around my body. I needed to harness it then push it towards the dragon.

Her eyes sharpened as I slowly rose to my feet, keeping my shoulders tucked in and my head low. In this situation she was still the predator. I wanted her to know she was in charge despite the fact I was a vampire. She lowered her head slightly and, like a magnet, we connected.

You were in the forest.

I winced. So this was the same dragon.

I've heard from the creatures that you help us. A doc-tor?

"I'm what we call a vet. I was trained to help animals. Supernatural and mundane," I said, my voice soft but firm. The dragon almost looked like she was smiling.

Wonderful. The forest hasn't been well and I wanted a safe place for my babies to hatch.

My heart ached. While I knew that the forest was ill, it hurt to think that there were so many other creatures probably suffering.

"Of course! We're working on a remedy for the forest actually. I have to warn you I do have other animals here. Ones that use this pen. You are the top predator here right now, other than me of course," I started. "So please don't feel threatened. A lot of them are recovering," I said.

I smell them. No worries Miss…

"Dr. Luna," I said. The dragon nodded.

Thank you Dr. Luna. You wouldn't happen to have anything to eat, would you? My stomach is bothering me.

I sighed in relief. Great. So I had two pegasi, two baby griffin's and their mom, a pregnant unicorn, a few kittens, and now four baby dragon eggs.

By the way… the man you were with last night is very beautiful.

My face flushed and I coughed awkwardly. Did every creature enjoy bringing up Flynn? Was he magnetic to them?

"What did she say?" Crystal asked, standing up. I shook my head.

"She's all good. I'm going to put together a healing tonic and some food for her. Thank you guys so much for being here," I said, smiling at them. My head briefly drifted back to leaving Flynn this morning. I flushed, a part of me wishing I was still with him. Sailor chuckled, shaking his head. I stared at him. There was no way he knew what the dragon had said.

Crystal nodded and waved at the dragon, who waved her tail back. I glanced at Sailor again who gave me a wink. I glared at him. He shrugged his shoulders.

"Not my fault you're easy to read," Sailor teased. Crystal looked between us, confused.

"Wait. What did I miss?" she asked.

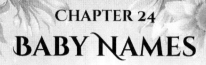

CHAPTER 24
BABY NAMES

FLYNN

I was antsy at The Drunken Fairy Tale Tavern. Lola had left in a hurry after our fun in the tent. I could make out bits and pieces from her phone call. Something about a dragon? I handed a customer a beer, my thoughts consumed with the beautiful vampire with the sunny disposition.

Our night together was incredible. It blew everything out of the water for me. Lola has always been someone stubborn, bright, giving, and confident.

And last night I got to see so much of that. The way we came together, the way we pushed and pulled at each other all felt natural. I stared at my hands, reminiscing on the way her soft body had given in to mine.

There was always an invisible force tugging us toward each other. We've been rivals, and we're great at that. Maybe the pull towards each other was for another reason entirely.

But what if by wanting more, I ended up fucking things up? Stars, I had a habit of always making her annoyed. I could easily push it too far.

"So, how was last night?" Bridget asked when she came to pick up some beers. I grimaced. Ever since Caleb broke his curse, we've been spending more time together as siblings and Bridget has loved being in our business.

"What do you mean, Bridge?" I asked, handing her two beers. She rolled her eyes.

"You realize your friends and I know about last night, right?" she said casually. My face grew hot. I didn't like people knowing my business. I was used to being the one to know things about everyone else. Being a middle child and a bartender made me good at listening and watching– not sharing.

"And how is that?" I asked, throwing a towel over my shoulder. Her eyes, which matched mine, twinkled.

"Small town big brother. Or have you forgotten that fact?" she teased. "Also: Fabian." I cursed. Now I understood why Caleb was constantly annoyed with Fabian. That little fox knew way too much.

"We got the flowers. I'm going to see Priscilla later and hopefully we can heal the tree and everything will be okay," I said. Bridget began placing the beers on the tray. She nodded.

"And what about you and Lola?" she asked. I paused at the mention of Lola.

"She'll lose our bet once we heal the tree, and I can continue to grow my flowers in peace," I said, wiping down the bar. Bridget stared at me, her brows furrowed in annoyance.

"Why must everyone in this town be *so* stubborn," she muttered.

"Stubborn about what?" I asked, curious.

"Everyone in this town has relationship problems," she said with a huff.

"Something you wanna talk about?" I asked, uneasiness in my stomach. While I knew my little sister had her fair share of relationships it didn't make hearing about them easier to stomach. She barked out a laugh.

"Please. No one in this town can handle me," she said, tossing her long blonde hair over her shoulder. I chuckled.

"Alright. Get back to work," I said. As Bridget walked across the bar the tension in my chest didn't ease. I *didn't* have relationship problems. I had friends, and then I had Lola.

What we had was a friendship of.... some kind. Nothing complicated. I *wasn't* trying to pursue any kind of relationship with her. I bit the inside of my cheek.

But now I knew how sweet she tasted and how soft her lips were. Now I knew that she slept at the clinic to take care of sick creatures, had an extensive knowledge of plants, enjoyed romance books, and had a smile that shined so bright it rivaled the sun itself. In these past few weeks I've learned more about her than in all the years I spent growing up with her.

Our relationship was changing. It was growing into something I wasn't sure I was ready for, or even deserved.

And while I constantly questioned myself around Lola, I found myself heading to the clinic after work with french fries and a cup of blood. Sailor had texted me explaining the dragon situation.

According to him, she had everything under control. Well, of course she did. She was Lola Sade Luna. She never backed down from a challenge and always saw a solution to everything. But in that, she had a tendency to push past her limits.

The clinic was empty when I walked in so I went around the back. No doubt she was probably checking in on the animals. The sun was high up today. Spring was definitely on its way, the humidity was trickling in.

I could feel sweat drip down the back of my neck. My eyes widened at the dragon curled up in the middle of the pen. Her tail was protectively wrapped around four eggs. I swallowed.

Her head came up and she stared at me as I lowered my head and averted my gaze, mimicking what I've seen Lola do. The dragon nodded and flicked her tail towards the barn. My lips twitched. She knew who I was looking for.

I made my way towards the barn and heard a soft voice muttering curses. The red door was slightly ajar and I smelled a mix of mint, hay and manure. Stepping in I noticed the pegasi relaxing in the back. To my right the unicorn was lying down, and next to her stall was the griffin with her two babies.

Both babies had pink feathers and a pale yellow peak. Their colors would most likely darken as they age. There were also two reindeer in the back. Each animal snapped their heads towards my direction. I gave them a pained smile. I felt like I walked into a horror movie. They were all staring at me, wide eyed. Either they were going to eat me or chase me out of here.

I heard another curse from up above. My heart raced. I glanced at the pegasi and one of them pointed upward with their muzzle. The other nodded and I headed towards the stairs on my left as instructed.

When I got to the top Lola was wearing pink scrubs with her braids in a bun at the top of her head. Her face was glistening with sweat and she was hunched over a desk clutching her finger.

"Lola?" I called out. She jumped back, eyes wide as she stared at me. She sucked in a deep breath.

"Flynn! You scared me," she said, regaining her breath. I rolled my eyes.

"How did I sneak up on a vampire?" I asked, jokingly. Her lips twitched.

"I was too focused on this," she said, pointing to the table filled with herbs, bowls and a cutting board. She licked her finger with a wince and I made my way over to her, taking her hand. There was a small cut on the knuckle of her middle finger. It was slowly closing up thanks to her vampire abilities.

"What are you doing?" I asked. She shrugged her shoulders.

"Since Priscilla is busy taking care of literally everything in town I didn't want to bother her with making some medicine," she said casually. I shook my head. *Of course.* The table was filled with ginger, mint, chamomile and bananas.

"Stomach problems?" I asked, recognizing the uses. She smiled wide, nodding.

"I wanted to add some of it to the food for the unicorn and the drag-on," she said. I softly handed her the fries and drink and pushed her away. She had a sink in the corner and I went to wash my hands.

"Is that dragon from last night?" I asked as I began chopping what she'd started. The air in the barn was warm. Lola began munching on her fries.

"It is. Apparently she's heard about me. She wanted a safe place for her babies to hatch since a lot of the creatures are getting sick," she said, taking a sip of her drink. "Her stomach has been bothering her, so I figured I could whip something up," she continued. "Mix it in with some meat from Griffin's Groceries."

I nodded, pouring the contents into the bowl. I sliced the bananas and mashed them up with the rest of the ingredients, creating a paste. Lola took a sip of her drink.

"You can give half to the unicorn and half to the dragon," I suggested. She smiled gratefully.

"Thank you so much!" She beamed at me and it sent a thrill down my spine. She set her stuff down before giving me a hug. My eyes widened. "Thank you, seriously," she said, her head in the crook of my neck. I let out a chuckle and wrapped my arms around her. She pulled away slightly, reaching back for the cup of blood.

She glanced out the window towards the forest. From this point we could see a few trees were struggling to maintain a vibrant green color. There was a lot on the line. Who knew that a tiny sapling could cause so much destruction.

When I checked the garden this morning everything seemed fine but the amount of raised bed gardens we needed to grow the number of flowers we needed, along with the delays of having to import soil were holding us back. Add in the amount of magic needed to protect and heal everything and the situation was exhausting.

"I'm heading to Priscilla's if you want to join me," I offered. She glanced at me, her eyes softening.

"Yes please. Hopefully she has everything she needs. I still have to stop at the garden too," she said, stifling a yawn.

"I can take care of the garden," I said immediately. Even though her vampire abilities kept her looking fresh I could see the toll that every-thing was taking on her by the droop in her eyes. She shook her head.

"I promised Eleanor and myself that we would work together," she said. I clenched my jaw.

"You're dealing with a lot Lola," I said firmly. She finished her fries before tossing the container into the trash.

"And so are you," she retorted. I scoffed.

"You're helping creatures give birth, on top of everything else," I pointed out.

"You're taking care of the garden which takes care of the town. Plus, I see you working on your whiskey for your family business. You're bartending and bringing me food. I'm helping you Flynn," she said, crossing her arms. We stared at each other in a silent battle. I sighed.

"What I hear is that we both have a lot on our plate," I said, my shoulders drooping. She nodded confidently.

"Exactly why we'll continue helping each other," she said. My lips twitched and I met her dark gaze. A ray of fucking sunshine.

"And making bets?" I teased. She smirked.

"Always Flynn Niall Kiernan," she said. My heart skipped. Maybe… this was okay. She reached for my hand, intertwining our fingers and tugging me towards the stairs. This *felt* okay.

"Speaking of bets," she said, before taking another gulp of blood. "Ready to name the griffin's babies?" she asked.

✳ ● ✳ ● ✳ ● ✳ ● ✳ ● ✳

I WAS STANDING in the stall with the griffin staring at me. Her feline-like eyes met mine. She was as tall as me when she was sitting down, and she was staring at me. Her babies nipped at my jeans. I could tell that Lola was fighting back a giggle by the way her shoulders trembled.

"You need to relax," Lola whispered.

"Sunflower, she's like moments away from my nose," I said. The griffin rolled her eyes at me. Griffin glares were scary.

"We're just visiting the babies, which she knows," Lola said. The griffin huffed and went to curl up in the corner. Lola hunched down and began running her fingers through the feathers of one of the babies. She looked up at me, a smile on her lips.

My heart rattled. She was comfortable in her element. She was so stunning when she was at peace, just working.

"Name?" she asked. I glanced at the babies. One kept nipping at my jeans and the other sat, staring up at me with big curious eyes. Their tails swished back and forth excitedly.

"The calm one is Nova," I said, scratching the top of her head. Lola grinned.

"And the other?" she asked. I knelt down and he butted his head against my chest. I let out a whoosh and pretended to get hurt. The little griffin jumped happily and tried again.

"Rebel," I said. Lola's face stared at me with so much warmth and serenity that I sat frozen. Her eyes almost seemed misty. I swallowed hard. This gorgeous woman was going to be my undoing and I was slowly becoming okay with that.

CHAPTER 25

A MOMENT

LOLA

T here was an awkwardness between us as we made our way towards Priscilla's Lotions and Potions. Ever since that moment in the barn Flynn had been quiet. I wasn't sure why.

After he named Nova and Rebel I smiled at him and I saw his eyes slowly shift. There was that wall between us again. I think? It was getting hard to tell, mainly because I think he is having a hard time keeping it up. I glanced down the street.

Eleanor was hard at work making sure the streets were lined with flowers and decorations in preparation for the festival. Pink and yellow bows were wrapped around the streetlights, and businesses were beginning to add flyers for all of the sales of the day.

I saw the purple of Priscilla's building and I smiled. I loved Priscilla's shop. It was always warm and inviting. Flynn held open the yellow door and I was immediately smacked in the face with the scent of citrus. Priscilla was waving off a customer when she noticed us.

"Don't you both look great," she said with a teasing grin. My cheeks were inflamed as I tried to control my reaction.

"We have the flowers," Flynn said with a grunt. Priscilla paid no attention to his tone.

"Beautiful. I'll start whipping up some herbal batches for the spell and I'll let you both know when it's ready," she said, turning away. She glanced back over her shoulder. "Lola, I'll be sending a few vitamins I made to your clinic soon," she said. I nodded, glancing at the array of herbs. She looked between us before shaking her head.

"You guys should check out the garden," she commented. Flynn took a step forward.

"Is something wrong?" he asked. She shrugged her shoulders.

"With everything that's happening, isn't something always wrong?" she teased. Flynn groaned and I let out a giggle. I looped my arm around his and tugged him towards the door.

"Thanks Priscilla!" I called out. Once outside Flynn pulled away from my grasp.

"Come on," he said, leading us to the garden. I rolled my eyes.

"Alright grumpy pants," I said, before smiling as he reached back to squeeze my hand. I was winning him over, one smile at a time.

✳ ✾ ✳ ✾ ✳ ✾ ✳ ✾ ✳

TWO RAISED beds worth of sunflowers had died. One bed of peppers and two beds of rosemary too. I glanced at Flynn as he stared at his sanctuary. This was his baby. He'd worked so hard to get the garden to be what it is today, and now it was decaying. He was fighting daily to keep it from dying.

I wanted to say something but I could tell by the way his eyes kept darting back and forth that he was still processing and coming up with a solution. If I reached for him now, he might pull away.

"I'll take the dead beds. Can you harvest as much as you can so it can be taken to Griffin's?" he asked. I nodded and moved to the side. He reached for my arm, pulling me back. I stared at him wide-eyed.

"I'm...happy you're here with me. I'm sorry about my attitude back at the shop," he said. I sighed, cupping his cheeks. The tips of ears pinkened.

"You tell me what you need okay? Remember: we're a team," I said.

"A team," he said, reassuring himself.

WE WORKED IN SILENCE. I had harvested about four buckets of daisies, five buckets of carnations and three of tulips. I had texted Eleanor to see if someone could pick up the flowers to take to Griffin's.

I would occasionally ask Flynn if he needed water but he always waved me off. His focus was on the dead sunflowers. Something about that filled me with worry. He almost looked helpless. There was some invisible weight pressing down on his shoulders.

I walked inside the greenhouse carrying the last bucket. The fans were on and spraying a cool mist everywhere. I was surrounded by flowers and herbs. It was a beautiful oasis that he'd created in this space. From the corner of my eye I saw a shelf under his work table that had the whiskey I had seen him carrying between here and the bar.

If I remember correctly the whiskey had smokey and sweet notes, with a hint of sage. It tasted like all of the things that I enjoyed. But I didn't want to delude myself with the thought that Flynn was making something for *me*. He was grumpy, but he also had a tendency to do sweet things that went unnoticed by everyone.

At the bar he would take extra shifts so that Caleb could be with Eleanor. No matter how busy it was I noticed that he would always double check my drink if someone else made it. He made sure no customer tried Bridget's patience. He was always one of the first people to lend a helping hand and an ear if someone needed to vent.

My brows furrowed. He flirted with the customers, but now that I thought about it I never saw him go home with anyone.

"Everything okay?" I heard his voice from behind me. "You were taking a while to come back out," he said. I sighed. He noticed me. I heard his footsteps behind me. I turned around quickly and smiled.

"Just marveling at what you've created here," I said honestly. He looked around.

"I guess. I just wish the outside was just as healthy," he mumbled. I placed a hand on his arm and looked at the color of his eyes, staring at the flecks of green and melted honey in them. His expression was solemn.

"What you've done here is magnificent, and what's happening out there would be a lot worse if it wasn't for you," I said, earnestly. There was a tick in his jaw. He didn't believe me. His head was clouded with doubt. I placed a tender kiss below his jaw. "Believe me," I whispered. Flynn swallowed and his eyes flashed with tenderness. He glanced around at his little universe. His arms wrapped around me.

"It is nice here," he said. Then he glanced at the buckets of flowers. "We are doing this," he said to himself. I squeezed him.

"Together," I reminded him. He nodded and my heart swelled. His scent didn't contain any nerves or worry.

"I have to lock up the greenhouse and head to the bar for a shift," he said, pulling away from me. I instantly missed his warmth.

"Okay. I told the girls I would meet them before I headed back to the clinic," I said, following him.

＊＊＊＊＊＊＊

AFTER WALKING Flynn to The Drunken Fairy Tale Tavern I headed to Lily's apartment. We were having another girls night, this time with pizza. Eleanor was in the kitchen plating our food while Lily was making lychee margaritas.

"Do you want some blood in yours?" Lily called out.

"Yes please!" I said. Lily always kept some blood in the fridge for me when we hung out. And after that night with Flynn and the griffin, I had gotten better about remembering to take care of myself. It also helped that Flynn and my friends were always reminding me to.

Crystal and I were curled up on the couch while Trixie was napping in the corner. Fabian sat a distance watching. According to Lily, Fabian has been attempting to flirt with Trixie but she is a stone cold princess. She was also feeling much better, so I knew there was another reason she was sticking around.

"How are things going?" Crystal asked as she finished her dutch braids. I shrugged my shoulders.

"Priscilla is making the remedies to heal the sapling, so everything should be back to normal soon," I said.

"That's amazing!" Lily called out. I stared at the coffee table which was covered in chips and popcorn.

"And Flynn?" Eleanor teased. I rolled my eyes as she handed me and Crystal a plate of Hawaiian pizza. Eleanor settled in the chair across from me. I took a bite before answering.

"He's..." I started. Eleanor motioned for me to continue and I felt my cheeks heat. "He's really fucking great," I confessed. Eleanor laughed and Crystal pinched my arm. Lily placed the tray of drinks next to the popcorn.

"Sip n' Spill everyone," Lily said. We all reached for our drinks.

"Well the spring festival is going great, as is my sex life with Caleb," Eleanor said. Crystal wrinkled her nose.

"Celestino and I are doing well," Lily said. We all looked at her. Lily had been going back and forth on whether or not she was ready to say 'I love you,' which we all understood. She was an overthinker. When it came to taking big steps, she liked to make sure whatever she thought or felt wasn't going to blow up in her face.

"I love him," she said quietly, her eyes springing with tears. We all looked at each other before bursting into screams. Crystal quickly covered her ears.

"Finally!" I said, clinking my glass against hers.

"Seriously, I don't know why you waited this long to figure this out," Eleanor said. Lily rolled her eyes.

"It's a really big emotion!" she said, defending herself. "I hope you realize I'm going to need your help to decide how to tell him," she said. Crystal leaned over to look at Lily.

"Can't you just say it?" Crystal suggested. Lily smirked.

"I may be an introvert but I'm extra in every possible way my dear Crystal. And that means my confession must be magical," Lily said, grinning. Crystal shook her head, giggling. We all continued eating and enjoying each other's company when an idea popped into my head.

"Flynn has been stressed lately. We all have been," I pointed out. The girls nodded. "Maybe we should have a night out? Do you think you can ask Caleb if he can have the night off?" I asked Eleanor. Her eyes narrowed and she smirked.

"We're getting the gang back together?" Eleanor said. She munched on a slice of pizza before her lips pulled up into a smirk. I took a sip of my drink, trying to figure out what Eleanor was up too.

"Everyone?" Crystal said nervously. Eleanor nodded.

"But let's do it at Highwayman Haunt," Eleanor said. And now I knew why she me gave that look. My apartment was right above that bar.

"Only if Crystal dances with me," I said, teasingly. Crystal groaned.

"I don't like dancing," she whined.

"But you'll be dancing with *us*," Eleanor pointed out. Like Lily, Crystal was an introvert but Lily knew when to let loose. I had a feeling Crystal was still getting used to being Crystal and not Ms. Hale, COO of Hale's Lumber Industry.

"The boys will be there," Eleanor offered. I bit back a smile. If the boys were going to be there then that meant Sailor would be there. I glanced at Crystal whose cheeks pinkened.

"Including Flynn," Crystal pointed out, trying to divert the attention to me. Her phone beeped. Eleanor glared at her little sister.

"Is that a work email? This late?" Eleanor asked. Crystal sighed, scanning her phone quickly.

"I'm working on a deal with the mayor of Coralia Coast, remember? He wants to fix up some of the shops and restore the town to what it once was. It would be a great look for the company," Crystal said, her voice slipping into a tone of authority. "We're hoping to establish more relationships with the supernatural towns on the east coast," she said with a grin. Eleanor's eyes widened.

"My little sister is so impressive," Eleanor said. Despite Eleanor not being involved in her father's company, she felt proud to see what her little sister was accomplishing there.

"I think we'll be closing the deal very soon," she said, her cheeks pink. I cocked an eyebrow at Lily who was sipping her drink with a grin. After finishing our pizza we decided to watch a movie. But before we could press play, Eleanor smirked.

"Remember Lola, if you feel like ditching us your place is just upstairs," Eleanor said, then I smacked her with a pillow.

CHAPTER 26
MAGICAL GAME NIGHT

FLYNN

I did my best to stifle a yawn as my siblings and I were playing Celestial Uno. The difference between this version and the regular version of uno was the fact that the cards moved themselves.

"I heard you guys got the ingredient needed for the potion," Greg said. My older brother stretched his arms over his head. I nodded, pouring my siblings glasses of my latest whiskey concoction. Caleb sniffed the glass.

"Smokey *and* citrus?" Caleb questioned. I nodded. Bridget made a face as she took a sip. She was never the biggest fan of whiskey, no matter what I made. She got up to grab a mixer.

"We did. This potion should heal the dark sapling, and then all will be well in Lavender Falls," I said, sighing and leaning against the couch.

I glanced at the table and tapped once on one of my red cards. It floated out of my hand and onto the table. Caleb grunted and tapped the deck of cards. I smirked. This meant he had no reds.

"You're not using the same spell as last time?" Greg asked. His next card was a draw 2 and Bridget groaned from behind me. She was losing badly.

"Slightly different spell," I said. I glanced at my cards. "The quicker this gets resolved the quicker my garden can get back to normal."

"How is it? I haven't had a chance to check it out but I've heard you and Lola have been doing great at keeping it alive," Caleb said. I nodded, my face warm.

"It's been okay– I mean, it's not easy. Between the shops needing the garden and the festival it's a lot. Then there's the clinic too," I began saying. "Honestly…stressful as shit," I admitted. Caleb nodded.

"I appreciate you still being able to provide the herbs I need. Tourism is picking up now that we're close to the festival," Greg said. I leaned my back against the couch. Tourism *was* picking up. The tavern had been busy this past week.

"How's Lola?" Greg asked. I glanced at him, my jaw set.

"Fine," I said. He hummed in response. Each of my siblings have been on my ass about Lola. Everyone was forced to grow up around us and our rivalry, but now they've been giving me smirks and finding every excuse to bring her up to me. Bridget scoffed as she sat down next to me.

"Flynn," Bridget warned. I bit the inside of my cheek. Growing up I was never the center of attention. I grew up as the middle child and while sure, there were times where I craved attention, this was not one of them. This was uncomfortable.

"Bridge," I said, using the same tone. Greg stared at me with his piercing blue eyes. He had a serious look that made me squirm. Greg was the brightest out of all of us. He was also usually the easy going one so I felt nervous under his gaze.

"You need to stop that," he said, his voice rough. I tilted my head.

"Stop what?" I questioned. Caleb and Bridget looked between us. Greg sighed and took a sip of his whiskey. He stared at the glass, gathering his words.

"I should have done better as the eldest," he confessed. We all looked at each other in confusion.

"What are you talking about?" Caleb asked. Greg ran a hand through his wavy brown hair, which had streaks of gray in it now.

"I should have looked out for you all more. Caleb, I should have figured out a way to break your curse sooner. Bridget, I should have hung out around you more, helped you out, and Flynn…" Greg stared at me, his eyes filled with regret.

"What about me?" I asked, defensively. I didn't like where this was going.

"Growing up, you were the one taking care of all of us, being there for us, working twice as hard as the rest of us," he started to say. My stomach twisted.

Did he notice? Did he see all the times I would stay up to help Bridget study and then go to work with dad the next day?

I thought I'd grown up flying under everyone's radar. "I should have been around more but I was so focused on finishing school and starting my career," he said.

"It's difficult to make it in your field. You needed to practice and perfect your craft," I said in understanding. And I did. It was difficult to make it in baking. Baking was a science, and I understood that. Greg shook his head. "You're amazing at what you do and that's due to all of the hours you've put in," I said.

"*You* are amazing too, Flynn. You helped me all those years in school. You make amazing whiskey even though I don't like it," Bridget said. I huffed out a chuckle. "The garden has done so much for the town. You help Caleb with the pub all the time," Bridget said. I swallowed.

"Guys-"

"You deserve happiness and love," Caleb grumbled. I stared wide-eyed at my grumpiest and quietest sibling.

"Are you drunk already?" I asked, fighting off the doubt that was poisoning my brain. My heart sank and my stomach twisted. I wasn't comfortable with praise. I was perfectly fine behind the bar, or alone with my hands in the ground.

"You and Lola are a good thing," Bridget said, placing a hand on my shoulder. I took a breath and stared up at the ceiling.

"Guys I came here to have a family game night and drink whiskey, not for a therapy session," I said, firmly. They all rolled their eyes.

"One of us here pointed out we needed therapy," Greg said. Bridget beamed.

"I mean look at us so far. We just had a sibling bond breakthrough," Bridget said. Caleb chuckled and I turned to him. He placed a hand on my shoulder and silently nodded.

"Thank you," he grunted, cheeks flushed in embarrassment. *Fuck.* Not Caleb being emotional.

"Thank you for taking care of the family," Greg said, holding up his glass.

"Thanks for being a hardass brother," Bridget said, mixing her drink. I knocked back my whiskey, using the burn as a distraction.

"I'm not a fan of this," I said. Caleb lightly slapped the back of my head.

"Shut the fuck up and accept our love," he grunted.

CHAPTER 27
SHOTS ALL AROUND

LOLA

Highwaymen Haunt was packed with beings. Tonight they had a live band playing. The lights were low and rock music blared throughout the bar. I had finally made my way downstairs and towards where my friends were waiting for me.

I had spent the majority of the afternoon going over flying exercises with the pegasi and giving the kittens a much needed bath. I waved at Alex and Thalia who were enjoying a night out as new parents.

At the bar Caleb had his arms wrapped around Eleanor while Lily was tucked into Celestino's side. Flynn was sitting on a bar stool nursing a beer. He wore fitted black jeans and a loose soccer jersey. Crystal was standing in front of Lily, watching everyone. I did my best not to laugh. It was obvious she felt uncomfortable.

"You okay Crys?" I asked, wrapping an arm around her. She snorted despite relaxing in my hold.

"Don't I look like I'm enjoying myself?" she teased. I threw my head back and laughed. From the corner of my eye I caught Flynn staring. I gave him a smile that had his ears turning pink. Eleanor patted my arm and handed me and Crystal a shot.

"To us?" Eleanor asked. My eyebrows furrowed.

"Where's Sailor?" Lily asked. Celestino kissed her temple.

"He's on the way. Just running a little late. He had to talk to Carrie about something," Celestino said.

"To us," Caleb said, raising his shot.

"To spring," Lily said.

"To winning," I said, smirking at Flynn. He cocked an eyebrow. Everyone glanced at us.

"We'll see," Flynn said with a smirk, raising his shot glass. We clinked our drinks and threw our heads back. The burn slithered down my throat and settled low in my belly. My body was tingling. I dragged Crystal onto the dance floor. I needed this break as much as everyone else. With our hands in the air we lost ourselves to the music.

✵ ⚹ ✵ ⚹ ✵ ⚹ ✵ ⚹ ✵

HANDS MADE their way around my hips. A chest pressed against my back. I tilted my head back to meet the eyes of a werewolf. He had an earthy scent to him and there was a gold band around his pupils that gave him away. He had shaggy black hair. I didn't recognize him which meant he was just passing through

"Dance?" he asked, over the music. I nodded as I wrapped my arms around his neck and let him dance my worries away. I glanced over and my eyes widened at Crystal who had allowed a man to dance with her. Her arms were around an elf, he was tall with brown hair.

I looked over at the bar to see Eleanor smirking at her little sister. Sailor stood off to the side, his eyes trained on Crystal. *This was going to be interesting.*

I turned my body around to face my dance partner. He was cute. He had a bit of scruff and full lips. I pulled our bodies closer. His eyes sparked with mischief and we leaned into each other, my chest brushing against his. Despite how attractive he was, my body didn't light up the way it did with Flynn.

190

At the thought of Flynn, my eyes made their way back to the bar. Flynn was busy talking to Caleb and Celestino, ignoring me. I bit the inside of my cheek.

A tiny part of me wanted him to be jealous. I wanted him to come over here, pull this werewolf out of my arms and dance with me instead; to claim me in front of everyone.

But this whole thing could be one sided. My thoughts soured and it felt wrong to be dancing with this stranger when the person I wanted was just across the way.

"Thanks for the dance," I said, patting his arm. He nodded, pulling away.

"If you want another dance later, I'll be here," he said with a wink. I headed to the back of the bar towards the bathrooms, needing to breathe. The whole bar felt hot with so many bodies pressing against me. I needed a moment. The back exit door caught my eye and I walked out. The air was cool but thick with humidity. I could hear crickets in the background, and the stars were out.

There was one light that illuminated the back of the pub. A few motorcycles were parked nearby. I leaned against the brick building, sighing. My phone buzzed and I checked it.

The unicorn was pacing around. It was happening soon. Even though I wasn't sure, something in my gut told me it would be soon. The door creaked next to me. A mop of brown hair came into view.

"Sunflower?" a deep voice called out.

"Here," I said, my voice sounding small. Flynn's eyes collided with mine and his shoulders dropped in relief. "What's wrong?" I asked. He walked to me and leaned against the wall. His warmth sank into me, urging me to move closer.

"Everyone wanted to know where you went," he mumbled as he took out his phone to send a quick text.

"Just needed to breathe," I said. Flynn leaned towards me, trying to catch my eye.

"What?" I asked, regretting the annoyed tone in my voice.

"You're lying," he said. I rolled my eyes.

"I'm fine, Rider," I said. He scoffed and moved to stand in front of me. My eyes lined up with his full lips. He frowned and his eyebrows were pinched in the middle.

"What do you need?" he asked in a rough voice. My heart skipped. I placed my hand on his chest, wanting to push him away but he took that as a sign to press closer, his arms caging me against the wall. "What do you need, Sunflower?"

His scent was shifting. The smell of pine and sunscreen was shifting to something spicier, something enticing. My fangs poked out and my body began tingling. I dragged my hand from his chest slowly up and into his hair. I gave a quick tug and Flynn's eyes fluttered close.

"I need oxytocin, dopamine and vasopressin," I said.

✳ ◦ ✳ ◦ ✳ ◦ ✳ ◦ ✳ ◦ ✳

WE STUMBLED into my apartment with my hands shoving Flynn's shirt up. His lips latched onto my neck, biting down. I cried out, my legs trembling. Flynn pressed me against the door. The smell of pine filled my nose and the air vibrated. I pulled away, glancing down in time to see my door lock. I swallowed, my heart beating excitedly.

"Did you just use your magic to lock my door?" I asked, my voice turning sultry. Flynn stepped away and lifted his shirt over his head. His jeans hung low on his hips. Something I enjoyed about Flynn was the fact he wasn't completely ripped, but rather soft and hard in all the right places. It made me want to dig my hands into him. He nodded silently.

"What else can your magic do?" I asked, walking towards him. He eyed the couch with a smirk and sat down. He spread his legs open and tapped his lap.

"How about we find out?" he asked, his voice rough. I shivered with anticipation. There was an invisible tug and I tumbled into his lap. I gasped at the force of his magic. His eyes glowed brightly.

My stomach twisted and my hips rocked. Flynn leaned his head back and groaned as I settled fully onto his lap. He was hard and I moaned at the feel of his erection.

I was already wet for him. Flynn muttered something in gaelige and one of the straps of my dress slid off my shoulder. I smiled as I rocked my hips.

"If you want the other strap to follow, you need to answer my question," he said. I swallowed, running my hands through his hair. I nodded. "What was the real reason you went outside?" he asked. I sat frozen. He cupped my cheek, keeping my eyes locked with his eyes. My heart pounded against my chest.

"I was dancing," I said.

"With the werewolf," he said. So he did notice and he did nothing.

"I wished it was you," I confessed. My other strap fell off my shoulder. Flynn's hypnotic magic slowly tugged down my dress. My nipples were pebbles when the dress slipped lower.

Flynn groaned deep in his throat at the sight of my naked chest. He took one of my nipples into his mouth, keeping his eyes on me. I gasped at the sudden scrape of teeth. I pressed against him, needing to feel more of his skin. Flynn whispered more words and there was a delicious pressure keeping me pressed against him. My eyes widened.

"What the stars?" I said. I looked down and Flynn was grinning. He continued to bite and suck my chest until I was a whimpering mess. I ran my hands through his hair and yanked him back, my lips smashing against his. Our tongues fought for control, our hands roaming each other's bodies. He lifted me up and laid me on the couch.

"I need you naked if you want to experience the chemicals that are released with an orgasm," he said, teasingly. With a few more hushed words my dress and panties slid off my body and fell to the floor.

Flynn placed one of my legs on the top of the couch, keeping me spread open. Once again the smell of pine caressed me and I felt a force keeping my legs open.

"Just enjoy," he murmured against my thigh. I nodded wordlessly. He kissed his way up towards my pussy. I did my best to lift towards him but his magic pressed me down. Flynn placed a kiss on my folds before spreading them open with his fingers. He stared at me, his mouth right above my clit which was begging for attention. I nodded, desperately.

Flynn's mouth descended on me. His fingers ran up and down on either side of my clit as his tongue flicked slowly. I kept squirming under his mouth. My hands dove into his hair, tugging him impossibly closer. His tongue teased my entrance and I rocked harder.

"Fingers *please*. Fill–" he cut me off, slipping two fingers inside me roughly. I cried out, my stomach tightening as Flynn orchestrated my body into a beautifully passionate melody. His fingers pumped in and out, harder and harder, his tongue flicking my clit. Faintly I heard a sensual drum beat from the bar below. My hand tightened in his hair and I found myself choking to get air in.

"Flynn, Flynn, Flynn," I muttered over and over again. He lifted his head.

"You're tight around my fingers Lola," he grunted. I whined, his words sending a thrill through me. Flynn kept the same pace, matching the beat from the band and before I could tell him what to do he placed his tongue flat against my clit and pushed. I came screaming his name against the sound of an electric guitar solo.

Flynn sat up, his fingers still rocking into me until I was whining. He pulled his fingers out and sucked them clean. I whimpered at the magnificent sight.

"Wow," I said. Flynn gave me a lazy grin before crawling on top of me. I wrapped a leg around him, pressing him against me. I shuddered at the feel of our skin. I kissed his temple as I brushed his hair back. "Thank you," I said, sighing happily. I hadn't realized how much stress my body was holding onto.

"Do you feel better?" he mumbled. I nodded, giggling.

"Want to head back down?" I asked. His eyes met mine before quickly glancing away quickly. His fingers caught one of the sunflower charms in my hair.

"Just a few more minutes," he whispered.

CHAPTER 28

PARENTAL ACCEPTANCE

LOLA

A steady beat lured me awake. There was something warm and firm beneath my hand. My eyes fluttered open. The sunlight was trickling in from my window. Flynn had his arms wrapped around me. My head was on his chest and when I looked up he was still asleep. His lashes were long and gently brushed his skin. His mouth was slightly parted.

I closed my eyes trying to remember last night. Flynn had followed me out and then we came up to my apartment. The couch– I remember him making me scream, but how did we end up in bed?

I went to scratch my head when I realized I had my bonnet on. I don't remember putting my hair up. Flynn twitched and his arms tightened around me. He mumbled something. I placed a kiss on his chest.

"Flynn I have to go," I whispered. His eyes opened slowly. I could see flecks of green today. He smacked his lips before turning away to yawn. He rolled us until he was spooning me. He placed a soft kiss on the back of my neck.

"A few more minutes," he said. I huffed out a laugh.

"You said that last night and I think we fell asleep on the couch," I said. His arms tightened around me and his morning wood pressed against my butt.

"Mhmm. We fell asleep," he said, his voice rough with sleep.

"Did you carry me to bed and put on my bonnet?" I asked, my heart hammering. He placed another kiss on my bare shoulder.

"Mhmm," he said.

"And then you stayed," I said.

"I should check on the garden," he said, pulling away. My stomach sank. One second I thought we were getting somewhere, and the next he was pulling away again. Ignoring the pain in my chest I got out of bed and headed to the bathroom. I knew I needed to be patient with him but that didn't lessen the pain of his rejection.

After brushing my teeth and washing my face I headed back out to see Flynn already fully dressed and clicking through his phone. His nostrils flared and his shoulders drooped.

"Priscilla is done with the potions. So I'm thinking later today we can all head over to the tree," he said. My eyes widened. *Dragon's piss*. This was it. We were near the end. The spring festival was next weekend and this mystery was finally coming to a close.

"That's amazing! Is there a time you want everyone to meet up?" I asked, pulling out my phone to check on the clinic's cameras.

"Four?" he offered. I nodded.

"Meet at the Boogeyman's swamp?" I asked. He nodded before yawning. His eyes darted around my apartment. He looked anxious, like a small rabbit trying to escape its cage.

"Yeah. I'll see you later," he said. I turned to go get dressed. Clearly Flynn wanted to avoid any emotions with me and that was fine. I would return the sentiment and then he would come to his senses. "Did you sleep well?" he asked. His question caught me off guard.

"Um..yeah, actually I really did," I said honestly. He nodded his head, his hands twitching at his sides.

"Good," he said, the tips of his ears pink.

FLYNN

I sat in my apartment, my knee bobbing up and down as I sat at my dining room table. The group had sent a string of text messages in the morning about how last night was fun and my brain spiraled.

Eleanor: so we need to do weekly hangouts that don't involve trivia

Lily: Agree

Caleb: you just don't want to lose

Crystal: I had fun!

Celestino: why don't we rotate?

Lola: Last night was amazing!

Last night was amazing. She said it was *amazing.* But could have it been if I walked out on her this morning. Was she referring to dancing with a stranger? Her night with me? All I could think about is the fact I fucked up.

I managed to leave Lola's apartment and make it home without running into anyone. I felt like I was doing the walk of shame. But I wasn't ashamed to have spent the night with Lola. I was ashamed of myself and how I made her react. She seemed hurt. I felt guilty for what I did.

Last night was the best sleep I've gotten in months. I knew something was off with Lola when she snuck outside the bar. Did I like seeing her dance with someone else? No, of course not. But we weren't exclusive, and even if we were it was just a dance.

Then I followed her out and when I saw the look on her face I just wanted to wash it away. I wanted to soothe her and make her smile. The

197

more intimate we were with each other the more real my feelings were becoming. It was terrifying.

We had fallen asleep on the couch and I was going to sneak out after placing her in her bed but…I selfishly asked if I could stay. She gave me a stunning sleepy smile and said she wanted my warmth. With my heart in my throat I pulled her close and we slept.

I grimaced, remembering my reaction from this morning. I was cold to her. Her eyes were wide with worry. She was tiptoeing around me and it hurt. But wouldn't that be how things would go? There would be dark days with her having to be careful around me. I didn't want Lola to be careful around me, or worry about me in general. I shook my head. I needed to get out.

※ ● ※ ● ※ ● ※ ● ※ ● ※

I SCRATCHED the back of my head and entered Coffin's Coffee Shop. I needed a giant coffee if I was going to push past my feelings and possibly save the town. I smiled as I walked up to Madame Coraline.

"Good morning Madame C. How are you on this lovely morning?" I asked. Madame C snorted. Her salt and pepper hair was braided away from her face and she glared at me. I offered her another smile. "And why the frown on that beautiful face?" I asked. Her lips twitched and she rolled her eyes.

"Black coffee?" she said, remembering my order. I nodded and paid for my drink.

"Oh Flynn dear," she said in a sickly sweet tone that had my stomach churning.

"Yes?" I said. Her eyes narrowed.

"Go say hi to your mom," she said. I sighed. *Really?* She'd nearly given me a heart attack. I thought she was going to bring up the fact we haven't been sending many supplies. She was known for her rosemary scones, but the rosemary's been rotting at the roots.

"I will. Oh, could you send a caramel macchiato to Lola at the clinic?" I asked. Madame C smacked her lips and she grinned.

"Why of course Flynn."

I looked around and found my mom sitting in the back by the window. But she wasn't alone. My mom's pale blonde hair was piled on top of her head and when her blue eyes met mine, they melted with motherly love.

"Mom," I said, placing a kiss on her cheek. "Mrs. Luna," I said, giving Lola's mom a hug. That's why Madame C was giving me that look. Mrs. Luna gave me the same smile that Lola always gave me: open and warm. She patted the chair next to her and I sat.

"How are you my sweet son?" My mom asked. My stomach twisted and I wanted to crawl out of my own skin.

Growing up I worked very hard for my mom not to worry about me. She had Greg, Bridget, Caleb, and her job as a preschool teacher to worry about. My skin prickled with awareness as I looked into my mom's eyes.

There was an itch to run away and lock myself in my greenhouse. I took a breath and gave her an easy going smile, one I spent years perfecting.

"I'm good," I said, masking my nerves. They both hummed at the same time and my stomach twisted again.

"Flynn, could I order more whiskey? We are planning a party for my department and you know how much my husband enjoys your brand," Mrs. Luna said. I nodded.

"Of course. Just let me know which kind and how many," I said. My mom reached for my hand. Her happiness seeped through my skin. She was using her magic to soothe my inner turmoil.

"You're such a sweet boy," my mom said. I rolled my eyes.

"Mom–"

"Take the compliment Flynn," Mrs. Luna said, cutting me off.

"Yes, Mrs. Luna," I said with a sheepish grin. Mrs. Luna glanced at her phone and there was a wrinkle between her eyebrows.

"What's wrong?" I asked. She let out a sigh.

"I worry about Lola," she confessed. My heart stopped. Did she know what was happening between us?

"She's doing great," my mom assured her.

"Why are you worried?" I asked as Madame C dropped off my coffee. I offered my thanks and turned to face Mrs. Luna. She shrugged her shoulders.

"She has so much on her plate. I'm worried she isn't taking care of herself," Mrs. Luna said.

"She's doing well," I said. Mrs. Luna raised an eyebrow, a small smirk on her lips. *Fuck.* I was in hot water. She was luring me into a trap.

"Oh really?" she asked. Both the ladies' attention were on me now and I squirmed under their calculated gazes.

"I'm just saying as someone who has been working with her. She's doing great. She's eating, drinking and sleeping," I said. They both hummed as I took a sip of scalding hot coffee hoping that the burning on my tongue would keep me from saying more stupid shit.

"Flynn," Mrs. Luna said, getting my attention. "You know I like you, right?" she asked. I gave out a nervous laugh.

"I think so," I said. My mother giggled.

"Flynn. Look at me," she demanded. I stared into her brown eyes that were firm and serious yet also hopeful. In spite of the fact that I wanted to look anywhere else, I held her gaze.

"I trust that you know my daughter is doing well," she said firmly. I swallowed. *Trust.* "And I trust that you will make sure she is," she said.

Without thinking I nodded. Instinctually I wanted Lola's mother to know that I would. I thought back to when Lola questioned if it was instinct for me to protect her. It was. And now, sitting before her mother I couldn't deny that fact. My heart spoke up before my brain could deny it.

"Good. I'm glad we have that understanding. Because I like you and so does Mr. Luna," she said with a teasing smile.

"Mr. Luna likes my whiskey," I pointed out.

"Lucky for him Lola has you," she said. I blushed furiously and willed my heart to relax.

"Um–" I began to say before she waved me off.

"That is all Flynn. I'll get what you need. Your mother and I have some gossip to discuss," she said, pushing me out of my seat.

"Bye my dear sweet boy. Remember," my mother started to say. I leaned over to give her a hug. "We are proud of you," she whispered in my ear before kissing my cheek and then she smacked the back of my head.

"Mom!" I exclaimed. She giggled.

"Be nice to your sister," she said with a grin. I rolled my eyes.

"Tell her to mind her own business," I said. She tsk-ed at me and waved me off.

"Mr. Hale went to apologize-" Mrs. Luna started to say as I turned to leave.

My thoughts were consumed by Mrs. Luna basically declaring me acceptable for her daughter. It seemed like everyone believed we belonged together except me.

CHAPTER 29
SPRING AWAKENING

LOLA

S *oon,* the unicorn said.

Her nostrils flared, sending hay everywhere. I waved my hand around, pushing it away. The baby was moving a lot more in her belly now.

Once again a feeling settled in my bones. My magic was sure of it. It *will* be soon. I recognized it now. There was a certainty that I felt deep in my bones and made my magic buzz. It was similar to the way that I knew that Flynn was mine and mine alone.

"I know. I'll be here to help," I said firmly. She nodded before moving to stand. I opened the stall so she could take a stroll around the pen with the pegasi. "Remember. Don't eat the grass, and we have the dragon outside," I warned. They all shook their heads, ignoring me. I rolled my eyes.

Who knew pegasi could be so sassy? Weirdly enough all of the animals were getting along. I even saw the kittens playing with Nova and Rebel. Maybe it was the spring air but I was eternally grateful for the peace.

The dragon seemed to be huffing and puffing at the griffin. I'm sure if I connected to them I could hear their conversation. They seemed to be enjoying themselves. The pegasi were on a walk with the unicorn and the sun was high up in the sky.

I quickly snapped a picture, not knowing when the clinic would have another moment like this. I sent it to Ms. Heinstein, knowing that while she was missing this season she was happy spending time with her family.

"Hey guys I'm heading inside to file some paperwork. Tap the door if you need me!" I called out. There was a chorus of snorts and whinnying.

* ❋ * ❋ * ❋ * ❋ * ❋

AFTER A DAY of cleaning all the cages and pens before filing a few patient charts, Flynn and I stood awkwardly at the edge of Boogeyman's Swamp. I glanced at him.

He wore a charcoal shirt that was covered in paint with some basketball shorts. He had a crossbody bag filled with bottles that clanged together whenever he shifted on his feet. His hair was pulled back with a headband and he'd recently shaved off his scruff.

The sun made his eyes melt into a warm honey color. My heart thumped in my chest. He looked so much like the boy I grew up with today.

We would always bicker in class over formulas. He would be stubborn about the rules and regulations. And yet, this Flynn wasn't the same. Growing up, my perception of Flynn was that of someone brilliant, quick witted and stubborn, with a charming smile.

But now I noticed the cracks in his mask, the way that he painfully clung onto things that were his because he was afraid to let go. The way he watched everyone else, always ready to offer an ear, a smile or a hand.

"Are you nervous?" I asked, breaking the silence. Flynn's jaw clenched. His hands tightened on the bag.

"I want to say no, but the Hollow Tree was difficult during winter," he said, swallowing. "Sailor, Eleanor and Caleb worked their asses off to get the ingredients for the healing potion," he glanced at the forest quickly. "But I'm sure we'll be okay this time too," he said. I watched him carefully. His ears were pink.

"It's okay to be nervous," I said, trying to catch his eye. He sighed.

"I'm trying to be positive like you," he said. My cheeks heated. "Are *you* nervous?"

"Actually…yes," I confessed. Flynn whipped his head to the side, finally looking at me. I was fidgeting with the end of my scrub top. I was anxious.

We spent this spring season fighting to keep everything alive. I've worked so hard for all the creatures. Feeding them, healing them, nurturing them. I had to watch every single thing they ate and drank. I had to double check that their waters were pure, double check their feces and bloodwork. All on my own.

"I need this to work, Flynn. I *need* it. The creatures are relying on *me* to keep them alive," I said. Tears pricked my eyes and my stomach twisted. *Fuck*. I was breaking under pressure.

But I couldn't break. They were all relying on me. Flynn's face fell. His hand came up to my elbow and he turned me to face him.

"It'll be okay Lola," he said softly. His words felt like a salve on my heart, soothing me. I brought my hand to hold onto his arm. My body on its own accord began leaning towards him. He took a step forward and I was ready to fall into his embrace. "I'm sorry… about basically running out of your apartment," he said.

"It's okay," I said, knowing that he did so because he was running from his emotions.

"No it's—"

"We're here!" Eleanor's voice caused us to spring a part. I bit back an irritated sigh. Lily's eyes looked between us.

"Have everything we need?" Lily asked, trying not to smile. Flynn crossed his arms and while he tried his best to look unphased his ears were still red.

"We have everything. Eleanor, are you ready?" Flynn asked. Eleanor reached for Caleb's hand. She had a special connection with the Hollow

Tree so it was safe to assume that this weird Dark Hollow Tree sapling would need her.

"I am," she said confidently.

"Sailor and Crystal?" I asked, noticing their absence.

"I have Sailor working on some furniture that Crystal needs to showcase to a client and Crystal is on a video call with said potential client," Celestino explained. I nodded. Flynn grunted, getting our attention.

"Alright. I just have to double check the location," he said, getting on his knees. A dirty thought skirted around my brain and I felt my cheeks heat again. I caught Eleanor's eye and she winked. I looked away quickly.

Flynn took a deep breath before digging his hands into the dirt. I've watched him do that a few times now. He took three deep breaths before his shoulders dropped and words I couldn't understand began spilling from his lips softly. It was beautiful to watch him use his magic.

His head twitched and I reached for him instinctively. My hand pressed against his shoulder and he relaxed. He breathed in sharply.

"The fucker likes to move its roots a lot," he muttered. I glanced up at everyone. Flynn tilted his head up to the sun, like a flower. The rays of sunlight made his skin glisten. My eyes narrowed.

If I stared intently I swore that I could see a faint yellow glow around him. I wish there was something I could do for him, like when Flynn helped me out with the animals. But I was helpless. All I could offer was a hand on his shoulder.

Flynn yanked his hands out and we all backed away, trying to avoid the flying dirt. "That fucker!" Flynn said, eyes wide and still glowing.

"What is it?" Caleb asked. Flynn stood up, clapping the dirt off his hands.

"This little tree has a tendency to move its roots around and apparently now it's by the garden," he grumbled. My eyes widened.

"Well that explains why the garden was affected first," I pointed out. Flynn nodded.

"It's also still a sapling and probably wanted nutrients from the garden," Lily pointed out.

"Let's hurry," Flynn said, walking away.

❋━❋━❖━❋━❖━❋━❖━❋

MY HEART STOPPED ONCE we got to the garden. We had a few flower beds that were wilting despite the fact that I had stopped by yesterday in the late afternoon. Flynn's eyebrows were scrunched together and I could tell that he was at a loss for words.

"I was here earlier today," he said in disbelief. My heart broke for him. Celestino placed a hand on his shoulder. They shared a look before nodding. Lily shook her head before rolling up her sleeves. She waved her hands at us.

"I can track with your help Flynn," she said. I bit back a smile.

"What do you need?" he asked. She pulled her wavy hair into a top knot.

"Dig your hand in and connect to the tree, and I'll hold your other hand. With the two of us connected I can try a tracker spell," she said, confidently. "You could do it too, but it recognizes you. My magic will mask yours," she said. According to Flynn, the little sapling didn't like him.

Eleanor squeezed my hand as she stared at Lily. It's been amazing to watch Lily grow closer to her magic. Flynn knelt down again and dug his left hand into the ground, his fingers slipping beneath the blades of grass. Lily gripped his right hand and took a deep breath.

Closing her eyes, she let her shoulders drop. I couldn't deny that a part of me was jealous that Lily could do this for Flynn and I couldn't.

"With our magic intertwined there is a tree that we must find," she said softly. A cool breeze that smelled like the ocean twirled around Lily, shaking her clothes and hair. Flynn's eyes widened. When Lily opened her eyes they were glowing.

Although she was looking at me, her eyes were unfocused. A trail of light broke out from where Flynn's hand was and zipped behind us towards the forest. Lily pulled her hand away with a sigh.

"And now we follow!" she said with a smile. Celestino wrapped his arm around her and kissed her cheek before whispering something in her ear that made her blush. We all moved, following Lily and Flynn.

We broke through the edge of the woods and after a few minutes of walking, someone gasped. My eyes widened at the sight.

There was a small sapling, its bark a darker brown than our Hollow Tree, with wilted branches and black leaves blooming. There was a circle of dead grass around that was slowly spreading. The trees surrounding it also seemed to be drooping, its leaves falling despite the season. In all honesty, it was beautiful in a haunting way.

"Holy shit," Eleanor whispered. My stomach tightened. *How did this little one stay hidden?* I glanced around my group of friends. Everyone was tense. But then there was Flynn. His face was calm. He pulled his bag off of his shoulders and dug for one of the potions.

"Eleanor, are you ready?" he asked her. Eleanor tore her eyes away from the tree to look at Flynn.

"I'm sorry I let this happen," she whispered, tears in her eyes. Flynn shook his head.

"You had no idea. None of us did," Flynn encouraged. I felt bad for Eleanor. She worked so hard to save the Hollow Tree during the winter. There was no way any of us could have predicted something like this.

Eleanor took the potion from Flynn and they both knelt in front of the tree. Eleanor gave it a tender smile. She placed a hand on the base of the sapling's trunk.

"Hey there my love. I'm so sorry we're late," she said softly. A breeze blew by. Flynn placed a hand in the grass by one of the roots.

"We're here to help you," Flynn said, his body trembling. Their magic caused the air around us to vibrate. Eleanor poured the potion onto their hands and on the roots of the tree.

"*In all this darkness, there is light. Let us heal you and make things right,*" Eleanor chanted. Flynn repeated the words and a gentle glow began emanating from them both. I sucked in a breath. There was magic pressing against my skin. The smell of cinnamon and sunscreen filled my senses and the light around them kept climbing higher until it encompassed the entire tree.

Lily reached for my hand and then Celestino's. The three of us moved to shield our eyes, trying to not let the magic blind us. I squinted, trying to see Flynn. I wanted to reach for him.

I took a step forward and the warm glow pushed me back. My bottom lip trembled as I heard Flynn grunt. "F-Flynn?" I called out. I dropped to my knees, pushing against the invisible force. I was *not* going to stand here while Flynn poured his soul and magic into healing this sapling. I needed to reach him.

"Please," I whispered out loud as I crawled towards him. The invisible field gave away slightly. With my eyes shut I moved until I bumped into Flynn. He was trembling and I wrapped my arms around his waist, pressing my face against his shirt. I breathed in his scent deeply, letting him center me. "I'm here," I said, pressing a kiss against the back of his neck.

Flynn's body relaxed against mine. I chanted the words alongside him, hoping somehow my magic could help them. There was a giant crack in the air that had me squeezing Flynn. I felt one of his hands brush my arm as he sagged back on his heel and I shifted backwards.

That's better

We heard a tiny voice around us. When the light dissipated Flynn and Eleanor were sitting on their heels with matching smiles. The ground was no longer brown. It was now a rich green color. The sapling's bark was brown, and green leaves were sprouting. Another strong breeze blew through as the trees around us raised their branches.

"Is that it?" I asked in wonderment. Flynn nodded, helping Eleanor stand up.

"We have another Hollow Tree," Eleanor said, beaming with a smile. "Twins, actually," she said, with a giggle.

"What?" Lily asked. Flynn handed his bag to Eleanor.

"Can you give this to Crystal? It's extra potions, courtesy of Priscilla. Your father and sister can keep it on hand for emergencies," Flynn said. Eleanor nodded.

"So as you know, a piece of rotten root had broken off and sprouted into a sapling Dark Hollow Tree. Both trees were growing at a similar rate. They were taking and giving to each other. But this bad boy was hungry for more nutrients," Eleanor explained.

"Hence everything that was happening to our vegetation," Flynn added.

"But now, our bad boy is feeling much better and everything should be back to normal," Eleanor said, confidently. I sighed happily.

Caleb wrapped an arm around Eleanor, pulling her close. She sagged into him. I couldn't imagine the amount of magic she must have used. When she healed the Hollow Tree she was out like a light. Flynn met my gaze. His lips pulled into a smirk.

"We've got a garden to fix," Flynn said.

CHAPTER 30
THE GARDEN OF LAVENDER FALLS

LOLA

I was covered in dirt and sweat. While it was gross I couldn't stop myself from smiling, because we'd healed the baby sapling the garden was no longer wilting. Both trees were working together to heal what was sick.

The sunflowers stood tall, the roses were vibrant and the garden was filled with fresh herbs and veggies. I glanced over at Flynn, who was harvesting some herbs for me.

I turned to the side to catch Eleanor and Lily staring at me. Everyone decided to stay around to help us with the garden. They made kissy faces at me when Flynn wasn't looking and I rolled my eyes every time.

Since we got back to the community garden Flynn had been in work mode. He was barking orders at Caleb and Celestino and hardly noticed me.

"Any more?" Caleb called out from the greenhouse. Greg was on his way to pick up all of our flowers and take them to storage. Celestino waved his hand and a pastel violet light wrapped around two bins of baby's breath. The bins lifted from the ground and made their way towards Caleb.

I separated the herbs into labeled bags to be taken to Priscilla's. I couldn't stop myself from smiling. *We did it.* The town was okay and it seemed like the spring festival was going to be a success.

A few earth fairies began strolling in. They would be using their magic to expedite the growth of flowers. Now that everything was fine and we didn't have to worry about spoiled dirt, infected water, or anything decaying, magic could flow without a second thought.

"So who grew the most flowers?" Lily asked. I glanced over to my six empty flower beds. The original bet of the season was who would grow the most flowers.

"I actually don't know," I said, sheepishly. The season was so hectic that I hadn't kept track. I shrugged my shoulders. Eleanor scoffed.

"You're not seriously telling me you don't know," Eleanor said. I wiped some sweat off my forehead. Lily came over with a basket of carnations.

"I don't. With everything that has been going on I didn't keep track. Plus with the influx of animals and the nights I spent sleeping at the clinic, Flynn was the one taking care of my share most of the time," I confessed. I believe Flynn won our last bet and that made me happy. He deserved it with how hard he's been working. Their eyes widened.

"Seriously?" Eleanor asked, glancing at Flynn. He was carrying a bag of dirt over his shoulders. His shirt was plastered to his chest and his muscles bulged. He looked delectable.

"Yeah," I said. Lily smiled.

"You guys are cute," Lily said. I rolled my eyes.

"Tell him that," I grumbled. Eleanor bumped my hip as we stood up.

"What's wrong?" Eleanor asked. I leaned my head slightly down. Lily and Eleanor crowded around me.

"He still pulls away and I don't know why," I said. Eleanor frowned.

"Maybe he just needs time," Lily said. I smiled at her optimism. "You saw how long it took me," she pointed out. I sighed. It took Lily forever to accept her feelings for Celestino. Flynn could be the same way.

But it hurt to think that he couldn't see how good we were together. Before I could say anything else my phone blared.

I pulled off my gloves and swiped open my phone to click on the cameras. One of the animals had set off a sensor. Swiping through the cameras my heart stopped. The unicorn was on her feet, pacing. Her breathing was labored. Her tail swished back and forth. Her eyes went to the camera as if sensing me and she nodded. My heart raced.

"It's happening," I whispered. They leaned over to look at my phone.

"She's going to give birth?" Lily asked.

"Yes. Fuck. Okay, I have to go guys," I said, staring at the two people I trusted most. They nodded.

"Go, go. Don't worry, we'll handle the garden," Eleanor said, already pushing me. I glanced back at the greenhouse where Flynn had gone inside. My heart was now pounding in my ears. A unicorn was going to give birth. I was going to help deliver a unicorn. Holy stars. Without another word or thought I raced out of the garden.

✳ ❀ ✳ ❀ ✳ ❀ ✳ ❀ ✳

I PUSHED through the barn doors to see the unicorn pacing back and forth. Our eyes connected and by the stars, I was met with a terrifying glare from the unicorn. I made my way over to her slowly.

Finally, she snorted. I needed to make sure that she and her baby were okay.

"I came as fast as I could," I said. I stepped towards the gate that separated us. "Is there anything you need from me?" I asked. Her tail swished violently back and forth and she snorted.

Come in, she demanded. I ran to the sink in the back and scrubbed my hands as quickly as possible.

I stepped into the stall, closing the gate behind me. She stood still, eyes on me. Bending over I checked her udders. They were leaking milk. This was happening. The unicorn snorted again. There was a noise behind me.

I turned around to see Flynn, who was running towards us gasping for air, hair wild. *Dragon's piss*. The unicorn whined and I quickly exited the stall.

"What are you doing here?" I hissed, my eyes darting back to the unicorn. Flynn took a deep breath.

"Eleanor said something about the unicorn. I came to make sure you were okay, and to help," he said, regaining his breath. My eyes widened.

"Help? What can you do?" The words slipped out of my mouth before I could take them back. I swallowed. I hadn't meant for them to sound so harsh. "Fuck, Flynn. I'm sorry. That was uncalled for," I said. The frustration of everything including us was getting to me. Flynn didn't flinch. Instead, he glanced over my shoulder to the unicorn.

"Should she be sitting down?" he asked. I gasped before turning back to the stall.

Time, Ms. Luna.

My heart stopped at her using my name. Okay. I was going to help a unicorn give birth. The hay under her was wet. The baby was going to emerge *now*.

"I'll sit right here. If you need something, let me know," I said gently. She was lying on her side and her legs kicked slightly. Turning my head, I could make out two legs in a sac emerging from her stretching vulva. My heart raced. "You got this," I whispered.

I kept my gloved hands on my knees. From the corner of my eye I could see Flynn standing by the gate. The unicorn let out a deep groan.

This could take anywhere from 12 minutes to close to an hour. I wasn't sure if she had given birth before. Sometimes new moms labored longer. But also, she was fucking unicorn. She lifted her head and turned to see her baby emerging. Her eyes connected with mine. Our link fully snapped and I felt a pain vibrating through my body. I grunted.

"Lola," Flynn hissed, stepping in. I waved him off.

"You got this," I whispered encouragingly. She laid her head back down, her breathing labored.

❋ ❖ ❋ ❖ ❋ ❖ ❋ ❖ ❋

AFTER TWENTY MINUTES the baby unicorn wiggled its head out, trying to break free from the sack. My eyes watered. The unicorn relaxed.

Ms. Luna, may you help with the sac? she asked. I nodded, moving carefully toward the foal with gentle hands to release it from the sac. The baby shook its head side to side. The foal began moving more, and I tried my best to look down to see if it was a boy or girl.

Girl, the unicorn said. My eyes snapped to hers.

"How did you know?" I asked. I could see a twinkle in her eyes. "Must be a magical unicorn thing," I said, with a smile. I sat back watching as she sat in a more comfortable position, gently licking her baby. It was a beautiful thing to see. A quiet moment watching a new mother and her baby. After a few minutes the unicorn gently pushed her baby to stand. My heart constricted.

This was an important moment. The baby needed to stand on its own, and walk. I stood up making my way over to the gate. Flynn stared wide eyed. The baby shook, stumbling to stand while the mother encouraged her.

"She has to stand already?" Flynn asked in a hushed whisper. He opened the gate and I came out, pulling off my gloves.

"Once she stands and walks, I'll be able to breathe," I confessed. Silence descended in the barn as we stood next to each other watching mother nature take its course.

It took over half an hour for her to begin walking around. Flynn's thumb brushed the side of my cheek, grabbing my attention. I stared at him. He offered me a small smile.

"You were brilliant," he said, gently. I rolled my eyes.

"I didn't do much," I muttered. "I am sorry about my attitude earlier," I said. Flynn shook his head and gripped my chin.

"Lola Sade Luna. You just helped deliver a *baby unicorn*. You're probably the first person to ever do that," he said firmly. "You've been under an enormous amount of stress while still finding the time to care so fucking much," he said. I swallowed, my heart in my throat.

He tilted my head up and pressed his forehead against mine. His scent washed over me, soothing the aches in my body.

"Do you know how unbelievable you are?" he whispered. Tears

pricked in my eyes. All the stress of the season was finally leaving my body and I found myself falling into Flynn's arms. He pressed a kiss against my temple.

"I do but you can still tell me. Preferably after a shower," I said, pressing my face against the side of his neck.

"No," he said, lifting me up. I was about to protest when he placed a scorching kiss against my lips. "I'll do it while we're both in the shower," he said, lifting me up in his arms.

Get a room, the unicorn said.

✳ ⚬ ✳ ⚬ ✳ ⚬ ✳ ⚬ ✳ ⚬ ✳

AFTER DOUBLE CHECKING on the unicorn and other animals Flynn picked me up again and carried me inside the clinic. My heart was stuck in my throat as he carried me to the back locker room, where we had a bathroom with a walk in shower. He stopped outside the door and with a wave of his hand the shower turned on.

"Towels," he said. I nodded and pulled out some that were situated inside of a cabinet. He glanced at my hair. "Do you have a shower cap?" he asked. I shook my head as I retwisted my hair into a high bun. Flynn moved to peel my scrubs off and tossed them into a corner. His hand moved to cup my cheek. His eyes softened.

"It's been a day," I said, pulling his shirt up over his head. He slightly crouched, allowing me to take it off.

"A very long day," he said as he pulled down his shorts and boxers. I placed a hand on his arm.

"Flynn. You're unbelievable too. You figured out what was wrong with the sapling. You helped heal the tree," I said. I wanted–*needed*– Flynn to know what an achievement he'd accomplished.

"We both need this," he said. I nodded. He grabbed my hand and led me towards the shower. Flynn stuck his hand behind the curtain under the running water, checking the temperature. He turned to look at me with a grin.

He stepped in first and I watched the water slide down his body. My stomach twisted and I clenched my thighs. He was breathtaking. He reached for my hand and I let him pull me in. The water was a welcomed heat against my skin.

I moaned, tilting my head as Flynn took a step back, letting the water wash over the front half of my body. He reached behind him for some soap and a small hand towel.

Flynn's hands were magical on my muscles. He slowly scrubbed my body, placing pressure in the spots where he felt knots. I couldn't stop myself from moaning.

He slowly moved behind me. His hands ran up to knead my soapy breasts. I could feel his erection on my ass. He placed an open mouth kiss on the side of my neck.

"Flynn," I hissed as he sank his teeth into me. He hummed. He pushed me a step forward, letting the shower wash away the soap. His hands began traveling lower. "Please," I begged. Flynn chuckled against my neck.

"Why do you feel so fucking good Lola?" he said, pressing his lips against my skin. He sucked and bit his way up and down my neck, coaxing whimpers out of me. His hand slipped between my folds and I moaned loudly.

Flynn's fingers teased my clit in slow circles and my legs trembled. He moved us a step to the left until one of the sprays of water was in direct contact with my nipple.

I gasped and began moving my hips. Between his hand on my clit, the other kneading my breast and the water teasing my other nipple I could feel myself climbing higher.

"More," I said. His hand dipped lower until I felt him push two fingers inside of me. Flynn let out a low curse.

"You're so wet and tight," he said, rubbing his cock against my ass. I moaned at the feeling. His fingers continued to work me over until he was practically holding me up. He curled his fingers, rubbing a spot that made me squeeze my eyes shut. My body trembled and a familiar feeling began zipping around.

"It's not enough Flynn," I gasped as he pulled his fingers out. I whimpered at the loss of contact. Flynn spun me around and pressed me against the cold shower wall. I hissed.

He cradled my face before pressing his lips against mine. His tongue swept into my mouth as my hands slid into his hair. He lifted his knee between my legs, locking me in place. I rub against his thigh, shamelessly, needing release. He bit my tongue, pulling slightly back and I snapped.

With my vampire strength I turned us around, pushing him against the wall. I dragged my mouth down his neck, my hand sliding down his wet body to grip his cock.

Flynn moaned loudly and it spurred me on as I stroked him hard and slow. He cradled the back of my head as I sucked on his neck. My fangs nicked his skin and his heartbeat raced.

My blood pushed me to sink my teeth into him. I pulled back immediately. I panted staring at the red splotches. I was about to bite him without thinking.

"No. Bite me Lola. Please," he said, panting. My eyes widened as he set a firm gaze on me. "Bite me," he demanded.

"I'll bite you on one condition," I said. My voice was a mix of desperation and lust. His head leaned back against the tile, watching me through his lashes. His cheeks were flushed and I could see his eyes were hazy as I continued to pump him. "I'll bite you but I want you inside of me," I said. Flynn's eyes widened and his nostrils flared. The smell of his arousal penetrated through the air. His whole body tensed.

"I'm not fucking you for the first time in a shower Lola," he said through clenched teeth. I dropped his cock and crossed my arms.

"Why?" I asked. He glanced away from me, hiding his emotions like he usually did.

"You deserve better than a shower fuck," he grunted. I rolled my eyes.

"I have fucked in a shower before. It's nice," I said. His eyes snapped back to me with jealousy. *Good.* Maybe the jealousy will snap some sense into him.

"Our first time shouldn't be-" I caught him off, shoving a finger in his chest.

"Our first time can be in a shower, in a tent, behind an alley. I don't care Flynn, as long as it's you," I said, pressing my palm against his rapidly pounding heart. I could hear his blood pumping faster. The smell of him mixed with the scent of my body wash was clogging up my senses.

"Are you sure?" he asked quietly after a few moments. I stared into his warm eyes with a smile, fangs and all.

"I want *you*," I said, softly.

"I- I want you too," he said, trailing his hand up my waist. I stepped away and we swapped places; my back against the shower wall and Flynn pressed against me. "Condom," he said. I cursed for not thinking that far ahead.

"I don't have one," he said, eyes tormented.

"It's fine. I take the enchanted birth control," I said. Forever grateful for the witches who figured out a birth control spell because I needed Flynn *now*, badly. His eyes wandered down my naked wet body, as if committing every single curve to memory.

"I'm going to pull out and come on your legs and I want it to be known that this is the only time I'm doing that," he said, his eyes serious. I nodded, wrapping my arms around his shoulders. "Next time: condoms," he said.

"So there's going to be a next time?" I teased.

"With the way you're begging me for it, you tell me," he said, leaning forward.

My lips hovered over the vein on his neck that was *begging* me to bite it. With Flynn's blood rushing and his body tight with anticipation it sang to me. My fangs grew and my fingers dug into his shoulders. I widened my stance and hooked a leg around his hip, my heel pressing into his lower back.

Flynn's hands dug into my ass and I moaned as he began to knead me. He placed his cock at my entrance. He glanced at me from the corner of his eye, a question lingering in the way his eyebrow arched up. I nodded slightly.

"Bite me."

My fangs sunk into his neck as he pushed inside me. For a brief second his body tensed. There's a sweetness to the metallic taste of Flynn's blood, it filled my body with a euphoric warmth that I knew he could feel too. He rocked back and forth until he was fully seated. He tilted his head to the side, allowing me more access.

"Fuck, Lola, you fee– *fuck*," he rasped as his hips bumped against mine. I moaned deeply, enjoying the rush.

He pushed me further against the wall until we were completely flushed together, the tile biting into my skin. He pumped into me faster, harder. I sucked and licked his neck. I felt high off of his blood and my impending orgasm was sending me higher.

I had never experienced such an out of body experience until now. This was heaven. I clenched around him and Flynn smacked his hips against me harder. This was pure ecstasy. Flynn's blood wasn't just calling to mine, it *was* mine. *He* was mine.

"Fuck, yes," he growled as he continued to slam into me, his fingers digging into my ass. I pull away from his neck, blood dripping down.

"F-Flynn- k-keep–" All my words died on my tongue as I exploded.

A string of curses flew from Flynn's mouth as he quickly pulled out. I sagged slightly and he replaced his cock with his fingers, pulling out the last bit of my orgasm as his cum dripped down my thigh.

We both stared at our lower halves, nearly joined. His blood was still singing through my veins. Flynn placed a tender kiss on my forehead as my heart tried its best to calm down.

"Wow," I whispered. Flynn set his hands on my hips, holding me in place as I dropped my leg and tried to steady myself.

"That was…" he trailed off.

"Amazing," I said firmly, trying to catch his eyes. We stayed like that until the water ran cold, silently holding each other as we tried to catch our breath. Looking into his eyes, there was a faraway look in them that made my heart sink.

Flynn was somewhere else, lost in the clouds he was always covered in. We quietly stepped out and dried off. I pulled on some of my emergency scrubs and handed him a clean pair that a male vet assistant had left behind.

I quietly went outside to check out on the animals. With each step away from Flynn I could see the space between us growing wider. The problem was that I had no clear idea *why*. After checking on the unicorn and the dragon (who was still curled up with her eggs), I headed back inside.

Flynn handed me a bottle of water and I took it, taking a gulp. The clinic floor was sterile and cool as I sat across from Flynn. He was fidgeting with his hands. The moment we'd shared together was wonderful, beautiful, like every other moment between us. His eyes skirted away, avoiding me.

"What's wrong Flynn?" I asked. His hands stilled in his lap. "Why do you keep pulling away? Is it me? Am I–"

"Don't you fucking finish that sentence," he growled, his head snapping in my direction, eyes burning. "There is nothing wrong with you. You- you are a blazing light." My cheeks flushed at his sincerity. He stood up abruptly and moved a step away.

"Then why?" I asked, standing and reaching for him. He stared at our intertwined hands with the same look from the campground. It broke my heart.

"Lola," he said, sounding scared. "It's not you," he confessed. I used my other hand to cup his cheek, forcing him to look at me. He shuddered, leaning into my touch.

"Then explain," I practically begged. We were good together–no, we *belonged* together. I felt it in my blood, in my magic, in the deepest part of my soul. *Did he not feel the same way?*

"You're too good for me," he said so softly that I almost missed it. I stared at him, wide-eyed.

"How could you possibly think that when you are my equal?" I said. He pulled away.

"But I'm not. You deserve someone who doesn't have so many days of feeling worthless and dejected," he said. I shook my head, not believing the words tumbling out of his mouth.

"Flynn, you are incredible, smart, kind. Why can't you see that?" I said, taking a step forward.

"Lola you are meant to live your life in the main stage while I belong behind the scenes. I'm fine with that, but you deserve someone who will walk in that spotlight with you," he said.

I was at a loss for words. I'd never noticed how insecure he was. How *lonely* he was. I took a deep breath. It wouldn't matter how much I praised him or loved him, he needed to love himself first. He needed to see that he was worthy.

"Then stop doing this," I said softly. He finally looked at me, hesitation clouding his eyes.

"Doing what?" he asked, reaching over to gently wrap a loose braid back around my bun. I huffed out a laugh and he went back to staring at the floor.

"*That.* Stop doing nice things for me. Stop bringing me food. Stop coming up with different remedies for the clinic," I said, reaching for his chin. I gripped it tightly, forcing him to look at me again. "Stop doing those things when you know how they make me feel," I said. Flynn's jaw tightened.

"Lola," he said, softly, pulling away. He gripped the back of his neck, shoulders hunched.

"Why do you do it Flynn?" I asked. He blew out a breath.

"Because…" he trailed off.

I waited a moment. His eyes flickered back and forth as he tried to find the right words to say. At least, I hope he's trying. I sighed. He needed to come to me. Just like wounded creatures who needed love, I was going to lay my heart out for him.

If he accepted I would be here with open arms. I moved to cup his stubbly cheek. He leaned into my touch and I felt tears in my eyes.

"Stop making me feel like a princess if you don't want to be my knight in shining armor. Stop making me feel like I'm living in a fairy tale if you don't want to be my happily ever after," I said, leaning to place a tender kiss on the corner of his cheek.

"I want it with you, Flynn Niall Kiernan," I said before leaving to check on the baby unicorn again.

CHAPTER 31
TRUTHS AND TALKS

FLYNN

I scrubbed the bar, Lola's words echoing in my head. Our shower was magical. It felt as if everything had clicked into place and that was terrifying. Lola was hurt, and while I spent most of the spring season trying to ease her stress it seemed like I was just adding onto it.

I groaned. Sometimes I wish I could get out of my own head. My heart wanted Lola's happily ever after. My brain was scared of ruining it.

But if I could make award winning whiskey, save my town, grow beautiful flowers *and* be there for my friends, then I could take care of Lola. Couldn't I?

Ba-bump.

My heart pounded in my chest as a giant tsunami of emotions washed over me. Lily, Celestino, and Eleanor came in and sat on the bar stools in front of me, breaking my thoughts. I eyed all three of them. They stared at me as I wiped down the bar. Caleb came up to my side. I sighed.

"Don't," I warned. Caleb crossed his arms.

"Don't what?" Caleb grunted.

"I know why you're here," I said, shaking my head. Eleanor smirked.

"And why is that?" Eleanor asked.

222

"You want to do the same thing Lola and Lily did to Caleb, and what you did to Tino," I said. Lily cocked her head.

"Wait, what did you do to Celestino?" Lily asked. Celestino snaked an arm around her waist.

"Don't worry about it *querida*," he said against her cheek. Lily blushed.

"So, if you already know, what are you going to do about it?" Eleanor asked.

"Nothing," I said, tossing the rag to the side.

"What the *fuck*?" a voice called from the left. I turned to see Bridget walking behind the bar with her arms crossed. My eyes widened. "Is everyone in our family dense?" she said.

"Hey!" Caleb said. Bridget rolled her eyes.

"We know what *your* issue was. What's yours Flynn?" Bridget asked, sitting next to Eleanor. I turned away. How could I tell them that what was wrong with me was something I needed to deal with alone? That it was *my* issue. Something I didn't need them worrying about.

"Nothing," I muttered.

"Then you can be with Lola," Celestino said matter of factly. My stomach dropped.

"Guys," I started to say.

"*Why not?*" Eleanor and Bridget said together. I bit the inside of my cheek.

"What is holding you back? It's not a curse. You're financially stable. Things are looking up for the festival. **What** is it?" Caleb pushed. Everyone's eyes were on me and an icky feeling began to spread inside me. They were right. There was nothing holding me back. Only myself.

But how could I explain to them that I wasn't good enough for Lola, that Lola needed someone who could brighten her day, who could fuel her light?

A warm hand pressed on mine as I gripped the bar. It felt like a cool ocean breeze had swept over me. My muscles began relaxing. I looked up to see Lily's warm brown eyes.

"I get it," she said softly. "But aren't you taking away Lola's choice

223

by taking yourself out of the equation?" she said. I swallowed. Celestino's eyes seemed to brighten in understanding.

"We all have insecurities, Flynn. We all feel like we're not good enough sometimes. I said 'fuck it' to my degree and opened a shop. Some days I feel like Lily is too good to be with me, that one day she'll figure out she can do better," Celestino said. Lily placed a hand on his shoulder.

"*Amorzinho*. No, I lo–you're it," Lily said, blushing. His eyes softened and he kissed her hand. "Sometimes I feel like *I'm* not good enough for Celestino. That he deserves someone who isn't as frazzled or who overthinks less," Lily said, her eyes watering.

"Eleanor is absolutely way too good for me. Sometimes I don't know how she puts up with my grumpiness. But she does, and she lights up my day every time," Caleb said. I wanted to gag at my older brother's words but my heart continued to thump against my chest. Eleanor reached for Caleb's hand.

"I feel like I'm too much for Caleb, that one day my dramatics and stubbornness will push him away," Eleanor said softly. *Fury fuck*. I coughed to mask the emotions that were beginning to choke me. Bridget squeezed my hand and I looked at her.

"We each have insecurities as people and in our relationships, Flynn. None of us are perfect, despite how hard we try. You might not see it but we all struggle mentally every day. What helps is finding the person and friends that will help hold your hand on the days you are struggling to get back up. We're your friends and family. We're here to help always, and Lola…" Bridget trailed off.

"Will be that special person to hold your hand," Eleanor said, finishing her sentence.

"And make out with," Fabian said, appearing on the bar.

"Not on the bar," Caleb grunted. We all broke out into laughter. Eleanor plucked Fabian off the bar and placed him in Lily's lap. Lily petted his head and the fox grinned.

I sighed, placing my head in my hands. Throughout this entire season in my moments of fear and weakness, Lola was right there. She never begged me to open up. She was just there for me, ready to hold my hand when I needed it.

I fucked up. I pushed her away. I've spent this whole time pulling and pushing, and yet she remained constant. She felt sure that I would eventually stop and just weather the storm with her by my side.

And I fucking pushed her away because I was too griffin shit to see it. I closed my eyes. Even when we made love in the shower she was there with me. I swallowed.

We made love. That day our body, our souls intertwined and it was the most alive I had ever felt. Our connection was locked in place that day.

Fuck, she's been so patient this is entire time.

"I fucked up," I admitted through gritted teeth. I left Lola in the clinic with a broken heart. We shared a magical moment, surrendering to each other, and then I *left* her.

"Well can you think of a way to un-fuck it up?" Bridget asked. I stared at my group of friends, my mind already racing with thoughts of how to win back the woman I loved. Because fucking griffin shit I did love that intelligent, strong, flirty vampire.

"How are you going to win your woman back?" Celestino said, pushing strands of hair out of Lily's face.

"My romantic confession was in a haunted house," Lily offered, glancing at her boyfriend.

"Mine was in bed," Eleanor said, causing my older brother to smirk. I wanted to gag again.

"*Of course* it was," Bridget murmured. None of that would work. Lola deserved more than just a confession. She wanted to be a princess. She *was* a princess which meant I needed to give her something straight out of a fairytale.

"I have an idea."

CHAPTER 32
WHAT WE'VE BEEN WAITING FOR

LOLA

"Lola, what you've managed deserves something far beyond praise," Ms. Heinstein said. Tears welled in my eyes. Ms. Heinstein had returned from vacationing with her family. I was in the middle of catching her up with all the reports when she'd paused to place a hand on mine.

"I was doing my job," I said. She shook her head and pulled her glasses off her face.

"Ms. Luna. You helped a multitude of creatures give birth, one of them being a *unicorn.* You have put together *at least* 10 effective herbal medicines that we can now distribute within the clinic. *And* you helped save the vegetation of this town," she said. I blushed at her praise.

"I had help," I mumbled. She sat back in her chair and gave me a look.

"Yes, **and** you still made a major contribution to each of those accomplishments. Which is why I'm making you partner," she said. My jaw dropped. *Partner? Me?* "Don't give me that look. You know damn well you deserve it. Plus, I'm getting old and I need someone I trust to take over," she said with a smile.

"Ms. Heinstein, I have no words," I said. She shrugged her shoulders.

"'Thank you' works fine," she said with a smirk. I rolled my eyes playfully.

"Thank you," I said. Ms. Heinstein stacked the folder of reports with a smile on her face.

"Now, if my timing is correct then the dragon eggs should be hatching today," she said with a knowing glint in her eyes. We both moved to head outside.

"You see *that's* what I want to be able to do," I said. Ms. Heinstein let out a laugh.

"You're halfway there Lola," she said with a smile. And that was true. It took awhile but I think I was finally getting the hang of working with my magic more deeply.

Outside the sun was shining bright. The grass was looking greener every day. Ever since we healed the sapling the spring season had sprung in full force. The unicorn and dragon were facing each other, snorting in some secret language. And the baby unicorn (who I've opted to name Rarity) was prancing around.

Not only was it rare for a unicorn to even connect with beings, the fact that I got to witness its birth was extraordinary. I let my eyes focus on the animals, magically connecting with them.

I believe they're hatching today, the dragon said.

You're lucky you lay eggs. My insides are still trying to move back into place, the unicorn whined. I did my best to suppress a giggle. Ms. Heinstein and I drew closer to the animals and they glanced at us.

I like her, the dragon said. The unicorn nodded.

She's feisty. Her man is cute, the unicorn said. I felt my mood drop at the mention of Flynn. We hadn't spoken in a few days. While I wanted answers I knew he needed time to think and process. My mind went back to Lily and how she struggled to accept her feelings for Celestino. We were in the same boat.

Before I could continue to think about Flynn, something began to rattle. Ms. Heinstein and I headed closer to the dragon, who unwinded her tail revealing four eggs that were beginning to crack. I held my breath as baby heads and tails began poking out.

"They're beautiful," Ms. Heinstein said. I nodded. One was a deep burgundy, the other violet, another was red, and the last one a burnt orange color.

"You did good momma," I said, beaming at the dragon. She leaned over to lick her younglings who were stretching.

Name them Dr. Luna. I want to bestow this honor upon you for all that you have done for me and every creature this season, the dragon said. Ms. Heinstein looked over at me with a knowing smile. She had a similar magic and could hear the words of creatures. She nodded and ushered me to sit down.

Sitting down in the fresh grass the baby dragons eyed me curiously. The burgundy one immediately began head butting my foot.

"That one is Rocky," I said, giggling. The violet one stayed sitting in its shell, all nice and cozy. "We can call that one–*her*," I corrected, leaning down to catch a glimpse of her lower belly as she rolled onto her back. "Cleo." The red dragon began trying to crawl into my lap and I gingerly picked him up. His eyes were like onyx and he licked my cheek playfully.

"Let's call this one Duke," I said, scratching the top of his head. The burnt orange dragon crawled over to its mom's tail and began nibbling on her. The mom gave a quick huff and her baby backed away.

"What about that one?" Ms. Heinstein said as she began petting Rarity, who had come over to see the babies.

"Sunny. I like Sunny."

* ❀ ❀ ❀ ❀ ❀ ❀ *

WITH MS. HEINSTEIN back in town she'd decided to give me the week off. When I tried to disagree she gave me that mother's look that made me immediately shut my mouth. I was tired. Not just from the festival and taking care of the animals, I felt drained in general.

My heart was still taking a beating from my talk with Flynn. The reason I was even *at* the tavern was because Bridget had told me that Flynn had the day off.

"Drink," Bridget said, setting down a whiskey cocktail. I gave her a pained smile.

"Well hello to you too, Bridge," I said. She snorted.

"How are you?" she asked, working on a few drinks. I shrugged my shoulders.

"Tired, but grateful for the week off. I can focus on the flowers for the festival now," I said. *And I'll use that time in the garden to avoid emotions and hopefully, Flynn.*

"How *is* that going?" she asked, moving to hand the drinks to another customer.

"Um…good. Ever since we figured out what the problem was, the vegetation has recovered quickly," I said. My chest tightened remembering how much magic Flynn had used, how much he was willing to give up for the town. He was always putting others before himself.

Bridget frowned and it reminded me of Flynn's; downturned, eyebrows scrunched in the middle. I bit the inside of my cheek, my heart aching. I wish he wasn't so worried about fucking things up. He couldn't, and even if he did we could fix it together.

"Okay I can't do this small talk shit anymore," Bridget said, reaching down. I stared at her in shock. I knew she had a tendency of being blunt but damn, what did I do? She tossed me a gift bag.

"Put on that dress and follow the clue," she said, crossing her arms.

"What?" I said. She shook her head with a smile.

"Smarty pants, put on the dress and read the *clue*," she said with a wink. "Trust me."

CHAPTER 33
SCAVENGER HUNT

LOLA

I stared at myself in the pub's bathroom mirror. The dress was a bright orange sundress with thin straps that went over my shoulders then criss crossed and tied in the back. It had a ruffled skirt that started to flare out under my breasts. It hit about mid-thigh and surprisingly matched the strappy brown sandals I was already wearing.

I licked my lips and my heart pounded. I was scared to jump to conclusions. I was feeling nervous and hopeful that this was something Flynn had planned. My hands shook as I reached for the note at the bottom of the bag.

Dopamine is released in areas of the brain to give you feelings of pleasure, satisfaction and motivation. It was at this location that the motivation to pursue what we've been harboring began.

I stumbled to the bar and stared at Bridget. I held the note in the air.

"Does this mean..." I trailed off, waiting for someone to tell me what I hoped and longed to hear. Bridget's lips twitched.

"One way to find out," Bridget said.

❊ ❖ ❊ ❖ ❊ ❖ ❊ ❖ ❊

"*WHERE THE MOTIVATION TO pursue what we've been harboring began.*"

He had to mean the Siren's Saloon. It was at trivia night when we'd placed the bet to see who would give in to the other first. That is where everything began. Flynn motivated me to make the bet. It's where his mask first cracked and I got a glimpse of his true desires. That is where the feeling of dopamine first flared between us.

I pushed open the wooden doors to see Caleb and Eleanor at a table. Eleanor beamed at me. My legs carried me over, the note clutched in my hand.

"Eleanor–" I began but she waved me off.

"I'm not going to say anything," Eleanor said with a grin.

"You just did," I said. She playfully glared at me.

"Don't ruin this. Anyway, what was your clue?" she said. I rolled my eyes.

"You know what it was," I said. She shrugged her shoulders and leaned against Caleb.

"Tell me," she said as she pretended to fan herself like a movie star. I shook my head, laughing.

"*Dopamine is released in areas of the brain to give you feelings of pleasure, satisfaction and motivation. It was at this location that the motivation to pursue what we've been harboring began,*" I said, clue memorized.

"And why here?" Caleb asked. My cheeks heated.

"We placed a bet here. A bet that made us– motivated us to step towards each other," I said. Eleanor smiled and tapped Caleb's chest. Caleb placed a piece of paper on the table and pushed it towards me.

Serotonin can affect your mood. One way to boost serotonin is sunlight. Do you remember where I mentioned that your smile was a shot of sunshine?

"Do you know where to go next?" Caleb asked. I nodded, my cheeks already hurting from smiling. Eleanor waved me off.

"You'd better go then," Eleanor said with a wide smile. Clutching both notes in my hand I raced to Boogeyman's Swamp.

✳ ❖ ✳ ❖ ✳ ❖ ✳ ❖ ✳

EVERYONE EYED me as I walked as fast as I could in the short dress. I could have used my vampire speed but we were already filling up with tourists. Boogeyman's Swamp was in view and I could see two figures sitting by the water. Sailor was petting Lucky, his pants rolled up to his knees as he stood in the water. Crystal sat next to him with a shy smile as her eyes went back and forth between Sailor and the baby.

She turned as I tried to catch my breath. Sailor turned around, blue eyes sparkling in the sunlight.

"Took you long enough," he teased. I rolled my eyes before bending down to pet Lucky.

"It was a walk and you should know that," I said. Crystal cleared her throat.

"So why did you come here?" she asked softly.

"Because here he told me my smile was like a shot of sunshine, clearing away his clouds," I said. Crystal's cheeks pinkened and she played with the ends of her cardigan. She nodded before pointing at Sailor. From his back pocket he pulled out a note. With a shaky breath I opened it.

Oxytocin can give you a rush of pleasure from affection and connection. It can also decrease levels of stress and increase trust. Can you think of the place where that connection spark? The place we first gave in to each other?

"You know where to go Lola?" Sailor asked. Once again I nodded. Crystal leaned over to give me a squeeze.

"Go," she whispered in my ear.

✳ ❀ ✳ ❀ ✳ ❀ ✳ ❀ ✳

I WAS TREMBLING as I made my way to the Lavender Falls community garden. I spent all afternoon walking around town, following clues to get to this place: the garden, his safe haven. The garden was the start of many things.

It's where my rivalry with Flynn began during potions class. Where my feelings grew as I watched him carry bags of mulch. Where our feelings for each other truly began to blossom. I cocked my head to the side as I noticed Lily and Celestino standing by the entrance of the garden.

"Hey guys!" I said. Lily's face flushed and she threw her arms around me. "Aw Lily," I said. Celestino pulled her back and nodded at her. She took a deep breath.

"You went around town collecting clues," she said. I nodded, holding up the pieces of paper. "What do those clues have in common?" she asked. My eyebrows furrowed.

"They're each chemicals that can be found in the body," I said. Lily's cheeks continue to flush. I bit back a laugh.

"And if you put those chemicals together what do they make?" she asked. My heart pounded. Suddenly my hands shook at the realization. This was too much. There was no way this was actually happening. "Lola, you know what it makes," Lily said as she nervously glanced at Celestino.

"Love," I said as my eyes watered. Lily let out a breath.

"Thank the stars you said it because I would have passed out," she said nervously.

"I'll get you to say it one day," Celestino teased. Lily bit her lip and looked at her feet before smacking his side. Celestino cleared his throat. From behind the adorable couple Fabian and Trixie appeared. Trixie was wearing a crown of sunflowers, daisies and sage.

"For you madame," Fabian said, glancing at his crush. Trixie bowed her head slightly and Celestino picked up the crown to hand it to Lily. Lily smiled and, with trembling hands, placed it on my head.

"A crown for a princess," she said softly.

"Go get your prince. I think you know where he's waiting," Celestino said, pulling Lily towards him.

FLYNN

My heart was beating erratically in my chest and I ate about five ginger candies. But nothing eased the knot in my stomach. Right now I was inside my greenhouse that was decked out in twinkling lights. The sun was setting, making everything sparkle. The window was slightly open allowing the breeze to filter in. There was a red carpet leading from the door to me. Sunflowers lined the carpet and soft jazz was playing.

On my workbench was the whiskey I had spent years perfecting. It was warm and sweet like honey with notes of sage running through it. It tasted like her. It was made with her mind, because as much as we bickered back and forth she was my constant motivation and muse. She occupied my thoughts in everything I did.

My phone beeped. The text was from Lily saying that Lola was on the way. In a few seconds the woman of my dreams would be walking in. Hopefully she would hear me out and allow me to prove to her that I could finally be her knight in shining armor.

The door creaked open and a gasp rang out. I turned around and the speech I had prepared went out the window.

Lola Sade Luna stood before me in an orange sundress, under a setting sun that made her skin glow. Her braids were decorated with sunflower charms that I knew were there because of me. Her smile was bright and showcased the fangs that drove me wild. Her dark eyes welled with tears filled with emotions I never thought I deserved to see directed at me.

"Flynn. What is all of this?" she asked, breathlessly. I reached out a hand, urging her forward. She began walking towards me.

"Dopamine, Serotonin, and Oxytocin make up the chemical formula that results in love. They're the chemicals that burst through me whenever I'm near you," I began. My throat constricted. *Fuck*. This was terrifying. Lola stopped halfway. She nodded, encouraging me to continue. I cleared my throat.

"I spent my whole life trying to prove my worth while staying behind the scenes. I helped my sister with school so my mom didn't have to worry. I helped Greg grow ingredients when he was training to be a pastry chef. I did everything I could to make the lives of my loved ones easier," I took a breath. "I don't regret those choices but I spent all my time wanting, *needing* people to see me. A contradiction, I am," I said, letting out a nervous chuckle. "I spent my whole life bickering with you because *you* made me feel noticed. You challenged me," I said. She resumed walking towards me as I took another breath.

"With you I can be grumpy. I can be a nerd. I can be sarcastic. I can be everything and nothing. I don't need to prove anything to anyone. I can just be me. You– *fuck* Lola," I said, my eyes watering. She cupped my cheek and encouraged me to continue.

"Honestly I don't feel like I deserve you. You're too smart, too kind, too brave. It's why I fought with you so much. So I could push this need for you away. You're everything I'm not and what I hope to be, confident and self-assured. I want to be your knight. I'll continue to learn every science fact imaginable if that means beating you at strip science trivia. I'll give you flowers and come up with new remedies." She giggled and wrapped her arms around my neck with a coy smile.

"I do like trivia," she teased. Tension eased off my shoulders.

"I can't promise that every day will be perfect. Some days I'll get insecure and moody," I said. "I've spent years keeping everyone away but I will work on it for myself and for you," I said, caressing her cheek. She nodded.

"We all do Flynn. I know how brilliant your mind is. I know how handsome and charming you are so there will be days where *I'll* be insecure. Where I feel like my love won't be enough to keep you. That you'll think I care more about the creatures than you because let's face it I take my work home with me," she said. I pulled her close to me.

"I think that's something we both do," I said. She nodded. "Sunflower, I promise to make our love like the fairy tales," I said, quietly. "I swear to work on myself for me and you." She pressed her forehead against mine. Her sweet perfume relaxed me.

"Flynn Niall Kiernan. I love how you quietly care for your friends and family. I love how intelligent you are. I love how you're willing to own your mistakes. I love how creative you are and that you push me to work harder. I love watching you garden, make drinks, and laugh. Fuck, I love your smile. And you know what else I love?" she said, knocking the breath out of my lungs. She cupped my face.

"I love that you think I don't know you're the only one who makes my drinks when you're behind the bar," she whispered. My eyes widened and I pulled back. Lola giggled.

"Wait how?" I asked. She walked over to my work bench and pulled herself on top. She grabbed the whiskey bottle and waved it in my face.

"You really think that with my vampire senses I haven't noticed that you've been trying to perfect this for my taste buds?" she said with a teasing smile. I threw my head back in laughter as I made my way over to her. I tapped her knees and settled myself between her legs, where I belonged.

"I guess you knew I loved you before I did," I said with a smirk. She rolled her eyes.

"Of course. I have vampire–" she began before stopping to read the label.

"What does it say, Sunflower?" I asked, my hands on her thighs, toying with the hemline of her dress. Her hands delicately brushed the bottle.

"*Anamchara*," she tried to say. I chuckled at her adorable attempt.

"It means soulmate," I whispered. A tear slipped from the corner of her eye and I wiped it with my thumb. I tilted her chin and her eyes met mine. They sparkled with love and disbelief.

"I feel it. You are my sunflower. The sun to my clouds. My soulmate. The one hand I'm supposed to hold as I walk in life. The person to challenge me to be a better lover, friend, son and all of the above," I said. "We have been intertwined since we were kids and I'll be damned if I get in the way of what the fates have blessed me with." Her breathing hitched.

"Fuck, Flynn," she said. I chuckled. "You know how to make a woman feel special," she teased. I pulled her towards the edge of the table and her eyes widened.

"Can I show you too?" I asked. "I'm more of a hands-on person."

"Let's pop open this whiskey and we can show each other," she said, biting down on her lip. I nodded, taking the bottle from her hand. I stepped away and she hopped off the table.

"Question is shall we have another round on this table or take it back to one of our places," I asked. A slow smirk spread across Lola's face and it made my dick twitch.

"There's a band playing at Highwaymen Haunt. They're typically very loud," she said, fixing her crown.

"Which means no one will hear you scream," I said, pulling her towards me.

"I won't be the only one," she teased, smacking my ass.

CHAPTER 34
MINE

FLYNN

We walked into her apartment hand in hand with my heart beating wildly. A smile graced her beautiful face. We kicked off our shoes and Lola turned to wrap her arms around me. Everything was right now. I had the vampire of my dreams in my arms.

"I'm sorry it took me so long," I whispered against her neck. She giggled slightly.

"I'm sorry it took so long for me to notice your pain," she said, pulling back to stare at me.

"My mental clouds might always be there," I said. Which was true. Life was full of sunny and rainy days.

"Some days I'll have clouds as well," she said. I placed a chaste kiss on her lips. It was a kiss of promise.

"I promise to be there with an umbrella," I said. She grinned widely and pressed her lips against mine. The soft kiss was tender and filled me with warmth.

"Can it have sunflowers on it?" she asked, pulling away. I let out a chuckle.

"Of course," I said. She nodded, and pulled out of my arms, walking towards the bedroom.

"You know…everyone is going to be happy that our rivalry has some to a close," she teased. I sighed, following her steps.

"I'd rather bet *on* you than *against* you Lola," I said. "And I *bet* we'll still have a rivalry," I said. Her cheeks flushed.

"There is always Thursday Trivia," she pointed out, tapping my nose. "Our parents will be happy about this," she said, motioning her hand between us. Once we were in her bedroom I shrugged off my shirt.

"While I must admit they've been sneaky with us, I do not want to talk about them right now," I said. Her eyes followed my hands as I unbuckled my pants. She licked her lips, her fangs already growing. My body heated and my cock strained against my pants at the sight. She reached back and undid the tie on her dress.

"Mhmm. Why's that?" she asked. Using my magic I slipped the dress down her body. I quickly learned that she enjoyed it when I used my magic behind closed doors. From the way her naked chest was rising and falling I knew I was right. She was a vision; tall, smooth brown skin and lean muscle that could throw me across the room.

"I want to make love to you, Lola Luna," I said, pulling her against me. I watched her pupils dilate. Her hands trembled as she snaked her arms around my neck.

"Make love? Why Flynn, you're becoming very comfortable with expressing your emotions now," she teased. I rolled my eyes and slapped her ass playfully. She pulled me towards the bed until we collapsed on the comforter. She rolled until she was on top of me.

Our mouths sealed against each other as my hands cupped her breasts. I craved every inch of Lola. My body needed her like it needed air to breathe. I tugged on her bottom lip and she opened willingly for me.

I slid my tongue into her mouth, and enjoyed teasing her fangs. Lola rocked against my hard cock. She whimpered as her hands tried to tug at my pants. I thumbed her nipples, eliciting sweet sounds.

I pushed her hands away and lifted my hips. With a whisper, my magic took my pants and boxers off. I gripped Lola's hips and slid her wet cunt back and forth on my cock. Lola's body trembled and I sat up to lick her nipple.

My mouth trailed wet kisses across each breast. Her nails dug into my hair and she cried for more. Her head was thrown back in bliss, her braids tickling the tops of my thighs.

"Lola," I groaned. She nodded, lost in her own bliss, pressing my mouth closer. I sucked and nipped her nipple with my teeth and she bounced on my lap. "Look at me," I demanded. Her lips were swollen and slightly parted as she stared at me. She raked her hands through my hair.

"I want to be inside you," I said. She nodded frantically, shifting herself. I opened my hand and a condom flew out from my pants. Lola grinned. "One condition," I said as I ripped open the package.

"I bite you," she said, already knowing where my mind was going. While I did want her to bite me, there was another condition. I rolled the condom onto my cock and gripped her hips.

"Yes, but this time leave a mark," I said. She sucked in a breath, her face beautifully flushed.

"A m-mark," she stammered. Her eyes rolled to the back of her head as the head of my cock teased her entrance.

"I want everyone to know I'm yours," I said. She lowered her hips until the head of my cock slipped in. She felt so fucking good on top of me.

"You're mine and mine only, Pretty Boy," she said, before sinking herself on my cock and her fangs in my neck.

Lola

The rush of his addictively sweet blood and his cock filling me up was a near blinding pleasure now that we had fully given ourselves to each other. He was taking space in every inch of my body and soul.

My nails dug into his shoulders and fuck, if he wanted my mark I was going to leave one everywhere and in every way I could think of. I'll use my fangs, my nails, my mouth.

Flynn bucked his hips, his tempo matching my bounce. I moaned into his neck as his hands gripped my hips, taking control over my body. My sex squeezed his cock. Flynn was at the mercy of my fangs and my body, and it drove me frantic with need.

"By the fucking stars Lola," he groaned. I shoved his hands away and pushed him to lay down, my mouth still latched onto his neck. I needed control. I needed to claim Flynn.

One of his hands cupped the back on my neck as I rode him. His other hand slapped my ass and I moaned. I pulled back and blood leaked from the puncture wounds. My fingers dragged the blood down his collarbone. This elf's blood was *mine*. He was my soulmate and everything in my magic was screaming in rapture.

Looking into his eyes I could no longer see the melted honey or flecks of green. His pupils were dilated, filled with lust.

"Fuck me Lola," he said. His hands came up to cup my breasts and I rode Flynn until I knew I would leave bruises against his hips. My name tumbled out his mouth over and over again.

"Mine," I murmured, slipping one hand down to play lazy circles on my clit.

"Yours," he grunted, his eyes trained on mine. He bucked once. "Mine," he said, staking his claim. I smiled down at him, showing my fangs.

"Yours," I growled, grinding myself deep, milking his cock. I gasped as he matched my rhythm. My hands dug half moons into his chest.

"*You. Better. Fucking. C-come. With. Me,*" he thrusted on each word. With his blood singing through my body, his heart in my hands and his cock inside me, a scream tore through me as I climaxed. He followed soon after with my name falling out of his mouth.

Flynn's thrusts turned slow and deep as I leaned over his body. He continued until we were both limp and satisfied. My fingers played with the spot where my fangs had sunk into his skin. His heart was still beating rapidly against my chest.

"Hey Lola," he said. I lifted up slightly to meet his gaze. His eyes were drunk on love, and a damn good orgasm.

"Yes, my Pretty Boy?" I said. His hands drifted down my back and kneaded my ass. I whimpered, already wanting more. His dick twitched inside me, hardening again.

"We were loud and the band hasn't started playing yet," he said. I barked out a laugh and Flynn groaned. "I can feel that Lola," he said. I rolled my eyes and sat up. We both hissed as I pulled out of him.

"I think we might have two hours before they start playing. So…we could shower, eat and then commence round 2," I suggested. Flynn got out of bed to get rid of the condom. Once he was back he leaned in for a soft kiss.

"You phone in the food and I'll go pick up more condoms," he said. I winked.

"I like the way you think, Mr. Kiernan."

CHAPTER 35
HAPPILY EVER AFTER

FLYNN

The spring festival was in full swing. The Drunken Fairy Tale Tavern was packed with people after the Flower Parade. Many shops and businesses created their own floats using the flowers we grew to decorate them. Flowers were scattered all over the town. It was like one giant garden.

Eleanor was talking animatedly to Ben Chaves, her boss. When it came to the seasonal events, Eleanor was the one that was *really* in charge.

I handed Celestino and Sailor a beer. The men had been building the floats since the end of the winter festival. For Celestino it was a great way to get his carpentry business out there. Crystal was off in the corner talking on the phone. She and Celestino had worked out a deal of providing him with lumber from Hale's Lumber Industry in a partnership.

Caleb smacked the back of my head and I growled. I glared at my older brother who pointed off to the side. I heard her laughter before I saw her. Lola Sade Luna. The woman of my dreams. Her braids flowed down her back and she wore a yellow sundress that made her skin shine and my hands aching to feel her curves.

Her eyes connected with mine and it was like we were the only two in the room. A cord was woven tightly around us and I finally felt at peace. She was the missing piece of my heart that made me feel whole. She offered me a small smile and made her way towards the bar.

Automatically I started making her a drink, topped with my special whiskey that I created for her. She leaned over the bar to offer me a sweet kiss and I caught the back of her neck with my hand. I needed more than just a brush of lips to survive the rest of the night.

"Oh no. Is this going to be like Caleb and Eleanor again?" Sailor whined. I rolled my eyes and tossed him a napkin. We all laughed.

"I don't know. Caleb and Eleanor are pretty wild," Lola said with a grin. Eleanor walked up next to her and threw an arm around her.

"Damn straight we are. Aren't we, Elfie?" Eleanor said, winking at Caleb who fought back a grin.

"Where's Lily?" Lola asked, looking around. Celestino sighed.

"She's still working. She'll join us later," Celestino said.

I looked at my friends and the clouds that covered my mind faded slightly. I knew they would be here for me. The tumbling thoughts would always be hanging around the outskirts of my mind, but I had people by my side that I could count on. Crystal made her way towards us, still on the phone.

"You think the summer is going to be like this?" Eleanor asked. We all groaned.

"Starburst, we're trying to get through spring right now," Caleb said, handing a tray of beers to Bridget.

"I don't want to know what you have planned after Sailor and I *just* had to build 12 floats," Celestino said, cracking his knuckles. I snuck a glance at Lola who smiled.

"We both deserve a break," Lola said, reaching for my hand. Eleanor sighed dramatically and tossed her hair back.

"Fine but expect an email by next Friday," Eleanor said, taking a shot of tequila from Caleb.

This spring season was chaotic. But this was a magical town and naturally we would have some adventures and amazing memories. I learned a lot about myself. I learned to trust others and mostly myself. I could finally see what I have always had and I was never going to let it go.

"Next week sounds perfect. I can't wait," Crystal said, sitting next to Sailor. Her cheeks were slightly flushed. "See you soon." She hung up the phone, a small smile on her face.

"Who was that?" Eleanor smirked. Crystal's eyes widened.

"Just a client," she said, hastily. I felt a tug on my hand. I looked over at Lola.

"Movie night?" she asked me. I smiled. I nodded, squeezing her hand. Her eyes widened. "Oh guys I have news!" She kept her hand in mine and turned to face everyone.

"Ms. Heinstein is making me partner," she said, beaming. We all exploded into cheers. I lined up shot glasses and began pouring a shot of tequila for everyone. Caleb helped hand them out. We each raised a glass.

"To another successful festival," Eleanor said. Lily pushed herself between Eleanor and Celestino.

"To Love," Lily said, raising an empty hand and blushing. Celestino kissed her temple and handed her his shot. Caleb poured him another quickly.

"To friends," I said, grinning.

"And to new adventures," Crystal said, cheeks still rosy. We threw back our shots and more people came in through the doors. We said our goodbyes and I got back to pouring drinks and taking orders.

From my peripheral I could see Lola staring at me. I caught her eye and she smiled wide, revealing her fangs before giving me a wink. I inhaled sharply. Flirting with fangs was becoming a weakness she was learning all too well.

Luckily I had a thing for biting.

The End

Sneak Peek of Book 4

CRYSTAL

CLAMMY HANDS. Erratic heartbeat. Light nausea.

This is how I always felt right before a meeting, and while my meeting was over I still felt anxious. The anxiety was like a monster just clawing beneath my skin, wanting and waiting to be released. On the outside I was the picture of calm and cool, just how my father had prepared me to be but on the inside I felt like a cracked egg on a sidewalk, burning up against the summer sun.

Sharp blue eyes captured me. I swallowed.

"I think this could be the start of a good partnership," Mr. Calder said, voice rough. He was taller than me with slicked back blonde hair.

Compared to our last face to face meeting in the fall he had a glow about him. He must have spent some time outside now that it was almost summer.

I gave him a practiced smile as I readjusted the strap of my laptop bag.

"I think so! We are looking forward to helping Coralia Coast rebuild its structures. I hear it's a beautiful seaside town," I said, earnestly. Ever since I was little I was fascinated with the ocean.

While my pixie magic was made for the Earth there was always something that drew me to the water. Maybe it was the way it was unapologetic with its emotions. It always brought me solace. Mr.

Calder's hand slipped beneath the strap on my shoulder as we made our way to The Drunken Fairy Tale Tavern.

"Let me," he said, nicely. My eyes widened slightly in shock. I nodded silently, afraid my voice would squeak. It's not that I was attracted to him. At least, I didn't think so but my experience was lacking so it might be hard to tell.

I spent so much time working for my father's company, Hale's Lumber Industry that I had little time to interact with others. Add in the fact that I was an introvert who was always a little lost when it came to interacting with beings.

As we continued to walk in silence I remembered how during the winter I got to reconnect with my sister, Eleanor. Eleanor was my older sister who was vibrant, warm and talkative. She loved being surrounded by people. She thrived on attention.

When she left for college and had a falling out with my father I felt like I lost a piece of myself. And now ever since being reunited with her and being introduced to her friends I've slowly felt myself break out of my shell. But now here I was walking with a business partner and at a loss for words.

"Well you'll be spending time in Coralia Coast soon," Mr. Calder said. I glanced up at him. Mr. Calder wasn't exactly cold but I've learned he's reserved and calculated.

We both agreed that I would help oversee the construction of the town's buildings and therefore I was going to be spending the summer there.

Honestly I was excited to start an adventure somewhere new, a place untouched by my family. It's not that I didn't love being back in Lavender Falls, it was just here I was Eleanor's little sister or Mr. Hale's baby girl. In Coralia I'll just be Crystal Hale Silva.

"My friends have visited before. Lilianna and Celestino, and then my sister Eleanor with her boyfriend Caleb," I commented. Mr. Calder sighed.

"I heard and I do apologize for my town's…cold behavior," he said. I bit my lip. That's what I'd heard. They had told me there was something off about Coralia Coast. The people there seemed to be wary but also lonely. We turned the corner and I could see the door to the tavern was propped open. I had been curious about the town ever since Eleanor visited.

"I hope I'm not prying but is there a reason why?" I asked, curiously. Mr. Calder's eyes flickered to me. There was a swirl of emotions in them. They reminded me of a tormented sea. They reminded me of Sailor anytime someone brought up Coralia Coast.

I wonder if Mr. Calder knows who Sailor is.

According to Eleanor, Sailor didn't like talking about his hometown and when they had visited to get some magical ingredients to heal the Hollow Tree and break Caleb's curse he'd needed to stay hidden. My cheeks warmed at the thought of Sailor. He was like the sun on a warm beach day. He was a friend that made me nervous.

But I don't think friends were supposed to make you nervous. I think in a way I liked that he did. He had the same warmth as my sister which is why I liked being around him. In a flash Mr. Calder's demeanor softened.

"It's okay Ms. Hale. I understand my town gives off a much different feeling to Lavender Falls. We lost someone important to us. Or shall I say they ran away from their responsibility," he said. I raised an eyebrow in confusion. He gave a slight chuckle that sounded rough, as if he wasn't used to expressing that emotion. "This person had a responsibility to the town, to his people. Because of that the ocean has been upset," he said cryptically. *The ocean?*

"Is this person like the heart of the town or something?" I asked. My cheeks heated. I bit the inside of my cheek in embarrassment. I probably sounded like a child. Mr. Calder gave a weak smile.

"He was the heart of the town and the family so yes," he said. I nodded as we stepped into the tavern. I noticed my friends in the back corner.

"Would you like to meet my sister and our friends?" I asked him. When I looked up at Mr. Calder, his eyes were elsewhere. He was staring at someone with a glare.

"Please introduce me to your friends, Crystal."

SAILOR

"But it's so hot!" Eleanor exclaimed. I leaned against the booth, laughing with my friends. Caleb dropped off our drinks and Eleanor was begging him to do a renaissance themed weekend which meant that Caleb would be dressed as a knight. Caleb glared lovingly at his girlfriend.

"I agree. I would love to see Flynn in some tights," Lola said grinning at Flynn, who was standing behind the booth, hands on his girlfriend's shoulders. I glanced at Lily who was staring at Celestino with a faint blush. I didn't need to read her energy to know what she was thinking.

"I honestly think it's a good idea," I said. Everyone looked at me.

"See!" Eleanor said. I chuckled.

"There used to be a renaissance festival that came through Coralia Coast every year and it was a lot of fun," I said as a pain ran through my heart.

The winter season was the first time I had been back home in a year. When I left, I'd packed up my things and walked away from my family and my town. I stared at the empty finger of my right pinky. I had left everything behind to come to Lavender Falls.

Here I was just Sailor. I was a bartender and a carpenter. I didn't need to hear everyone's problems. I didn't need to be in ridiculous meetings making stupid decisions. Here I could just be me. Just Sailor.

"Sailor," Lily called. My eyes widened.

"Sorry, spaced out," I said, sheepishly. While everyone rolled their eyes and laughed, Lily's eyes were filled with worry.

Although she couldn't read energies the way I could, she was good at reading people. I looked around the group of friends I found for myself. People who liked me for me and not my last name. They all knew I was hiding a secret, and I *wanted* to tell them. I wanted to tell them the truth but I was afraid they would look at me differently.

"I think you should do it. I know I look good in tights," I said, hoping to lighten the mood. I smiled as my friends joined in laughter.

"*This* is where you have been?" a familiar cold voice said from behind. I froze. Everyone's eyes stared behind me. *No.* This couldn't be happening. He wasn't really here. "Turn around," he ordered. I closed my eyes briefly. Turning around I saw a pair of hazel eyes first. My heart thumped. *Fuck, what was Crystal doing here next to **him**?*

"Sailor?" Crystal hesitated. I finally looked at him. He was still tall with broad shoulders. His blonde hair was a bit longer and pulled back. I see he finally decided to let himself grow a beard. And his eyes were stormy. Eyes that matched mine. Eyes that screamed brother.

"Sailor? That's what you call yourself? Really? Couldn't have been more creative?" he grumbled. Crystal placed a hand on my brother's arm, stepping forward. I looked between them. *Why was she touching him so openly? What was their relationship?* I noticed her patchwork laptop bag was around his shoulder. I grinded my teeth.

"What's happening?" Eleanor said from behind them. My eyes were still glued to the hand on my brother's arm. *Why was she touching him?*

"Sailor?" Crystal said again, much softer. I swallowed. Her voice was like the whisper of a sea breeze, pulling me in and I was unable to resist it. My brother crossed his arms.

"I hope you know this means you're coming home," he said. I clenched my fists.

"No," I said sternly. My brother's eyebrows shot up in surprise.

"Yes, you will. You need to," he said, his voice laced with authority. I looked at the floor, away from his compelling eyes.

"Don't even try. It won't work on me," I said. I had spent years building up a tolerance to a siren's voice. I refused to let our own people's magic be used against me.

"You need to come home," my brother's voice softened for half a second. I glanced at Crystal quickly.

"Why are you two even together?" I asked, ignoring what he said. I couldn't mask the tone of jealousy even if I'd wanted to. My brother must have sensed it because his lips twitched.

"Ms. Hale and I have an agreement," he said, placing a hand on her shoulder, a little too close to her neck. Crystal didn't flinch. She didn't shrink away from his touch, not like she usually did around people. My stomach churned. *What fucking agreement was he referring to?*

"She'll be coming to Coralia Coast with me for some time," he said, nonchalantly. My blood boiled.

"Oh! Wait, you're Mr. Calder!" Eleanor said. My brother nodded and gave a practiced smile.

"Yes, I am. I'm Ronan Coralia Calder. I'm the Mayor of Coralia Coast," he said, facing my friends before turning back to me. "Now, Cas. You need to return home," he said, refocusing the conversation.

Return home.

Return to the life I never wanted. Return to the life of having the responsibility of my people on my shoulders. But not *just* my people, the ocean and every living creature there. I ignored him and instead took Crystal's bag from his shoulder and placed it on my own.

"You know what this year is," my brother said. I sighed. I knew what this year was, which is why I wanted a year to myself. A year for me to live how I wanted to. This year marked something important, and every Calder had to be there to perform the ceremony. I needed to do my duty no matter how much I hated it.

"Cas?" Crystal asked, confused.

"Are you going to tell them or shall I?" my brother asked. I felt another twist in my stomach and a pang through my heart. I sucked in a big breath and stepped away from the booth. I faced each of my friends. I didn't want the truth to come out, and even if I did I didn't want it to be this way. There were so many opportunities for me to tell them the truth.

But I'd shied away. A small part of me had hoped I'd never have to.

Although deep down I knew it would come to light eventually. I finally glanced at Crystal who'd taken a step towards me. I gave her a weak smile. *Would she still think of me as her friend after this?* I hope they all would.

"My name isn't Sailor. It's Prince Caspian Coralia Calder. Second prince of Coralia Coast, and of the Atlantic Ocean."

Acknowledgments

Another book! Im still in awe that I get to write these love stories and people read them.

I knew I was going to have so much fun writing Lola. Lola and Eleanor have been the easiest to write since they are two women who are confident, loving and love what they do. Writing women like that (the opposite of how I feel) is easy because they are who I want to be.

But Lola and Flynn's story was one of the hardest stories to write despite it being short. In all honesty it was Flynn that I struggled with. I was so worried about writing a male character who while strong and sweet was riddled with insecurities. Flynn and Lilianna have been the characters closest to my heart meaning I was worried about writing them and then people not liking them and in-turn not liking me.

Despite that I'm so happy with the story I wrote. Two people who want love, who give love and are what the other person needs. They own up to their mistakes and promise to do better not just for the other but for themselves.

This book wouldn't have happened without so many people. Thank you to Mel and the Steamy Lit family for always supporting me.

Thank you to Jennette for designing my cover once again and listening to my rants. For being my number one supporter. I started this journey with you and I can't wait to see where we go from here.

Thank you to Michelle for fixing all of my comma mistakes because I can never get it right. I'm so excited for our journey together. And thank you to Ash for making sure that Lola was written with the love and care that she gives others.

Thank you to Alise for your constant support. You have no idea how much your light has pushed me to keep going.

Ruby, my writing partner in crime. Thank you for reading my endless screenshots, giving me ideas and pushing me. I hope you know you're stuck as my sprint partner. I'm also so proud of YOU! Please ready Ruby Rana's books! It's hockey, it's hot and you'll laugh and cry.

A big thank you to Bear for making sure I eat and drink water. You teach me about love every single day and I'm thankful that when I'm scared you're willing to hold me in the dark.

Thank you to my mom. Thank you for helping me fall in love with books. I promise one day it'll be worth it and you'll rest easier. I know I'm not where I should be but one day I'll be able to repay you. I promise. *Te amo.*

And lastly to me. I know 2024 was hard on you mentally. I know you struggled a lot with depression but you did it. Woman, you wrote another book! Something little Isabel never thought she would. So be proud.

Also who even reads these? If you read this, remember to drink water.

About the Author

Isabel Barreiro is an anxious bookworm who loves being a dork and knowing random facts. Did you know a bumblebee bat is the world's smallest mammal?

During the day she's a freelance social media manager and at night she's binging anime shows or kdramas. Her brain has five hamsters running around on fire which makes the day to day interesting.

Despite being born and raised in Miami she prefers mountains and the fall/winter season. Maybe one day she'll have her small town life that she loves writing about. (Please it's my dream). She loves cooking and crafting and being an extroverted introvert.

You can follow her on Instagram/TikTok:
@authorisabelbarreiro
You can receive my newsletter on substack:
A Bookworm's Diary by Isabel Barreiro

You can also check out the first book in the Lavender Falls series, Falling For Fairy Tales on Amazon! A workplace romance between two childhood best friends who reunite to put on a magical pub crawl.

Want something a bit darker? Isabel also has a mafia book under a penance! Check out: The Mafia's Seamstress by Isabel Catrina on Amazon!

Made in the USA
Columbia, SC
10 June 2025